A WELCOME MURDER

ALSO BY ROBIN YOCUM

A Brilliant Death

A
WELCOME
MURDER

A NOVEL

ROBIN YOCUM

SEVENTH STREET BOOKS®
AN IMPRINT OF PROMETHEUS BOOKS
59 JOHN GLENN DRIVE • AMHERST, NY 14228
www.seventhstreetbooks.com

Published 2017 by Seventh Street Books®, an imprint of Prometheus Books

Cover image © Shutterstock
Cover design by Nicole Sommer-Lecht
Cover design © Prometheus Books

Inquiries should be addressed to
Seventh Street Books
59 John Glenn Drive
Amherst, New York 14228
VOICE: 716–691–0133 • FAX: 716–691–0137
WWW.SEVENTHSTREETBOOKS.COM

21 20 19 18 17 • 5 4 3 2 1

Library of Congress Cataloging-in-Publication Data

Names: Yocum, Robin, author.
Title: A welcome murder / By Robin Yocum.
Description: Amherst, NY : Seventh Street Books, an imprint of Prometheus Books,
    2017.
Identifiers: LCCN 2016051813 (print) | LCCN 2016059183 (ebook) |
    ISBN 9781633882638 (pbk.) | ISBN 9781633882645 (ebook)
Subjects: LCSH: Murder—Investigation—Fiction. | GSAFD: Mystery fiction.
Classification: LCC PS3625.O29 W45 2017 (print) | LCC PS3625.O29 (ebook) |
    DDC 813/.6—dc23
LC record available at https://lccn.loc.gov/2016051813

Printed in the United States of America

For my mother, Carroll Yocum
A great proofreader, a better mom. (Sorry about the profanity.)

PROLOGUE
JOHNNY EARL

You know things have taken a hard left when even the corpses are conspiring to further screw up your life. Sadly, I never needed help from the living or the dead. For nearly four decades, I had done a grand job all by myself.

The forces that conspired to keep me trapped in Steubenville, Ohio, in the summer of 1989 were not of my devising. For once, I was not guilty of the stupidity and poor decisions that had defined my entire adult life.

It was solely the fault of that festering, bullet-ridden corpse.

My guilt or innocence aside, I became the primary suspect in his murder. For those of you unfamiliar with the justice system in this country, that is very bad for a guy who has just walked out of a federal penitentiary. I quickly became what law enforcement officials like to call a "person of interest."

All I wanted was to put the Ohio River Valley in my rearview mirror and start my pathetic life over some place where they had never heard of Johnny Earl. But I couldn't.

When I was six, my mother bought me a hamster at J. G. McCrory's five-and-dime in Steubenville. I named him Herman, and that little guy was the first thing in my life that I loved more than myself. I carried him around the neighborhood in the pocket of my sweatshirt and played with him for hours. Mom bought a hollow plastic ball in which I could put Herman so he could run around the house on our hardwood floors.

I took him outside in his plastic ball one hot afternoon to let him run around on the garage floor. The kids next door were playing Wiffle Ball, and I went over to get in the game, forgetting about Herman. The poor little guy rolled himself off the driveway and got stuck in the grass, where he cooked to death in the afternoon sun. I was devastated.

I thought of Herman often that summer of 1989. Not unlike Herman, I was trapped in a ball, the metaphorical heat coming in from all sides. If there is a God in the universe that cares about small animals, this was Herman's revenge.

CHAPTER ONE
JOHNNY EARL

I t was never my life's ambition to be a cocaine dealer. My goal in life, from the time I was old enough to hold a baseball bat, was to play in the major leagues, make a boatload of money, and be inducted into the Hall of Fame. When I was in high school I would practice my induction speech by standing in front of the bathroom mirror holding a hairbrush for a microphone. I became a cocaine dealer by accident. Unfortunately, I was every bit as adept at dealing cocaine as I was at hitting a baseball, and I was the greatest baseball player to ever come out of Steubenville, Ohio. That's a fact. The biggest difference between the two is this: To the best of my knowledge, no one has ever been sent to a federal penitentiary for booting a ground ball.

I've really screwed up my life. That's also a fact. I had it all. I mean, so far as Steubenville was concerned, I was the king. I was the best-looking kid in our school. I'm not bragging—just telling you the way it was. I'm bald now, which I hate even more than the idiotic tattoos I allowed a white supremacist to ink into my biceps with a sewing needle while I was in prison. But in high school, I had thick, dark hair that I parted in the middle and feathered back over my ears. My eyes are pale blue, I have a little cleft in my chin, and I had the most perfect set of teeth you ever saw. They're still nice, except now I have a partial plate that fills the gap where that black son of a bitch, Andre Edwards, a psychopath who should have been in permanent lockdown, smacked me with a piece of pipe and knocked an incisor and an eyetooth down my throat.

There were probably some girls in my class who would say that Jimmy Hinton was better-looking than me. His family owned the big lairy and cattle farm out on County Road 724 near New Noblesville, and they had, as my dad liked to say, more money than God. Jimmy always dressed up for school—never wore blue jeans or sneakers like he rest of us—and he drove a very cherry, midnight blue '55 Ford with blue lights under the wheel wells. He wore nicer clothes than me, and ie had a much sweeter ride, but no way was he better-looking. He was a pretty boy—curly blond hair, a baby face, and sleepy eyes. Hell, I always igured he wasn't interested in girls. After all, he played the clarinet in he marching band, for Christ's sake.

I also dated the most beautiful girl in the school—Dena Marie Conchek. That's another fact. If you want proof, look at my senior yearbook. She was the head cheerleader, she was the homecoming queen, and she had the most incredible ass in Jefferson County. I was tapping that action every Friday and Saturday night and getting head on Sunday afternoons when her parents were visiting her grandmother at the nursing home. Since we weren't married, Dena Marie thought it was sinful to have intercourse on Sundays but apparently didn't think God had a problem with oral sex. It was typical Dena Marie. She was as crazy as she was beautiful, but putting up with her lunacy was a minor sacrifice in exchange for such great sex, especially when you're eighteen years old and sporting a perpetual boner.

If I had spent any time at all studying, I would have been valedictorian, too. Maybe. Lanny Chester was pretty damn smart, but I would have given him a run for his money. I was smart. Well, book smart, anyway. Most people would tell you that I never had a lick of common sense, and, given my recent track record as a guest of the Federal Penitentiary at Terre Haute, Indiana, it's hard to put up a strong argument to the contrary. But I was pretty close to straight A's, and I never cracked a book. I finished in the top ten in the class—eighth, I think.

Grades were never a big concern, because I was the best athlete in the storied history of Steubenville High School. Again, I'm not bragging—I'm just telling you the facts. You can find people who will tell you that little limp-dick Jimmy Hinton was better-looking than me, and that Lanny Chester was smarter, but no one will argue that I wasn't the best athlete to ever wear the crimson and black of the Steubenville Big Red. I was first-team all-Ohio six times. Six times! Three times in baseball, twice in football, and once in basketball. Now, I'll be the first to admit that being all-state in basketball was probably a gift—name recognition from my baseball and football accomplishments. But that doesn't matter. It still counts. First-team, all-Ohio, six times. You can check it out if you like. Photos of the all-staters hang in the front hall of the school. I'm the only one up there more than twice. At least, I think I'm still up there. After the drug conviction, they might have decided that I was too big of a disgrace and taken them all down.

I was five foot ten, a hundred and ninety-five pounds, and built like a statue of one of those Greek gods. My belly was rippled so tight you could hardly pinch the skin. And I was born to play baseball; I swear I was. I had twenty-three home runs my senior year. No one in the history of the school had ever hit twenty-three in a career, and I hit them in one season. I was a dead fastball hitter. You could sneak sunrise past a rooster easier than you could sneak a fastball past me.

I have always been very competitive. My friend Fran Roberson was at a high school debate competition and a kid from Mount Pleasant High School asked him what I was like. Fran said, "If you met him on the street, you'd think he was a nice guy. But he hates to lose, and he's an absolute prick between the lines." To this day, I consider that the highest compliment I've ever been paid. It was true. I would do anything to gain the advantage, including getting under the skin of an opponent. I was pretty good at it, too.

My senior year, Jefferson Union had a pitcher named Harry Bantel—a lanky kid who wore horn-rimmed glasses that made him look like Buddy Holly. Before the game, he yelled into our dugout that he was going to challenge me. I yelled back, "Give it your best shot, Buddy." Everyone laughed, and that pissed him off. He tried to blow the first pitch by me, and I hit it over the bus barn behind the center-field bleachers. I touched home plate and asked, "Hey, Buddy, when are you going to start challenging me?" Next time I'm up, he gives me a dick-high fastball and I hit it into the tennis courts beyond the left-field fence. I said, "Do your ovaries hurt today, Bantel? You don't have your good stuff." Now, he's furious and I start singing "Peggy Sue" while I'm circling the bases. Next time up, he tries to put one in my ear. I dodge it, give him a wink, then hit the next pitch through a shop-class window. Take that, Buddy. Three swings, three home runs. I laughed all the way around the bases.

The Baltimore Orioles drafted me in the second round. I was pissed because I thought I was a sure first-rounder. Still, any thoughts I had of going to college ended when the Orioles flashed a fifty-thousand-dollar signing bonus in front of me. It was more than my dad made in two years at the steel mill. I went right over to Ohio Valley Chevrolet and bought a new Camaro and drove straight to Jimmy Hinton's house. I raced the engine until he came outside. "Whatta ya think of this?" I asked.

He shrugged. "It's okay."

"Okay?!" I couldn't believe it. "Better than that piece-of-shit Ford you're driving. They're going to pay me a lot of money to hit a baseball, Jimmy boy, which is lots better than shovelin' shit and tuggin' on cow tits for the rest of your life." I laid rubber a hundred feet down County Road 724. Jimmy Hinton was as nice a kid as you would ever meet, and he had never done a thing to me, but I was so scalded that some girls thought he was better-looking that I had to show off.

Admittedly, there were times when I was a first-class horse's ass.

Most everyone in Steubenville was real excited when I got drafted, with one notable exception—Dena Marie Conchek. The day I signed with the Orioles, she wouldn't stop crying. Ultimately, though, I asked the question to which I already knew the answer. "Dena Marie, what's wrong?"

"If you leave, we'll never get married," she blubbered.

"Dena Marie, I never said we were going to get married." That was a fact.

"You don't want to marry me?"

"I want to play in the major leagues." The wailing began anew.

A week before I left for my minor-league assignment, I said, "Dena Marie, we need to break up." She was still bawling when I left her house, and I didn't talk to her again for more than eight years.

Here's another thing, and it's a stone fact. When I got to the Orioles' rookie league team, I learned very quickly that there are a lot of guys outside of Steubenville who can play the game. I was a fastball hitter and that was great in high school, where you get a steady diet of fastballs. That wasn't the case in the pros. They had the most unbelievable breaking balls I had ever seen. I flailed away at curveballs and missed so mightily that it was embarrassing. And here's another thing: Once word gets around the league that you can't hit a breaking ball, and you can trust me on this, that's *all* you see.

I was basically a career minor-leaguer. I hit some mammoth home runs, but my average was about two-twenty, and I struck out seven times for every home run I hit. For those of you unfamiliar with the statistics of baseball, that is not good. The Orioles were patient, but I only made it to double-A ball, and after six years I was traded to Pittsburgh. In the middle of my second season in the Pirates organization, the left fielder at their triple-A affiliate got hurt and I got moved up. All of a sudden, for reasons that I cannot explain, I started hitting the ball like Babe Ruth. It looked like a cantaloupe coming in there, and I was spraying line drives all over the park. That was the year I got the call to the majors. It was an end-of-the-year call-up, a cup of coffee, but it still counts. I, Johnny Earl, was a member of the Pittsburgh Pirates and a major leaguer.

My claim to fame was hitting an off-the-wall triple off of Nolan Ryan. That's right, *the* Nolan Ryan, and I rocked his ass for a three-bagger. A big crowd from Steubenville had come up in a couple of charter buses to see me play, and they were all on their feet, cheering. I was standing on third, grinning, all proud of myself. That's when Nolan Ryan looked over and said, "Enjoy it, rook. It won't happen again." And it didn't. The next three times up, he struck me out on three pitches.

I thought I had finally gotten the hang of professional pitching. The Pirates thought it was a fluke and traded me in the off-season to the Detroit Tigers. My agent said they wanted to unload me because they thought my sudden ability to hit a curveball had been an anomaly. Unfortunately, they were right. By the time I got to spring training,

I was again floundering, flailing away at curves like a blind man at a buzzing fly.

My career ended on a damp evening in July of 1979 in Toledo. I sent a loopy fly ball down the right-field line and blew my knee rounding first. I crumpled into a heap ten feet from the base. The pain was excruciating; I felt like I'd been shot and my leg was on fire. The right fielder threw the ball to the first baseman, who leaned down and said, "Sorry to do this to you, pal," putting the tag on me as I rolled around the infield. That was the last time I ever stepped onto a ball field. I had reconstructive surgery and went back home to rehabilitate and consider my future.

In a little more than eight years, I went from signing bonus to *sayonara*. At age twenty-six, the only thing on my résumé was 158 minor-league home runs and a major-league triple off of Nolan Ryan. I was depressed and humiliated by my failure. When I was in high school, you couldn't have told me that I wasn't going to play in the major leagues. If you had, I would have laughed in your face. I was Johnny Earl, goddammit. You get a distorted view of the world growing up in a place like Steubenville. I had had such great success in my little pond that I thought I couldn't fail.

But I had.

Most Jefferson Countians had a similarly hard time understanding my failure. They didn't realize the level of talent out there and assumed that because I had been a stud for the Steubenville Big Red that I was a lock for the big leagues. Hell, even I thought that. Not long after the knee surgery, Bubbie Szismondo, who worked with my dad at Weirton Steel, walked by the house and saw me sitting on the porch with my leg in a brace. "How's the knee?" he asked.

"Not good," I said.

"Gonna try again next year?"

"Nope. I'm done."

He shook his head, disgusted, and sent a spray of tobacco juice into my mother's zinnias. "I knew you should have taken one of them football scholarships," he said, already walking away.

Everything in my life had been a competition. It wasn't that I loved winning, but I loathed losing. The victories in my life were never as sweet as the defeats were bitter. Why else at this point in my life would I still be upset that some people thought Jimmy Hinton was better-looking than me back in high school? It's great to have a competitive fire as an athlete, but it can lead to problems if you don't control it off the field. I am the poster child for that last statement.

For the first time in my life, I didn't have some kind of athletic season to get ready for. I moped, worked on model cars, and generally felt sorry for myself. This was a major blow to my ego. (Once upon a time, my mammoth ego was my most dominating characteristic. That's not so much the case anymore. Seven years in the penitentiary and going bald in the process will knock the swagger right out of you.) I was pushing twenty-seven, my baseball career was over, I was driving a rusting Camaro with 180,000 miles on it, I had thirteen hundred bucks in my checking account and no education beyond high school, and my only job prospects were the steel mills or the coal mines. Tell me that isn't depressing.

And, just to prove that God has a sense of humor, three days after I got home from my knee surgery, Dena Marie Conchek rapped twice on the front door and then just came in. I was sitting at the dining-room table putting together a model of a '64 Thunderbird. "Hey there, Dena Marie," I said, my first words to her since I left her crying in her living room.

She stopped in mid-stride, her eyes widened, and she said, "Oh my God, you're going bald!"

"Thanks so much for noticing. It's nice to see you, too."

She sat down at the table next to me and said, "Johnny . . ." She waited until I looked up from my model. "I knew that you'd come back to me."

"I know this will come as a big surprise to you, Dena Marie, but I didn't come back to Steubenville looking for you. My knee exploded, the Detroit Tigers fired me, and I needed a place to live." She pretended not to hear me, but I knew Dena Marie, and I'll bet the minute she heard I was coming back home she had started planning our wedding. "Besides, aren't you still married to Jack Androski?" I knew she wasn't. My mom was the most spectacular gossip in Steubenville, and I had received regular updates on the town's sins and sinners. Jack had divorced Dena Marie a few years earlier, after he caught her with Alan Vetcher.

"I'm divorced. It was a bad marriage from the start," she said in a whiny tone. "I couldn't help it. I was so upset when you left that I married the first man who asked me."

"Well, I knew it would somehow end up being my fault."

"Johnny, is it my fault that I never stopped loving you?"

It was my turn to pretend like I hadn't heard her, and I went back to working on the Thunderbird. Dena Marie sat at the table for an hour, telling me everything I didn't want to know about everything I didn't want to hear about. I was exhausted just from listening. I was ready to ask her to go when she said she was late for her job at the grocery store and left.

She stopped by the next day.

And the next.

On her fourth visit, we had sex.

I hadn't been with a woman in months, and my willpower was at low tide. Granted, my moral compass spends a lot of time at low tide, but I got a good whiff of her perfume, and when she touched the inside of my thigh while inspecting my surgery scars it became readily apparent that although my knee was out of commission, other body parts were fully operational. A stiff dick has no conscience. I hobbled up the steps on my crutches and we had clumsy sex in the twin bed in my bedroom, which was still adorned with trophies and plaques from my high school days. Once again, I was back to ignoring Dena Marie's lunacy in exchange for sex.

I have the morals of an alligator.

Things got worse. I was five weeks post-surgery when Rayce Daubner showed up at my door. I hated Rayce Daubner. I had pretended to like him when we were playing football together, even though he smelled like piss and used to call me "Hollywood" with a sneer because he was jealous of all the attention I received. The last time I recall ever talking to Rayce was when he was named second-team all-Ohio in football. He was upset, of course, because I was first-team. I said, "Second-team all-state is a hell of an honor."

"Really? Do they put your picture up on the wall for second-team?"

I shrugged. "No, but . . ."

"That's right. They don't. I bust my ass blocking for you, Hollywood, and what do I get—second-fucking-team. That's nothing."

Until the minute he walked through my door, those were the last words that we had spoken to each other, but he acted like we had been best friends for years. "John-eeee Earl!" he yelled, holding up a hand to give me a high-five. "How the hell are ya?" His hair was long and black, drawn into a ponytail that somewhat disguised his lopsided head, and he had a thin goatee. He was wearing a yellow shirt with green paisleys and a hard pack of Marlboros in the pocket, blue jeans, and sandals. He was thinner than he had been in high school, but still muscular and broad across the shoulders. It was an odd look for someone who had aspired to join the Marine Corps and boasted of having uncles who were card-carrying members of the Ku Klux Klan. He still smelled like a wet diaper.

In yet another bad decision, I started going out with Rayce to the Starlighter Bar, otherwise known as the Star Bar. The Star Bar was the hangout of many of my buddies who had mentally and emotionally never left high school. You could hear the same stories about the same high school heroics night after night at the Star Bar. The regulars would buy me beers and ask me to tell stories about home runs or touchdowns that I could barely recall. The first night I was there, Chico Deter asked, "Johnny, do you remember that block I threw on that linebacker from Warren Harding that sprung you for that touchdown just before the half our junior year?"

"Oh, hell yes, I remember that, Chico!" I said. "You lit his ass up." Chico smiled, slapped me on the back, and bought me a beer. I have absolutely no recollection whatsoever of the block or the touchdown, or the game, for that matter, but it made him happy.

After a night of drinking, just as I was starting to walk without a noticeable limp, Rayce said, "Let's swing by the house and do a line of coke."

I had never done cocaine. I was mostly a beer man, and on rare occasions, reefer. "Ah, I dunno, man. I've never done coke."

"Come on, try it. Once. You'll fuckin' love it."

He was right. I fuckin' loved it. The minute that powder hit my nose, I was hooked. My eyes watered, my dick got hard, and I thought a kettle of popcorn was going off in my brain. I turned to Rayce and said, "I'm gonna call Dena Marie and ask her to marry me. Maybe even tonight."

He laughed and said, "Why don't you wait and rethink that in the morning?"

I did cocaine every night for a week and drained my checking account. It didn't take a rocket scientist to see that I was heading down a path that was not conducive to a promising future. Cocaine was going up my nose at an astonishing rate. I was borrowing money from my parents to buy cocaine from a man I didn't trust as far as I could throw him. I was sleeping with Dena Marie, and she was starting to talk about what color drapes she wanted in our living room. I had no job and no prospects. I had to get out of town and find some work.

I went to Pittsburgh and landed a job with a construction company owned by Geno Bartelli, who had been a Pirates season-ticketholder and had once told me to call him if I ever needed work. Because my knee was still tender, Mr. Bartelli had me train to be a backhoe operator. I quickly got the hang of it. When my knee healed to the point where I could walk and kneel, Mr. Bartelli said he wanted me to be an apprentice mason. I liked the backhoe, but he assured me that there was a better future in masonry.

As I stated earlier, I didn't start out to be a drug dealer. After two months with Bartelli Construction, I figured I owed myself a reward, so after work on a Friday afternoon I drove back to Steubenville to visit Rayce's supplier, a guy I knew only as Squirrel. He was a disgusting little man with oily, shoulder-length hair, an unwieldy moustache, and a perpetually runny nose, but great cocaine. I bought four grams and, as luck would have it, ran into Rayce on my way back to the car. "Where the fuck you been?" he demanded.

"Pittsburgh. I got a job."

"You couldn't say something?"

"It came up kind of sudden."

"You fuckin' prima donna. You still think you're better than everyone else." Rayce Daubner was a prick once again. My universe was back in alignment.

That night I went to a club downtown that I frequented when I was with the Pirates. Yes, I went there hoping that someone would recognize me as a former Pirate. Perhaps someone was at the game when I tripled off of Nolan Ryan. Either they had faulty memories or the game had been poorly attended, because no one remembered. I was no longer Johnny Earl. Now, I was simply Johnny the backhoe guy.

My first cocaine sale was that night at the bar. A brunette with a couple dozen earrings rimming each ear squeezed up to the bar next to my stool and ordered drinks for her and some friends. As she waited, she turned and her eyes locked on my face. *Finally*, I thought, *someone remembers*. After a few moments, she asked, "What's your name?"

"Johnny Earl."

"Uh-huh. Johnny. I'm Samantha. Can I give you a little advice, Johnny?"

"Sure."

She put an index finger in her mouth, wetting it with her tongue, and swiped it under my nose. She held out the finger for my inspection. It was smeared with a thin film of white powder. "Don't let this stuff go to waste," she said, putting the finger back in her mouth. I grabbed my cocktail napkin and began furiously scrubbing my face. "Relax, sweetie, I got it all." I kept rubbing. "Got any more?"

I leaned toward her and asked, "Could we have this conversation outside?" She followed me to the parking lot and that's how it began. I sold her a half gram of cocaine for double the amount I paid for it. It seemed ridiculously easy. "I have friends who'll buy coke from you," Samantha said. "Can you get more?"

I thought it over for a moment and said, "I'll be here next Friday." The next week, I doubled my purchase from Squirrel, then doubled it again the next week. At first, I just sold to Samantha and her friends. Eventually, I had Samantha and one of her friends selling for me. I found out that I'm a damn good businessman. I kept my overhead low and my profit margins high. I didn't sell on credit and was real strict about getting paid. No money, no coke. I started sleeping with Samantha, and she thought this would entitle her to free cocaine. When she found out otherwise, she was livid and stood naked in the middle of my apartment, screaming and throwing empty beer cans at me and calling me a greedy bastard and a greedy prick and a greedy son of a bitch, all of which were arguably true, but that didn't change my cash-and-carry policy.

I used to wonder why people would take the chance of going to prison for dealing drugs. It didn't take me long to figure it out. Dealing was lucrative as hell. Within a couple of months, I had upward of $80,000 hidden in my apartment. I kept working my job with the construction company, because I was smart enough to know that no one grew to an old age in the cocaine-dealing business. You either get arrested or someone who wants your business hits you over the head with a two-by-four and they find you floating in the Mononga-hela River. My plan was to make enough money to buy a backhoe and dump truck and start my own excavating business. The problem was, as Samantha noted, I'm a greedy son of a bitch. I worked all day for Bar-telli Construction and made coke deliveries at night. Eventually, I took on the drug-dealer image. I shaved my head, grew a lip beard, wore lots of gold, and got an earring. I liked the persona. Mr. Bartelli saw me one day and said, "You're not going faggot on me, are you?" I recruited some lieutenants to keep me away from the action. I'm sure they were stealing from me, but I was still making a ton of money, so I let it slide. I expanded my business and found another supplier, which reduced my costs but really pissed off Squirrel.

After about three years, I knew I was running on borrowed time. Too many people knew I was a drug dealer, and that meant it was just a matter of time before a cop or a competitor put a stop to my business.

Adding to the angst was the fact that beneath the floor of my closet were bricks of hundred-dollar bills. I had to find a better hiding place, but where? Depositing the money in a bank would set off an alarm at the Internal Revenue Service, and I didn't want to put it in a safe-deposit box because if I was ever arrested my ill-gotten gains were a mere search warrant away from being confiscated.

By this time, I was still an apprentice mason with no enthusiasm for the work. This aggravated the masons, who perceived themselves as being above the other crafts, and certainly above a heavy equipment operator. They gave me menial jobs, like mixing mortar, or building trivial shit, like brick walls in front of buildings or the little vaults that held corner-stone documents or time capsules. Basically, I did jobs in which a mistake would not cause an entire building to come crashing down.

As I was considering getting out of the cocaine-dealing business, I got a phone call and the guy on the other end says, "Hey, Hollywood."

My stomach knotted up. "Rayce?"

"Yeah, dude, it's me. I need some help. You seen Squirrel?"

"Squirrel? No, I haven't seen him in a year or so."

"I got to find him. I got a fuckin' opportunity here that you can't believe."

"I can't help you, Rayce. I don't know where he is." My curiosity and greedy nature got the best of me. "What kind of opportunity?"

"A big-time deal. Big time. I got a guy from Cleveland, some lawyer, who says he knows these rich cokeheads who will buy anything he can get his hands on."

"How much you looking for?"

"Six kilos."

"That's a lot of dope. Squirrel's a small-timer. He couldn't get you that much."

"Goddamn, dude, I've got to have it. This guy's got more money than good sense. I can make a shitload of money on this. Can you help me out?"

Now, here's the thing: I'm smart enough to know that I shouldn't have gotten involved with any of Rayce Daubner's brainstorms. Warning sirens should have been going off in my head. But I was thinking that unloading a steady stream of dope on Rayce would be easy money and expedite my exit from the trade. "When do you need it?"

"Yesterday."

"It'll take some time to line it up. Give me a number, and I'll call you back."

Four days later, I had the coke and called Rayce. I told him to meet me at a restaurant along Route 22 in the West Virginia panhandle. I was having a cup of coffee when he arrived. "I'm in a hurry," he said. "You got the coke?"

"Good seeing you again, too, Rayce."

"I told you, I don't have the time for chitchat. You got the coke?"

"Maybe. You got the cash?"

He slid the newspaper he was carrying across the table. I pulled an envelope out of the sports pages and, holding it in my lap, slit the flap with my finger. It was stuffed with crisp hundred-dollar bills. I put my foot behind the gym bag that was on the floor and slid it between his feet. "Don't open it here. It's all good. Your lawyer friend will be pleased."

"Good. Let me get out of here first," he said.

"When are you going to want more?" I asked. "I never keep this much in stock. You've got to give me more time."

"I'll let you know." And he booked.

I pushed the envelope into my pants, paid the bill, and walked outside. I never made it to my car. Unmarked cop cars came in from everywhere. Guys in baseball caps and black jackets with "FBI" across the back jumped out, pointing pistols and shotguns at me, screaming, "Get your hands in the air! Get on your knees, get on your knees, goddammit!" I was screwed. The feds had the dope, and I was carrying an envelope full of marked bills. I found out later that a guy who had been sitting across the restaurant had a video camera in his briefcase. They had me dead to rights.

The headline in the Steubenville *Herald-Star* the next day read:

Former Steubenville High Star Arrested for Cocaine Trafficking

Before my arrest, not one person in Pittsburgh remembered my brief stint with the Pirates. Afterward, however, every news story in every paper carried the phrase, "former Pittsburgh Pirate Johnny Earl." Once upon a time, I would have been proud to see that in the paper. Now, it was just humiliating and a reminder of how far I had tumbled.

Everyone in Jefferson County looked at each other and said, "Oh, that's why he didn't make it to the major leagues. He was on cocaine." Rayce was a federal informant. He was working off some minor drug rap and had told the feds he could get them a major dealer. Mainly, me. He testified before the grand jury that he had asked me why I wasn't afraid of getting caught and I had said, "I'm a former Pittsburgh Pirate and a six-time all-Ohioan. Who's going to mess with me? I'm untouchable."

Bull crap. I never said anything of the kind. He invented that just to make me look bad, as though being charged with cocaine trafficking wasn't bad enough. But that was it. That whole all-Ohio thing had sat in his craw all those years.

After I was indicted, I asked my lawyer, "So, what do you think my chances are?"

"Of what?" he asked.

"Of getting off."

"Zero. Maybe less than zero. You're totally screwed." Not exactly the words I was hoping to hear. "It's your first offense. Let's cop a plea. You'll get out of prison while you're still a young man." It is a sickening feeling knowing that you have only two options—prison or more prison. Before my sentencing, my lawyer said, "How about we soften up the looks a little? Let's lose the lip beard and grow some hair."

Seemed reasonable. Then, adding insult to injury, it turns out that while I was dealing drugs and shaving my head every other day I had gone bald. And I mean completely *bald*. Perhaps this says something about my psyche, but I was more upset about going bald than I was with the prospect of a lengthy prison term.

Not far from Steubenville is the village of New Rumley, the birthplace of General George Armstrong Custer. Each year, fourth-graders from the Steubenville elementary schools take a field trip to New

Rumley to see Custer's statue and hear an impersonator tell the story of the general's life—his glorious victories, his fearlessness in battle, and his death while trying to save America from the godless red horde at the Little Big Horn. Historians may think Custer a lunatic, but he's still a hero back home.

I told you that in order to tell you this, and it's one of those little ironies of life that wasn't lost on me. By the time I pleaded guilty to cocaine trafficking, limpy Jimmy Hinton was no longer shoveling cow shit at the farm, as I had predicted. He had gone to college and was the chief editorial writer for the Steubenville *Herald-Star*. I was still at the Allegheny County Jail in Pittsburgh, awaiting my transfer to the federal penitentiary, when a smirking deputy stopped by my cell. He was carrying a manila envelope that looked like it had been opened and had its contents inspected. "Here's something for your scrapbook, big shot," he said, flipping the envelope to me between the bars.

It was a copy of the *Herald-Star*—sent, most likely, by Rayce Daubner—opened to the editorial page.

Steubenville's Fallen Star

Not since the fateful day in 1876 when this paper carried the news of the slaughter of General George Armstrong Custer and the Seventh Cavalry at the Little Big Horn has such a pall hung over eastern Ohio.

On that day on the plains of Montana, a star fell.

Today, another star has fallen.

Johnny Earl, arguably the greatest athlete to ever graduate from Steubenville High School and a hero to many, yesterday admitted to being a cocaine dealer and was subsequently sentenced to seven to twelve years in the federal penitentiary.

That's all I could read. I threw up in the stainless steel toilet and wondered whether limpy Jimmy had recalled the day I stopped by his house to show off my new Camaro and squealed my tires down the road, and thus had chuckled to himself the entire time that he was writing the editorial.

CHAPTER TWO
SHERIFF FRANCIS ROBERSON

I love being the sheriff of Jefferson County. I love the uniform and the badge and the pistol hanging at my side. I love leading the Fourth of July parade in my cruiser and tossing bubble gum to the kids on the curb. I love walking into the diner for breakfast and seeing heads turn and hearing men say, "G' morning, Sheriff."

I love all that.

It's being a cop that I hate.

Admittedly, that's an unusual confession for someone who has spent his entire professional career in law enforcement and who dragged his family from a comfortable life in Minneapolis to take a job as sheriff in the hardscrabble hills of eastern Ohio. But, it's the truth. I hate it. It's a disgusting, dirty job in which I am forever dealing with idiots with beer on their breath and vomit on their shoes. No fewer than a dozen guys have either pissed, vomited, or defecated themselves in the back of my cruiser. And, this isn't a great trait for a lawman, but I get nauseated at the sight of blood. Always have. Someone starts bleeding and I start gagging. When I was at the FBI Academy I had to watch an autopsy, and I threw up in a sink. The room started whirling and I thought I was going to pass out. My instructors said I would eventually get used to the sight of blood and intestines and it would no longer bother me. They were wrong. It still makes my stomach churn.

I try to hide it from the men. My chief deputy, Toots Majowski, knows. He's seen me hurl several times. An elderly woman near Dillonvale died in her house a couple of summers ago, and by the time a niece got around to checking on her she had been dead for a week. The thing is, she had six dogs and a couple dozen cats. The corpse was bloated and half eaten. There were piles of feces everywhere. The smell was so overwhelming that I vomited on what was left of the old woman.

Toots laughed and said, "Francis, why don't you just wait outside?" We're a small county, and I am not exempt from making runs. I'm not so much a lawman as I am a babysitter for drunks, derelicts, and wife-beaters. I liked being an FBI agent. You got to deal with a better class of criminal. They were basically gentlemen who let greed or cocaine or a mistress get the better of their judgment and cause them to defraud their clients or embezzle from their banks. When I walked into a business to arrest one of these sad sacks, they would just start crying and saying, "Oh no, oh God, no, no, no." Then they'd stand there and put their arms behind their backs and let me cuff them and walk peaceably out of the building. I never had to worry about arresting someone who might have lice and a bad attitude. Generally, the white-collar criminals were very well-groomed and didn't want to fight.

But every time I go to some bar to arrest one of the drunks, usually an unemployed steelworker with too much time and not enough work on his hands, the fight is on. Some are guys I went to high school with who don't like getting arrested by a classmate. Sometimes it's an older guy my dad pissed off somewhere along the line. They slide off the bar stool, stagger for footing, try to focus in on me, and say, "Why, you're Edgar Roberson's boy. You're a sumbitch, just like your old man." And then they take a wild swing and miss. "You motherfuckin', cock of a son of bastard, fuckin' ass wipe . . ." That's generally when I hit them with the Mace. I got a call to the Hoot 'n' Holler Bar out on County Road 12 one night when "Dimebag" Dave O'Connell was crazy on mescaline and tearing up the inside of the bar. Dimebag threw a few wild punches, and when I hit him with the Mace he kept coming. I laced him across the side of the head with my nightstick, and it sounded like I had hit a bowling ball. He dropped to his knees, swayed left, swayed right, and then fell on his face. I struggled to get him to the cruiser and asked if he needed to get sick before he got in. He said no. He waited until I shut him inside, then sent a stream of vomit through the wire mesh divider and into the front seat. I dragged him out of the car and smacked him again.

After several weeks of listening to me complain about this and the number of prisoners leaving bodily fluids in my cruiser, Toots dragged me with him on his next drunk run. "This is a very easy problem to remedy, partner," he said as we climbed into his cruiser. We drove to the Blue Swan near Smithfield, where Tiny Puet, who was six foot three—and two hundred and fifty pounds of mean drunk—was causing a ruckus. As soon as we walked in, Toots, who wrestled in high school and has huge hands, grabbed Tiny by the nape of his neck and marched him outside. Tiny was crying and squealing and begging to be let go, but Toots never broke stride, banging him through the door and marching him to the cruiser. He cuffed Tiny and sat him in the backseat with his feet still on the gravel parking lot. "Look at me, Tiny," he said in a calm tone. When Tiny looked up, Toots reached down and grabbed a handful of Tiny's privates. It sounded like he was squeezing a bag of potato chips. I don't know how bad it hurt Tiny, but I instinctively cupped my balls and doubled over. With his balls in a vise grip, Tiny's eyes and mouth opened wide, though only a faint squeak emitted from somewhere deep in his throat. Toots said, "Tiny, you're going to jail. If you piss, shit, or vomit in my cruiser, I'm going to stop the elevator between floors and whip the living dog out of you." Toots tightened his grip, and Tiny moaned. "Understand?" Tiny looked up and nodded furiously, his eyes starting to roll into the back of his head from the pain. Toots looked at me and smiled. "Any questions?"

I shook my head. "No, I think I've got it."

The bar runs still aren't as bad as the domestics. You never know what you're running into, and I'd just as soon break up a fight between a couple of rabid Rottweilers as get involved in a domestic scrap. The old man can be whipping the blue Jesus out of Momma, but as soon as you show up and put a hand on Daddy, all bets are off. All of a sudden you're everyone's enemy. You're trying to arrest the old man and the next thing you know, Momma's jumping on your back. Most of the time, the women don't want you to arrest the husband; they just want you to make him stop beating her. I'd like to bottle the magic potion that would make that happen.

We made regular domestic runs to the Goins place out on Kenton Ridge. Richard Goins was a vicious drunk, and his wife was this homely little thing who served as a punching bag every time he got a snootful, which was four or five nights a week. He'd get hammered, then go home and whale on Mildred, who couldn't have weighed ninety pounds. As soon as the old man stopped to catch his breath or take a piss, Mildred would call us before he got out of the bathroom. We'd send a cruiser out, but she never wanted to press charges; she just wanted us to referee. Ultimately, little Mildred took care of the problem. We went out there one night and Richard was dead on the floor—shot right through the heart. Mildred demanded a lawyer and wouldn't talk to us about it. She told the grand jury that Richard was beating her and at one point he had his hands around her neck and threatened to kill her. She got away, grabbed his shotgun out of the gun case, and fired. The grand jury ruled it self-defense.

You have to put up with a lot of crud as sheriff. But that's okay. It's not forever; it's just a means to an end. Someday, I'm going to be president. I know that sounds like pretty big talk for a guy who's only the sheriff of Jefferson County, Ohio. My wife, Allison, hates it when I talk about becoming president. She says I shouldn't do it because people are always suspicious of those with great ambition. I don't think that's true. Take my deputies, for example. They all know that I want to be president, and they actually admire me for it. My wife's heart is in the right place, but she worries way too much. These are my people, and they respect me.

My campaign for the presidency of the United States began when I was in the sixth grade. We were at the dinner table, and I announced that I had been elected president of my homeroom. This pleased my dad immensely. He loved politics and, working through a mouthful of pork chop, he said, "You know, with my connections, one day you could be a United States congressman."

I responded, "Why not president of the United States?"

It was as if the skies opened and the angels sent down a hallelujah chorus. He was never more proud of me. His brain was just whirling—Edgar Roberson's son, Francis Delano Roberson, president of the United States of America. My father is the most self-absorbed, scheming human being I have ever met. If my dad told you "good morning," you had to analyze your response for fear he was going to find a way to use it against you.

No sooner were those words out of my mouth than my mother was boring in on me with one of those withering looks, the kind I would get if I was fidgeting in church and she needed to stop it from several seats away. The brows dropped and the lips puckered. When my father had left the table, she sat down across from me, rolling a coffee cup between her palms, and said, "Why do you do this to me?" Even at the tender age of twelve, I knew exactly what she was talking about. She meant my dad would make her crazy with talk of me being the president. I was Dad's biggest trophy, and when I said I wanted to be president, he immediately began charting the course. When he wasn't busy promoting himself for president of the ironworkers' union or for mayor of Steubenville, he was busy promoting me. In the years before I returned to Steubenville to take the sheriff job, at least once during every telephone conversation he would ask, "You working on the run for the White House?"

I'd been working on it all my life. I ran for president of every club in high school, from the debate team to the chess club. I read every self-help and public-speaking book I could find. My experience in the FBI would set me up as a no-nonsense, law-and-order candidate. "Yup," I'd say. "I'm going to be the next Republican senator from Minnesota."

This would make him spew venom. "Republican?" he would yelp. "Minnesota?" he would whine. "Minnesota doesn't produce presidents. They come from Ohio and they're Democrats, goddammit! You need to come back here to get started."

My father put his plan into overdrive the day Jefferson County Sheriff Beaumont T. Bonecutter abruptly resigned after he became the target of a federal investigation for dereliction of duty and taking kick-backs from drug dealers. Jefferson County sheriffs accepting kickbacks was nothing new; it was a practice dating back to the day when the mills and the mines were booming and the prostitution and gambling businesses were extremely lucrative. When those industries thrived, law officers up and down the river earned a tidy sum accepting payoffs to ignore the illegal operations.

Bonecutter's resignation opened the door for my dad to get me back to Steubenville and take control of my political career. Dad said that Sheriff Bonecutter's demise and my return to Jefferson County was "divine intervention." I always referred to it as "Edgar interven-tion." Dad was an ironworker at Weirton Steel, but he lusted for the political power that always seemed just beyond his grasp. While he had been the longtime chairman of the Jefferson County Democratic Party, he had lost two bids for mayor of Steubenville and one for county com-missioner. However, Bonecutter's departure created a unique oppor-tunity. Federal investigators were swarming all over Jefferson County, and the sphincter of every elected official with good sense was puck-ered up tight. Once he had their collective testicles in hand, Edgar Roberson offered to deliver his boy, the FBI agent, back to Jefferson County to clean up the mess and get the feds out of town. In return, he wanted a commitment from every elected official—Republican and Democrat—that they would support me for sheriff in the next two elections, then back me for the US House of Representatives, and then help finance a run for the governor's office. They were only too happy to oblige.

I'm now in my second elected term as sheriff. It will be my last. I'll run for Congress in the next election, and I'll be a lock, barring a scandal. That, however, may be a bit of a problem, because as of late I've been having trouble keeping my pecker in my pants. I'm having an affair with Dena Marie Conchek Androski Xenakis. This is bad on several fronts. I'm gambling my political future by sleeping with a woman who has the stability of a case of nitroglycerin. But I can't help myself. I can't remember a time in my life when I wasn't in love with her. I told her I liked her in the second grade, and on Valentine's Day I gave her a homemade card and a pack of Sugar Babies, but she scorned me for my best buddy, Johnny Earl. I was crushed. While I fantasized about being married to Dena Marie, I was never so much as a blip on her radar.

That was until I ran into her at the A&P a few days after I moved back to Steubenville. Dena Marie ran across the store, threw her arms around me, and kissed me square on the lips. It was typical Dena Marie. She knew I was married, happily, and she knew I was the new sheriff, so suddenly I seemed a lot more attractive than in the days when I was Johnny Earl's athletic inferior and captain of the debate team. Unbelievably, Dena Marie was married to "Smoochie" Xenakis. If you had asked me in high school to create a list of the hundred males most likely to marry Dena Marie, Smoochie would have been a hundred-and-twelfth.

I made regular stops at the grocery where Dena Marie worked, just to buy gum or a soda, because I enjoyed flirting with her. One day last spring, I casually asked her, "So, how's married life?"

"So-so. It's difficult to be married to Smoochie when I'm in love with someone else."

I nodded and said, "I heard Johnny will be getting out of prison later this summer."

She slowly shook her head. "No, not Johnny. You."

It was a lie. I knew it was a lie the instant the words left her mouth. But when the girl you've dreamed about since the second grade says she loves you, you'll make up reasons to believe her. I remember sitting in Mrs. Ferwerda's first-grade class, looking across the room at Dena Marie and hoping that I would someday marry her. But the only guy she's ever loved, and ever will love, is Johnny Earl. I knew that. Anyone who got involved with Dena Marie would be playing second fiddle in her heart to Johnny. Still, I accepted her lie as the gospel. Logic should have told me to stay the hell away. She was a checkout girl. She was crazy. She was married. She would never truly love me. I knew that, but I could not stay away. I was never going to leave my wife, and even if Allison left me, did I honestly think Dena Marie would be an asset in a political campaign? Hell, no. She would be a liability of the highest order. Dena Marie is easy on the eyes, but she couldn't spell politics if you spotted her the P and the O. She talks too much, cracks her gum, and has bad grammar, and funeral directors don't put as much makeup on accident victims as Dena Marie trowels on every morning.

Yet, as I stood at the checkout counter at the A&P with all of these negative factors running through my head, my loins were tingling up into my chest, and the next words out of my mouth were, "Maybe we should get together sometime."

"You know where to find me," she said.

I also knew—without a shred of doubt—that the instant I dropped my pants in the vicinity of Dena Marie, the entire city would know about it. There were no secrets in Steubenville. I had lived here long enough to know that. Even so, I was surprised that word spread so quickly. I met Dena Marie three times, always at night, at the River Downs Motel in Wheeling, West Virginia, which was about a forty-five-minute drive. I learned that word had gotten out the day my dad came storming into my office and slammed the door behind him, as mad as I've ever seen him. "What in the name of Jesus, Mary, and Joseph is wrong with you?"

I played dumb. "What?"

"You want to blow your chance at getting into Congress over a crazy piece of ass like Dena Marie Conchek?"

"Her name's Xenakis now."

"Right, Xenakis, because she's married. She's crazy and married. And you're married. And you must be crazy, too, or you wouldn't have gotten within a mile of that loon on legs."

"How'd you find out?"

"How do you think? The same way everyone else in town is finding out. That stupid bitch is telling everyone she checks out down at the grocery that the two of you are getting married."

"Married?" I rubbed my temples. "I should have my head examined."

"You'll get no argument from me, junior. You need to break it off, now."

"I will. I will. Right away. It's done."

I didn't. I couldn't. I still loved her. We met two more times. I told her that she had to quit talking or it would sink both of us. She promised she would, but I knew it wasn't her nature. Two days after our last meeting, Allison walked into my office, calm as can be, and asked, "Are you screwing Dena Marie Xenakis? Don't lie to me, Fran."

I thought my face was going to combust. I lied. I denied it—looked her square in the eye and lied my ass off. I said I was friends with Dena Marie, and that she had always been in love with me and she was devastated when we had gotten married and she had never gotten over it and she was always pleading with me to get a divorce and marry her but I would never, ever be unfaithful. It was a lie of titanic proportions, but I took psychology courses at the FBI Academy and I know how to relax under intense questioning. Allison got upset, but I know in her heart she believed me. It's not something of which I'm particularly proud, and I haven't seen Dena Marie since.

CHAPTER THREE
JOHNNY EARL

I did my time in several different prisons, but the majority of it was spent in the federal penitentiary in Terre Haute, Indiana. My first roommate was an accountant who had gotten busted in an interstate insurance scam that bilked the life savings out of a couple hundred elderly people. After he was released, I had a single for about a month before two guards showed up at my cell with the biggest son of a bitch I had ever seen in my life. He was six foot six, with a flattop, a scar running from the corner of his left eye to the bottom of his jawbone, a protruding brow, and deep-set eyes. His head was made up entirely of right angles and was the size of a toaster oven. His jawbone protruded on each side like a pair of giant fish gills, and I swear I could have grabbed hold of it and done chin-ups. He was carrying his bed sheets in his massive hands.

After you're in the penitentiary for a while, you get a feeling for which inmates are bluster and which ones could really hurt you. It took me about two seconds to determine that this monster fell into the latter category. If I had hit him in the head with a baseball bat, I don't think it would have fazed him in the least.

No sooner had he walked into the cell than he said to me, "Do you cater to Jews and niggers?"

And I said, as though I had a mouthful of dog piss, "Cater to Jews and niggers? Not in this lifetime."

One of the guards, a black man named Oscar Davenport, who I liked, turned and glared at me, his lip curling in one corner. I was sorry to upset Oscar with that kind of talk, but I didn't have to share a cell with him. I had to share one with this Cro-Magnon, and I didn't want to get off on the wrong foot.

He smiled, revealing a gold-capped tooth on a lower incisor, and said, "Excellent." He reached out to shake my hand, and it felt like I had put it inside a first baseman's mitt. He had hands like hams, with cracked and rough knuckles that looked as though they could do a lot of damage. "I don't hanker to live with no Jew- or nigger-lover." Then he pointed at my lower bunk and said, "You're sittin' on my bed." In one quick swipe, I stripped off the sheets and then set up residence upstairs.

For the record, I don't have anything against blacks or Jews. I spewed some venom after Andre Edwards knocked out my teeth, but I'm pretty much a live-and-let-live kind of guy. But here's the thing: When you get to prison, they don't care that you once tripled off of Nolan Ryan or how many touchdowns you scored in high school. Every other prisoner in the place looks at you and thinks, "How can I take advantage of this sumbitch?" When I got to prison, I was scared witless. I also was bald, so the instant I walked through the doors I was singled out as a skinhead, and every black guy in the place put a target on my back. I had to pick a side, and I certainly didn't fit in with the brothers, so I picked the white supremacists.

My new bunkie's name was Alaric Himmler, which I'm sure wasn't the name his mother had given him, but I never questioned him about it. He said Alaric meant "ruler of all" in German, or something like that, and it was a sign that he was destined to be the leader of a new and great country.

I said, "Uh-huh. Got one in mind?"

He claimed to be a general in the army of the New Order of the Third Reich, which the best I could tell consisted of a bunch of similar-minded nut jobs roaming the wilds of Utah or Idaho or Montana in a "country" that he called the Aryan Republic of New Germania. Not only was he the supreme commander of the army, he also was the president of the Aryan Republic of New Germania. "Where exactly is New Germania?" I asked.

"The *Aryan Republic* of New Germania," he corrected me.

"Sorry," I said. "Where is the Aryan Republic of New Germania?"

He put an index finger the size of a kielbasa to his lips. "I can't tell you. It would put your life in danger," he whispered.

"Thanks," I whispered back, thinking that he didn't know for sure, either.

Because he considered himself a citizen of his own country, the general believed that his imprisonment was a violation of international law. Some days he claimed to be a political prisoner, and other days he recited violations of the Geneva Convention because he was a prisoner of war. His imprisonment actually had something to do with the possession and transportation of illegal firearms, which I heard were rocket launchers, but the general was always vague on the details. He said he couldn't discuss issues of state because he was sure a listening device had been implanted in the cell and agents of the federal government of the United States were eavesdropping.

Over time, the general, as he demanded that he be addressed, took a liking to me. For this, I was grateful, because absolutely nobody fucked with him, and that gave me a degree of protection. When Andre Edwards smacked me with the pipe, for no damn reason other than he didn't like my looks, the general beat him within an inch of his sorry life. In return, all I had to do was enthusiastically agree with every word he uttered about blacks, Jews, Hitler, and Germany. And I did. I agreed with every single word, and with great gusto.

Six months before my release, the general grabbed me by my shoulders and said, "You have been very faithful to me."

I blinked, having no idea what he was talking about, and said, "You're welcome."

"I am rewarding you with a position of power in the New Order of the Third Reich."

I was thinking, *Oh, sweet mother of Christ, this is a fucking nightmare.* But I said, "I'm honored, General."

He smiled and said, "You are hereby inducted into the army of the New Order of the Third Reich and granted the rank of colonel. You will report directly to me."

I didn't know what else to do, so I saluted him and said, "Thank you, sir. That is a great honor." But I was thinking, *I've got to get the fuck out of here.*

He shared his belief that my genes would make an excellent addition to the gene pool of the Aryan Republic of New Germania. Actually, what he said was, "You will make excellent breeding stock. It's critical that we preserve the white race." He draped a heavy arm around my shoulder and said, "Two of my wives have sisters who will make fine wives for you. Are you good with that?"

"Two wives, you say?"

He grinned and arched his brows. "Sounds good, doesn't it?"

To give you a better idea of the type of genius I was dealing with, the general was walking past the chapel one day and overheard Marshall Goldman conversing with a rabbi in Yiddish. Marshall was a scrawny little guy who took an Internal Revenue Service agent hostage and drove her across six states trying to explain why it had been his constitutional right not to pay taxes for seven consecutive years. The general cornered Marshall a few days after overhearing the conversation, used a massive hand to pin him against a wall by his neck, and said, "I want you to teach me to talk German."

"I don't speak German," Marshall said.

The general squeezed up under Marshall's chin, lifting him off the ground. "Don't lie to me, Jew boy, I heard you talkin' to that preacher of yours the other day in German."

The general was cutting off Marshall's air, but he eked out, "You're right. I'm sorry I lied. It was German. I'd be happy to teach you."

Marshall began teaching the general Yiddish; the general believed he was learning German. At one point, Marshall had the general saying, "*Ich bin a shtum tuches un,*" which the general believed to be the German phrase, "I am a man of destiny," but was actually Yiddish for "I am a flaming dumb ass." The general also learned, "*Ich hob de klenster poz in dem alvelt,*" which he believed to be German for "Our people will someday rule the world," but was actually Yiddish for "I have the smallest pecker in the universe."

"You realize, of course, that he will kill you if he ever figures out what you're doing," I said to Marshall.

"Oh, for sure," Marshall said. "But in the meantime it is so damn much fun."

In the months before my release, I was charting out a plan that would make me only a vapor trail by the time the general was released. I was receiving counseling from a prison minister, the Reverend Wilfred A. Lewis. Although it was his job to help prepare me for my return to society, when he questioned me about my past and future plans, he acted disinterested. Under a pair of untamed eyebrows, I'd often catch him staring into space for long moments at a time.

During one of our meetings, the Reverend Lewis looked at some notes scrawled on a legal pad and said, "In our last meeting, you said you wanted to start your own excavation business. Is that still the case?"

"It is," I said.

"Have you ever run your own business?" he asked, running his fingers tiredly through his thinning, greasy hair.

I grinned and said, "I sold about two million dollars' worth of cocaine the year before I got busted. Does that count?"

He gave me an icy stare down the barrel of his beaked nose, from which I gathered that drug dealing didn't count, at least not with Reverend Wilfred A. Lewis. "How will you start the business? It will take money."

"I was able to stash a little cash before I got arrested."

"How much?"

"Why do you want to know that?"

"Just curious."

"Enough to get an excavation business started."

"That will take a lot of money, will it not?"

I shrugged.

"Is this drug money?" he pressed.

"Some of it, maybe . . ."

"Put your faith in me, son. How much money are we talking about?"

I told him, but not because I wanted to cleanse my soul or relieve any guilt. You know why I told him? Well, for one thing, because I'm a damned idiot. But mostly because I wanted to brag about how much money I had stashed. I had never told anyone about the cash, because the guys in prison would slit your throat for fifteen cents. Since he was a preacher, I assumed it was like talking to a lawyer: he wouldn't repeat it. "Four hundred and seventy-two thousand dollars," I proudly announced.

He didn't flinch. "That's a lot of money," he said calmly.

"Yes it is. I was a good drug dealer."

"You should donate that to a worthy cause and start fresh."

I smiled. "You're kidding, of course."

"I most certainly am not. It's tainted. It's drug money. Dirty money. Give it away. Start your new life with money unsoiled by your criminal past."

I nodded and said, "Okay, I'll give that some thought." A nano-second later I was done thinking; there was no way in hell that was happening.

Two hours later, the general stormed into our cell and said, "Colonel, what's this I hear about you having four hundred and seventy-two thousand dollars stashed away?"

I swallowed and made a mental note to strangle the preacher. "Is that important?"

"Of course it's important. As a colonel in the New Order of the Third Reich, you are obligated to contribute all personal goods and money to the cause."

"I don't recall seeing that in the enlistment papers."

He laughed and whispered, "That kind of money will go a long way toward the purchase of weapons, fortifications, and air defense."

"And you'll get it, General, every last penny."

He grinned and said, "Excellent." He slapped me on the back and went off to lunch; I went looking for Lewis. "Hey, goddammit, what are you doing telling another convict about my money? You're a preacher; aren't you supposed to keep that kind of stuff to yourself?"

"Ordinarily," he said. "But I believe in the cause. When the general gets out, I'm going with him to the Aryan Republic of New Germania to be chaplain of the state."

"You realize, of course, there is no such place as the Aryan Republic of New Germania?"

"Not yet, but there will be."

I stormed off, kicking myself in the ass for telling the chaplain of the state about the money. That bastard was the first person I ever told, and damned if it didn't come back and bite me in the ass. The good pastor was a white supremacist.

A month before I was to be released, the general sat me down in the cell and ordered me to roll a sheet of paper into my manual typewriter. "You type fast. I'm going to tell you my manifesto. You type it down." As always when dealing with this beast of a human being, I did as he ordered. He dictated and I typed. It made me nervous just to have those words spilling forth from my fingers. He called his manifesto "Operation Adolph Lives." He was going to assassinate the president, his cabinet, and every member of the US Congress. He would then declare war on the United States. He planned to poison the water supply in Washington, DC, and overtake the military. He would lynch every black man in the country. He would resurrect the concentration camps of Germany and enslave the Jews. What Jews he couldn't work to death, he would gas. He would become president for life of the Aryan Republic of New Germania, which would occupy all of the current United States. At times, he would stop and say, "Read that back to me." Then he would ask, "What do you think?"

"Brilliant," I would say. Or, "You are a born leader, General," all the while thinking of how far I could be from the prison by the time he was released.

He dictated his plans in painful detail. Dictated until my fingers cramped. Dictated such vile, hateful venom that I hated that my grandmother's Underwood was being used for such a purpose. Dictated so that I had to change my ribbon twice. It was so terrifying that I pinched the clean sheets of typing paper with my fingernails so as to not leave fingerprints. After each page was typed, he would rip it from my typewriter and read it. As he read, I would carefully reload the Underwood and get ready for more details on the overthrow of the country.

After nearly four days, he handed me three sheets of notebook paper, on which were scrawled the names of men and the cities in which they lived. "These are my compatriots across the country," he said. "They are my loyal followers. When the time is right, they will form the heart of the New Order of the Third Reich. Type 'em up."

I did, alphabetically, and in the middle of the "D" list I added a name of my own—*Daubner, Rayce; Steubenville, Ohio*. Someday, hopefully, the general would be arrested on the front lawn of the White House with a rocket launcher. When they looked through his belongings, Daubner's name would be found as an associate. Oh, wouldn't that be delightful?

The general took the stack of papers—it must have been sixty pages, single-spaced—and slipped them to the preacher for safe-keeping. "When I get out and return to the Aryan Republic of New Germania, I will hold a meeting of my top colonels. That's when our plans will be revealed and Operation Adolph Lives will begin."

I hated the way he called them "our plans."

As I was leaving the cell the day of my release, the general said, "Now, Colonel, you stay in touch. I'll be out in about six weeks."

I saluted and said, "Oh, I will, General. You can count on me."

My parents drove to Terre Haute and picked me up. It was Monday, July 10, 1989. I hadn't seen my folks in three years; they had aged dramatically while I was in prison, which was largely my fault. I hoped they lived long enough to see me right the ship. I'm humiliated by my past, but, mostly, I'm sorry about the pain that I caused my parents. They were so proud and thought they had raised a future major-league-baseball player. Instead, they had raised a career minor leaguer and a convicted drug dealer. Not long after my conviction, they bought a house in Dunedin, Florida. They said they wanted to escape the cold weather, but I think they wanted to escape the embarrassment.

Mom was crying when the final set of steel doors swung open and I walked into the foyer. I had a gym bag in one hand and my Underwood in the other. Perhaps, I thought, I would have Dad pull off the road near a bridge so I could pitch the Underwood into a river: it was sullied by the words of the manifesto, and if the general's hateful piece of trash was ever made public, I wanted no association with it. The cocaine conviction was bad enough; I didn't need a treason charge, too.

As I climbed into the backseat of the Buick, I spotted a bag from Mosblack's Hobby Shop. In it were four car models, a set of model paint, a tube of glue, and a hobby knife. "This is thoughtful," I said. Mom turned and smiled; I knew it was her idea. I slumped in the backseat on the way back to Steubenville, chatting easily with the folks. I was certainly glad to be out of prison but also nervous about going back home. I was a disappointment not only to my parents but also to the entire community. All I wanted to do was keep a low profile and avoid adding to my humiliation by running into people who had known me when I was the great Johnny Earl of the Steubenville Big Red.

Mom said we were going to stay with Aunt Connie on Pleasant Heights. Aunt Connie had said I was welcome to stay in the garage apartment behind her house, rent free, until I got my feet on the ground. I didn't tell Mom that I didn't plan to be in Steubenville long enough to get my feet on the ground. My plan was to visit with the folks for a few days until they headed back to Florida, then get my cash and put Steubenville, Ohio, in my rearview mirror before the general came looking for me.

Of course, my luck ran true to form and things began going awry two minutes after I got back to Jefferson County. We stopped at the Town & Country Market outside of Wintersville on the way home because Mom wanted to make city chicken and mashed potatoes for my return.

"You want to come in?" she asked as we pulled into the parking lot.

"I'll just wait in the car," I said. I took one of the models out of the bag and sliced open the cellophane wrapper with the hobby knife. Finally, I was starting to feel free. The window was down and the air fresh; the sights were familiar. Unfortunately, the first voice I heard was a familiar one, too.

"Free at last, free at last. Thank God almighty, he's free at last." Placing both hands on the side of the Buick and leaning toward the open window was Rayce Daubner. I looked up briefly, then back to my model. "Why, just the other day, I was thinking..."

"There's a rarity," I said.

He squinted, and his nostrils flared. "I was thinking it was 'bout time for ol' John-eeee Earl to be getting out of prison."

I nodded. "I've been thinking, too, Rayce. Thinking about how much I'd like to see this hobby knife buried in one of your eyes."

"You don't have the balls. You never did."

He was carrying a six-pack of beer in a cardboard carton. He leaned down and put both palms on his knees, the beer carton dangling from the fingers of his right hand. "I know you just got out, but do you think you can score me some coke?" He started laughing. I pulled on the door handle and pushed out with all I had, catching him right across the bridge of the nose with the top of the door. He flew backward and landed on his ass, and beer bottles went flying, sending frothy explosions and amber glass skittering across the asphalt. As I hopped out of the car and started toward him, a Jefferson County Sheriff's cruiser pulled into the lot. I was fresh out of prison, with a hobby knife in my hand, and the guy who had set me up was sprawled on the asphalt, bleeding from a gash across his nose.

Chief Deputy Toots Majowski got out of the car, pinching his temples with one hand like he was fighting off a migraine. "What the hell's going on here?"

"I accidentally opened the door into Rayce's nose," I said, slipping the knife into my pocket.

"Accidentally?" Majowski asked.

"We were talking, and a bee flew into the car and I panicked. I'm allergic to bees."

Rayce stood, wobbled, and blinked me into focus. "You're going to be sorry, Hollywood," Rayce said, walking past me toward his car, dabbing at the cut with the sleeve of his T-shirt.

That was the last time I ever saw that worthless piece of shit alive. He got into his car, swearing, blood dripping down his face. He peeled out of the parking lot. Majowski shook his head and said, "Welcome home, Johnny. Good to see you. Try to keep your ass out of trouble."

CHAPTER FOUR
ALLISON ROBERSON

My great-aunt Mae had breath that smelled like her insides were rotting away, and wild, white whiskers that spiraled away from her upper lip and chin. Yet she insisted on greeting me by wrapping her spindly fingers around my head, the fingernails of her thumbs pressing against my cheeks. She would then pucker up and deliver a foul kiss right on my lips.

For my fourteenth birthday, she gave me a diary. By the looks of the yellowed box that held the diary, I suspected that she had regifted something that had been in her attic for twenty years. But I actually liked the diary, which had a section in the front with such categories as *My favorite foods are:* . . . , *The names of my pets are:* . . . , and *When I grow up, I want to be:* . . . . Under this last category, I wrote that I wanted to be a movie star, a famous singer, a veterinarian, a model, and married to Mark Lindsay, who was the lead singer of Paul Revere & the Raiders.

When I was sixteen, our English teacher, Mrs. Graeter, had us compose a term paper on our future plans. I wrote that I wanted to be a pediatrician and, perhaps, an English teacher. I didn't really want to be an English teacher, but I thought that might ingratiate me to Mrs. Graeter. I made no mention of wanting to be a movie star or a singer or of wishing to marry Mark Lindsay. Although I still harbored those dreams, under no circumstances would I commit them to paper and risk the possibility of having it read to the entire class.

By the time I was eighteen and a senior, our guidance counselor, Mr. Jankowski, pulled me into his office and asked me what I wanted to do with the rest of my life. It was a heavy question. I told him that maybe I wanted to be a secretary or a dental hygienist or a dietitian. I was clueless, but I needed to give him some answers so he could fill out my file, feel as though he had done his job, and more importantly, get off my back.

I am the first to admit that I have never been the most focused or most directed person in the world. However, I can tell you with absolute certainty that not in my diary, not in my term paper for Mrs. Graeter, not in my conversation with Mr. Jankowski, and otherwise never in my life did I say that my dream job was to be the chief dispatcher for the Jefferson County Sheriff's Department. Yet, at age thirty-five, that is exactly where I find myself, seated in a room of blaring scanners and squawking police radios, while my ass grows daily, straining against the seams of the hideous, department-issued gray slacks with navy and gold piping. I never had great aspirations, yet it pains me to admit that I am without talent and possess not one quality that would qualify me for anything more than the position I currently hold.

The building that houses the administrative offices of the Jefferson County Sheriff's Department, on Market Street, was built in 1898, just as the steel and mining industries were hitting a peak that would last for the next seven decades. It's a three-story, Victorian-style building constructed solidly of red bricks that were made at the Steubenville Brick and Tile Company, just a quarter mile away. It was built to house both prisoners and the county's chief law enforcement officer and family. In days long past, the jail occupied the first floor of the building, while the sheriff and his family lived on the upper two floors, though prisoners and family alike used the same front door and it was the job of the sheriff's wife to cook meals for the prisoners. A separate jail was constructed in 1961, and the original building was converted to house the radio room, the detective bureau, and administrative offices.

At least once a day, twice if things are slow, I escape to the third floor of the sheriff's office where an alcove hides a recessed porch behind a widow's walk. I go out to the alcove to smoke a cigarette in peace, free of the mayhem of the office. Prisoners are shuttled through the office en route from their jail cells to the courthouse, and I am sick of seeing unkempt men in jumpsuits and handcuffs who reek of urine, vomit, and alcohol. They leer at me, flipping a nervous trigger that makes me crazy for a cigarette. My children hate that I smoke, and I do my best to hide it from them, but I have no intention of stopping. It's a release for the edgy case of nerves I've developed since moving to this godforsaken town. The alcove provides a refuge where I can unwind for a few minutes and enjoy a smoke, hidden from view of the street, and scan the patchwork of rooftops that dot the hillsides that slope toward the Ohio River.

Steubenville is a dingy, gray city that is dying a slow death. On many mornings, the fog rolls up out of the Ohio River Valley, covering the city until all that is visible is the yellow haze of the streetlights. From the far edge of Steubenville—Pottery Row, as it is still called—comes the occasional whistle of a passing freight train. Across the river in West Virginia, the Weirton Steel Corporation kicks out sooty, black smoke that hangs throughout the valley. Even on cloudless days, Steubenville is a gray lady. Its old homes, built into the steep hillsides at a time when the town boomed and steel and coal were twin kings, now sag under their own weight, stripped by the acrid smoke and bleached by years of neglect.

Along Market Street are the brick buildings that once housed the heart of a vibrant business district. There were theaters, five-and-dimes, bakeries, grocery and butcher shops, and clothing stores jammed together all along the avenue. Now, people drive to the mall in St. Clairsville or Pittsburgh, and the buildings along Market Street are vacant or house secondhand clothing stores or craft shops that open only on weekends.

I first visited Steubenville a week after Fran and I were engaged. We flew in to Pittsburgh and rented a car. By the time we drove up windy Sinclair Avenue and got to his boyhood home off of Lover's Lane, I was so sick that I made him stop the car so I could throw up in a ditch before meeting my future in-laws. We spent three days in Steubenville; I couldn't wait to leave. The town was depressing and dirty, and everyone spoke with a hillbilly twang and called us "yunz guys." It's a place where they keep their chipped-chopped ham in the icebox, where they drive "Chivies," and where every plant with a petal is a "flahr" and every plant with a thorn is a "jaggerbush." It was like living in the lyrics of a bad country song. I couldn't believe that someone as articulate as my future husband, Francis Roberson, had grown up in the Ohio River Valley. Never did I dream that I would someday be living here. In fact, had I any idea that we would someday come back here to live, I would have dumped Fran and run like my hair was on fire. I would have gone back to Washington and married Alfred Vincenzio, no questions asked.

I'm a city girl, having grown up in a Baltimore suburb. My mother was a stay-at-home mom, and my dad worked for the US State Department. Dad was only a mid-level dignitary, so we never hosted kings or presidents, but every undersecretary of agriculture from every Third World country you can name came to dinner at my parents' home. They were always little dark men with bowling-ball heads, thick accents, impeccable manners, and obedient wives. Many evenings when I would rather be hanging out with my friends, I had to sit at the table, listening to accented prattling on the best methods of harvesting sugar beets.

After graduating high school with no clear direction, I enrolled at Towson State University as a history major. I have no idea where that motivation came from, but it didn't last long. Towson gave me the boot after a year of mediocre attendance and worse grades. I enrolled at community college for two years, accumulating a jumble of credits in no particular area. Finally, my father said he wasn't spending another dime on my education unless I enrolled in what he called a "real college" and began working diligently toward a degree. I told him that I didn't have much interest in college, real or pretend, and so he pulled a few strings and got me a job as a secretary at the FBI Training Academy in Quantico, Virginia. That's where I met Fran.

I noticed him the first time he walked past my office. He was handsome and had the arrogant swagger of every rookie FBI agent in the academy. It was a couple of days before he summoned up the courage to stop in and introduce himself. He was friendly and said that he was just completing his FBI training, but the FBI was a temporary job until he could figure out how to become president of the United States.

I laughed politely.

"I'm serious," he said.

I laughed harder. "Sorry," I said, still unsure whether he was serious. After a few minutes of idle chatter, I said, "Well, Mr. President, I have work to do."

He left, but he stopped by the next day and asked me out. "I'm not sure if I'm allowed to ask out other FBI employees," he said.

"It's totally against the rules," I said. I knew that because I had been secretly dating one of Fran's classmates, Alfred Vincenzio. I frowned and said, seriously, "I'm afraid I'm going to have to report you."

His eyes widened and he started to sputter, but I couldn't hold a straight face. When he realized the bluff, he grinned and said, "You got me."

After one date with Fran, I broke off my relationship with Alfred, who was enraged. I don't think he liked me all that much, but it was a slight to his Italian masculinity that he would get bumped for Fran Roberson. Alfred never spoke to me again, and things became very cool between him and Fran.

We got engaged a year to the day after our first date. We were married in a small ceremony at the United Methodist Church that I had attended since I was a child. We lived in Atlanta, Dallas, and Minneapolis over the next eight years as Fran began his climb up the ranks of the FBI, becoming a star in the bureau's white-collar crime division. He appeared to have a bright future in the agency, though he never quit talking about the presidency. He was always reading self-help and motivational books, and at the most inopportune times he would call me to his den and read me some stupid passage and ask, "What does that mean to you?"

"It means you have too much time on your hands, Francis," I finally told him. "While you're sitting there reading, I'm trying to get dinner ready, check homework, and clean the wax out of Bennie's ears."

"You can't get to the White House without being able to speak inspirationally," he answered.

"You can't get to the White House by reading a book, either," I countered. After a while, I just ignored his talk. We had two beautiful boys, Fran had a great career, and I was very happy in Minneapolis. I humored his talk about the presidency, but I couldn't imagine any scenario, any bizarre set of circumstances, that would place Francis Roberson on the path to the Oval Office.

Then that dunderhead Beaumont T. Bonecutter became the first sheriff in the corrupt history of Jefferson County, Ohio, to become the target of a federal investigation for taking kickbacks from drug dealers.

It was no secret in the valley that lawmen took payoffs from the mob to turn a blind eye to their gambling and prostitution operations. But as the steel mills and coal mines began losing purchase in the valley, people moved away in search of work. Without the steelworkers and coal miners, organized crime lost its loyal customer base and the traditional vices of gambling and prostitution disappeared. Drugs became more prevalent and, to offset their lost gambling and prostitution revenue streams, lawmen began accepting payoffs from small-time drug dealers.

Thus, Jefferson County wasn't nearly as lucrative for dishonest sheriffs as it had once been. This was a major disappointment for Beaumont T. Bonecutter, who had run for sheriff believing he would become rich from the illegal payoffs. When he found out how meager the payoffs were, he began squeezing the drug dealers for more money.

Things began to unravel for Bonecutter when he arrested a marijuana dealer named Chinky Leonard for possession of drugs with intent to distribute. The arrest occurred after Chinky could no longer manage the exorbitant payoffs that the sheriff demanded. Chinky had anticipated that such a day would come, and he had surreptitiously taped several telephone conversations with Bonecutter. After the arrest, Chinky handed his lawyer a micro tape of the telephone conversations. In one of those conversations, Bonecutter threatened to castrate Chinky if the payoffs didn't increase. Two weeks later, the headline in the *Herald-Star* read:

Bonecutter Target of Federal Probe
for Accepting Illegal Drug Payoffs

Despite the sheriff's bluster about a witch hunt, he crumbled under the pressure of the federal investigation. He developed a mysterious illness—some type of rare heart, kidney, and prostate disease that he invented—and resigned. That night, I got the phone call from Fran's father. We chatted for a few moments, exchanging pleasantries, before I handed the phone to Fran. This was followed by my husband saying, "Really . . . That's interesting . . . No kidding . . . That's great . . . Yeah, sure I'm interested . . ." He looked over at me, swallowed, and said, "Of course, I need to talk it over with Allison."

At that moment, I instinctively knew that I would soon be living in Steubenville, Ohio. A week after Bonecutter resigned, the three Democratic commissioners appointed Fran the interim sheriff. You would have thought the Messiah himself was returning to Steubenville. Fran Roberson, the former quarterback of the Steubenville Big Red, Ed and Francine's boy, who had graduated with honors from Bethany College and went on to become an agent of the Federal Bureau of Investigation, was coming back to Jefferson County to straighten up the mess left by that damn Republican, Beaumont T. Bonecutter.

Now, just for the record, Francis Delano Roberson leans somewhere to the right of Attila the Hun and was no more a Democrat than I was the Queen of Sheba, but he became one the minute he got the call from his dad. Edgar Roberson was a Roosevelt Democrat—thus Francis's middle name of Delano—a former union steward at the steel mill, and the undisputed leader of the Jefferson County Democratic Party since 1965. Fran had never voted for a Democrat in his life. Once we moved back, he told people that he was the best kind of Democrat— "one that had been a Republican, but had seen the light and the error of his ways." He could barely say it with a straight face.

Fran was the appointed sheriff for one year before running for the position in his first election. He was unopposed in the primary and then soundly thrashed the Republican nominee, a township constable who was little more than a sacrificial lamb. The landslide victory reignited his talk of becoming president of the United States. I said, "Francis, I love you with all my heart, but you've just been elected sheriff of a backwater Ohio county by defeating an opponent with a harelip and an eighth-grade education. Don't you think it's a little early to be talking about the presidency?"

"It's a step, my dear, it's a step." Fran explained that his father had negotiated a deal for him. In exchange for serving two terms as sheriff, the Jefferson County Democratic Party had promised to support him in a run for the US Congress on a platform of returning jobs and prosperity to the Ohio River Valley. If this proved successful, the party also would back him for a bid for governor. "And you know, Allison, it's a short leap from the governor's mansion to the White House," Fran said.

Unfortunately, I wasn't the only one to whom he told this. Behind his back, his deputies called him "Mr. President" and "Honest Abe." I pleaded with him not to tell anyone else about his political aspirations.

"Why not?" he asked.

"Fran, people get suspicious of those with great ambition," I said.

He nodded and said, "Okay. Yeah, you're right."

In reality, I just didn't want people making fun of him.

I love my husband. He is mostly loyal—there was one indiscretion of which I know—and a dear man. He is a good provider, he doesn't drink to excess, he doesn't take drugs, and, to the best of my knowledge, he has never taken a bribe or a kickback. And he treats me like I *am* the Queen of Sheba. But he scares me because he thinks he's a lot smarter than he is. When I first took Fran home, my dad said, "Nice boy, but he's got more ambition than brains, and that's a very dangerous combination." That's true. Fran gets careless because he thinks he's smarter than everyone else. This is the attribute that's going to get him in a peck of trouble someday.

Shortly after we moved to Steubenville, I was bemoaning the fact that our youngest boy would be heading off to kindergarten in the fall and I would have nothing to do. Fran said, "How would you like to go back to work?"

"I'd love to. Do you know of something?"

"In fact, I do. You're going to be my chief dispatcher."

"You can't do that," I protested. "That's nepotism."

"Nepotism is a long-standing tradition in Jefferson County. You're my wife. It's expected that I'll give you a job in the department."

I took the job, and I can tell you the exact time and date that I decided that my days in the synthetic leather chair were numbered. When the revelation came to me, I looked at my watch to note the moment—10:13 a.m. on Tuesday, April 11, 1989. I was taking my morning cigarette break in the alcove, huddled against the back wall, shivering in the morning wind, and avoiding the cold rain that was slashing in from the west. The sky over Steubenville was its usual gray, and the air was pungent with sulfur from the Koppers plant across the river in Follansbee. The events of the previous night had pushed me over the edge. We'd been attending the Daughters of the American Revolution pancake supper in the Presbyterian Church basement when I looked across the room at my husband, a man who for as long as I have known him has had the posture of a Marine, and he was slouching, his belly beginning to protrude over his belt. This man, who used impeccable grammar and corrected our sons' misuse of the English language at every opportunity, was speaking with that cursed Ohio Valley twang, and I swear to Jesus that I heard him say, "Ain't no way I'm gonna stand for that."

Two nights before the pancake dinner, Fran and I had gotten into a horrendous argument—perhaps the worst of our marriage—because I wanted to take the boys out of the Steubenville School District and enroll them at St. Paul Elementary School. "Why in God's name would you take them out of Steubenville?" he asked.

"Oh, I don't know, maybe because it's the academic equivalent of a Nazi death camp?"

"I graduated from Steubenville High School."

"I rest my case."

"Well, they're not transferring, and that's that. I'm the sheriff, for God's sake. How will it look to the voters if my kids aren't in school in the community?"

"I'm glad you're able in good conscience to sacrifice the education of your children in order to further your political aspirations."

This came within a week of a downpour that flooded our basement and we were informed that we would have to jack up our house and rebuild the entire foundation. I cried for two days. It was another disaster in our ordeal to rehabilitate the old Kensington house. Shortly after we moved back to Steubenville, we bought the grand structure at the crest of Church Hill. It's three floors of red brick with six bedrooms and a ballroom on the top floor. By the time we bought it, the old place had been sectioned off and converted to apartments and allowed to fall into disrepair. At first, I romanticized about how wonderful it would be to return the house to its former splendor. I was a damn fool.

We've replaced the roof, front porch, back porch, eaves, windows, wiring, light fixtures, plumbing, doors, and walls. We've stripped to the studs and remodeled the entire kitchen and the three bathrooms. We've endured tens of thousands of dollars in cost overruns, hundreds of excuses from incompetent contractors, and invasions of bats, rats, sparrows, raccoons, mice, mud daubers, termites, chipmunks, squirrels, and black snakes. Dirt, drywall dust, sawdust, and plaster have taken turns covering my food, hair, and furniture and seeping into my body crevices ever since Dave Delaney and his crew of mouth-breathers entered my house. The dirt and dust were so bad that some days I would blow my nose and find a glob of black goo in my tissue. When longtime Steubenville residents came up to me and said, "Oh, you're doing just a great job fixing up the old Kensington place," I wanted to thank them and then rake them across the teeth with a backhand.

The continual repairs to the house, the arguing over the schools, his posture, and his grating accent all contributed to my decision to get Fran to the United States House of Representatives and get me out of Steubenville. But the real spark was when Fran had an affair with Dena Marie Conchek Androski Xenakis. There was a two-week stretch earlier in the year when he started making excuses and going out in the evening, supposedly to check on his patrols. It seemed unusual but not totally out of character.

Bella Figerelli was my afternoon dispatcher. She had a platinum hairdo held in place with a gallon of hairspray; sharp, harsh features;

and a corrosive voice graveled by forty years of sucking down two packs of non-filtered cigarettes a day. She had been married to four different Jefferson County deputies. Three of those unions had ended in such spectacular divorces that they were still gossip fodder at the Starlighter Bar. One day, she strolled into the radio room, looking more sinister than usual, and leered at me with a little smirk, and said, "So, Princess, I hear there's trouble in Camelot."

I could feel one corner of my lip curl, and I asked, "What are you talking about?" though in my heart I knew she would only confirm my suspicions. Bella didn't like me as much as I didn't like her, and I knew she loved slapping me with bad news.

"Under no circumstances can I be your source. I don't want to lose my job."

"Agreed."

"Say, 'I promise.'"

My jaw tensed. "I promise."

She couldn't wait to blurt it out. "Your husband's screwing Dena Marie Xenakis."

I could not believe my good fortune.

I realize that most women would have been outraged to learn that their husband had been unfaithful. Not me. It was a gift from heaven, and I was so giddy that I could hardly catch my breath. I felt like the luckiest woman in the world. Now, I had Francis Roberson's balls in a death grip, and I planned to twist them until the day he got me out of Steubenville. I had never wanted to move to this godforsaken place, but Frannie wanted to chase his political aspirations, and I had played the dutiful wife. Not anymore. His ass was mine.

I marched right into his office, closed the door, and asked, in an extremely civil tone, "Are you screwing Dena Marie Xenakis? Don't lie to me, Fran."

His face went ashen. Then, with all the phony indignation he could muster, he stuttered, "What? No, no, of course not. That's ridiculous. Where did you hear that?"

He would make a terrible president, because he's such a bad liar. "It had better stop, Francis, and I mean today. I'm taking the car and going home. I'm not hanging around here and waiting for another lie to come out of your mouth."

I walked out of the office, got in my car, and drove to the A&P, where Dena Marie was a checkout clerk. She was snapping her chewing gum and looking bored, pretending not to see me coming. I leaned over the counter, put my nose within two inches of hers, and said, "If you ever see my husband again, I'm going to call Children Services and tell them you're an unfit mother and you neglect your kids."

She looked bored with the confrontation. I doubt it was the first time she had been in that type of situation. "I don't know what you're talking about. I'm a married woman. And I'm a good mother, too. They won't—"

"You're missing the point, chicky. I don't give a shit if it's true or not. I'm the sheriff's wife, and by God they'll listen to me, and I'll have them all over your ass. I'll make sure it gets in the newspapers, too. Stay away from my husband."

When I finally got home, I locked the door and danced. Now, I had a legitimate reason to make his life miserable. It was too lovely, too delightful. He was going to stand up straight and use proper grammar. He was going to run for Congress, and so help me Jesus, he was going to get me the hell out of Steubenville.

Thus, at ten thirteen that morning, while standing in the alcove and pulling on a cigarette, I began planning our escape. I vowed to lose some weight, get my teeth straightened, and quit smoking. Ultimately, I would resign as the chief dispatcher, too, because I would need the time to organize my husband's campaign for Congress. And after I had gotten him elected to Congress, I would start on his campaign for governor. I must admit that the idea of becoming Ohio's first lady was growing on me. Did I think he was going to be president of the United States? No, of course not. But governor? That seemed doable. For the first time in my adult life, I had direction and purpose. I was getting the hell out of Jefferson County.

CHAPTER FIVE
JOHNNY EARL

It was a beautiful day in the Ohio River Valley. The blue sky stretched across the windshield of my battered Camaro, the sun warming my face. It was good to be alive and free. I had spent the day alone, cruising around and thinking of black widow spiders. Following the mating ritual, female black widow spiders frequently devour their mate. You would think that over the millions of years that black widows have scurried over the earth, the males would wise up. Perhaps they understand this and consider being consumed alive an acceptable exchange for sex, but I doubt it. The natural calling is simply so overwhelming that the male black widow simply cannot control its urges.

Dena Marie was my female black widow. I wanted desperately to climb into her web. The only real difference between me and a male black widow is that if I did have sex with her, I would *want* someone to kill me.

It had been more than eight years since I'd had sex with a woman. Okay, just for the record, it had been more than eight years since I'd had sex with *anyone*. Things never got that bad in prison. There were many times, however, when the mental vision of Dena Marie helped get me through the night. I didn't crave her because I was in love with her. I craved her because she was close and because I knew if I made the first move she would be readily available. Availability is very important to someone who hasn't been with a woman in more than eight years.

I would not, under any circumstances, go see her, but I secretly hoped—and feared—that she would come visit me in Aunt Connie's garage apartment and I would bed her on the inflatable mattress. I fantasized about sliding between her thighs, and that mental image gave me an erection harder than the bars of my prison cell. My dad used to tell me, "Be careful in life, because God gave you a penis and a brain, but not enough blood to operate them both at the same time."

It was time to say good-bye forever to Steubenville. I would slip out of town weeks ahead of the crazy behemoth of a white supremacist who wanted my money and to whisk me off to God-knows-where, Montana, and position myself far from any happenstance meetings with Dena Marie.

Once upon a time, I wanted to get out of Steubenville because I believed it couldn't hold me. It was too small for my rising star. I would leave to become a major leaguer, and when I came back they'd have a parade in my honor. I'd sit in the back of an open convertible, and it would pass a baseball-shaped sign that read, *Hometown of Johnny Earl—Major League Baseball Star.*

I knew what a disappointment I had been to my parents, my friends, and myself. I had been the guy everyone looked up to. Now, I was the guy people pointed at and said to each other, "There's what happens when you think the rules don't apply to you." I was embarrassed about that. Even though I hadn't made it in the major leagues, I could have been the guy they pointed to and said, "You should have seen him play ball." I could never have that. No matter what I did with the rest of my life, people were going to walk through the halls of the high school, point to my photo, and say, "Hell of an athlete, but dumber than a post hole. Boy, did he screw up his life." When I was in prison, I received an unsigned letter that read, among other venomous lines, "You should just kill yourself and relieve your parents and all of Steubenville of the embarrassment you have caused us."

It was hurtful but true.

Two days before I planned to leave town, after my folks returned to Florida, I heard Aunt Connie trudging up the outside staircase. She was panting when she opened the door and said, "telephone."

"Who is it?"

"I didn't ask."

It was my old classmate, Jimmy Hinton, who had become the editor of the *Herald-Star*. He wanted to do an interview with me on my time in prison. "Are you kidding me, Jimmy?" I said. "Hell no, I'm not doing an interview."

"A lot of kids could learn from your mistakes, Johnny," he said.

"I don't want them to learn from my mistakes. I'm not sure that *I've* learned from my mistakes, and don't quote me on that, goddammit."

"Well, think about it."

"I don't need to think about it."

"If not an interview, then maybe you could do a first-person column about your life."

"You know, Jimmy, I want to take this opportunity to apologize to you for being a dick with ears and squealing my tires on you that day back when I was eighteen. That was the wrong thing to do. But just so there aren't any hard feelings or misunderstanding, the next sound you're going to hear is me hanging up on you."

CHAPTER SIX
ALLISON ROBERSON

Three months later, my plan was moving forward. I had braces on my teeth, I had lost fifteen pounds—though I still wasn't happy about the dimples in my ass—and I had cut back to about four cigarettes a day. I was still the chief dispatcher, and I planned to hold the job until the end of the year, when Fran announced his candidacy for Congress.

Then one day at work I got a call from a woman in an absolute panic, screaming about a dead body at Jefferson Lake State Park.

"Ma'am, you need to calm down," I said.

"Oh, God, all we wanted to do was have a picnic lunch and there's a body. I think my daughter might have touched it."

"Ma'am, I need you to—"

"My son said, 'Mommy, there's a man sleeping over there in the weeds.' I'm thinking it might be a child molester, so I ran over and my daughter's squatting down beside it, poking at him with a stick."

"Ma'am, how do you know that he isn't sleeping? Or passed out?"

"Because he's riddled with bullet holes and covered with flies!" she screamed. "That's why. Do you think I'm an idiot?"

Jefferson Lake State Park is a nine-hundred-and-forty-five-acre park outside of Richmond in the far western part of the county. The park is several miles off the main road and, frankly, the ideal place to murder someone or dump a body.

"Where are you calling from, ma'am?"

"The convenience store in Richmond."

"Okay, I'm going to send a cruiser out. Stay there, please."

I radioed Fran's chief deputy, Toots Majowski, and sent him to the convenience store. "The lady says she is going to take you to the location of a ten-nineteen," I said, using the police code for a corpse.

I grabbed the phone book and called Minelli's Restaurant. The owner's wife, Millie Minelli, answered the phone. "Millie, this is Allison Roberson. I need to talk to the sheriff, ASAP."

This is going to sound crass, but after making the decision to get Fran elected to Congress, I didn't want him to miss a media opportunity. A murder was big news in Jefferson County. The newspapers from Steubenville and Wheeling would be out, and maybe so would the television stations.

"Roberson here," he said.

"I just sent Toots out to Jefferson Lake State Park. A woman called and said there's a man lying in the weeds, shot to death."

"Suicide?"

"I don't think so. She says there are multiple wounds."

"Okay, I'm heading that way."

In the old days, when the county was full of miners, steelworkers, potters, beer joints, and whores, shootings were a lot more common. Now, they are rare. Most of the calls to the sheriff's department were either nuisance calls—barking dogs or loud music—or domestics. A favorite pastime in rural Jefferson County was getting drunk and going to a Friday night football game. Another favorite pastime was getting drunk and beating the living bejesus out of your wife or girlfriend.

There had been fewer than thirty homicides in the seven years that Fran had been sheriff. The only time I ever saw my husband waver in his belief in justice was during the investigation of one of those homicides. Bella Figerelli called the house one night and said there had been a shooting on Kenton Ridge. "The Goins place?" I heard him ask. He hung up the phone and asked, "Want to ride along?"

Richard Goins was a dump-truck driver in his mid-fifties who was a mean drunk and a regular guest of the Jefferson County Jail. Deputies had made countless trips to his house after getting calls that he was beating his wife, but she was so terrified of him that she never wanted to press charges. When we got to the house that night, the emergency squad had already left. There was nothing they could do for Richard, who was on the floor in the living room with a deer slug in his chest. His little wife, Mildred, a pinch-faced woman with big ears pushing through stringy, dishwater hair, was sitting at a kitchen chair, puffing on a cigarette and sipping a cup of coffee. She was wearing a dirty, flowered housecoat and red slippers with holes in the toes.

"Mildred, why didn't you call us right away?" Fran asked.

"I was afraid that if you got here too quick, you might be able to save him."

Fran frowned and looked at the corpse. "He has a deer slug where his heart used to be, Mildred. Did you think he would survive that?"

"I just wanted to make sure, was all."

"Was he beating on you again?"

She shook her head. "No. But he would have, and I didn't want beat no more."

"Had he been drinking?"

"You knowed him, Sheriff, he was always drinkin'. He'd drink and beat on me, and I didn't want no more of it."

"Was he coming after you or threatening you when you shot him?" Fran asked, giving her every opportunity to claim self-defense.

But, again, she shook her head. "Nope. I didn't give him that chance."

Fran looked at me and then at Toots, who besides being Fran's chief deputy also was his most trusted friend. "Did you take a statement from her?" he asked Toots.

"No. I only got here a few minutes before you."

Fran nodded, rubbed the stubble of his chin for a moment, and said, "Mildred, I want to explain something to you. If you shot your husband because you were afraid for your life—say, he was threatening to kill you or even coming at you—then the prosecutor might look at this as self-defense. But if the shooting was unprovoked, if you killed him because you thought he *might* beat you, that's murder and you will go to prison for a very long time. Do you understand?"

She looked up, at last a faint hint of understanding in her eyes, and said, "Maybe I better talk to a lawyer."

"I think that would be a fine idea," Fran said.

Fran thought this was a noble move, but it made me extremely nervous. Richard Goins was a pathetic and despicable human being. But little Mildred was known to drink and run her mouth, too, and it seemed like a big chance to take. In the end, the case was taken to the grand jury; the shooting was ruled self-defense, and they refused to indict her.

Fran, Toots, and Deputy Phillip Gearhard worked the shooting at Jefferson Lake State Park. It was just after five when Fran left the park. The crime scene search unit from the Stark County Sheriff's Department in Canton was processing the scene, looking for latent clues. The body had been loaded into a commercial ambulance and was heading to the Franklin County Morgue in Columbus for an autopsy. Deputy Gearhard stayed at the scene to assist the crime scene search unit. Fran and Toots were back in the office by five thirty.

I was in the radio room with Bella when Fran and Toots stopped by. Without preamble, he said, "Rayce Daubner."

"Oh my God," Bella said. "Rayce Daubner? I can't believe it. He used to be in my nursery school class at church."

"Church?" Toots snorted, reaching for the coffeepot. "That must have been a hell of a long time ago."

"I just can't believe it," she said. "Rayce Daubner. I'm shocked. Just shocked."

"Why on God's green earth would you be shocked?" Toots asked. "He was a drug dealer, a thug, and a snitch. As potential murder victims go, he'd be a prime candidate. There've got to be a hundred people out there who would like to see him dead."

"It's just a shame. He was such a cute little thing in nursery school."

"That was thirty-some years ago, Bella," Fran said. "He may have been a cute kid, but he turned out to be a miserable adult."

"So what's the plan?" I asked.

"There's no short list of candidates, and we'll need to start talking to some of them tonight," Fran said.

"I'm going to run down to the Star Bar and grab a couple of fried bologna sandwiches," Toots announced. "You want anything, boss?"

"No thanks," Fran said, disappearing into his office.

I pulled a five-dollar bill from my purse and handed it to Toots. "Get him a cheeseburger—mustard, pickles, and onions—and an order of fries." I followed Fran into his office. "You're not hungry. That's a first."

"I'm starving, but my stomach is in such a knot that I don't think I could get anything down." He looked up from his desk, his face not unlike that of a child who has been wrongly accused but has no viable defense. "Rayce was shot with a thirty-eight."

"How do you know?"

"We pulled a slug out of the ground. It was a thirty-eight. He was shot four times—once in the knee, once in the shoulder, once in the chest, and once right in the middle of his forehead."

"Did you find the gun?"

Fran shook his head. "It was not a professional job—I can tell you that much. There was blood everywhere."

"Do you think he was shot with your gun?" I finally asked.

"No way to know. Could have been. Jesus only knows."

Earlier this year, Fran had lost his service revolver. Actually, it was stolen out of his office, and the last person whom he knew to be in the office was none other than Rayce Daubner. Fran wears his revolver in a holster that fits inside the waist of his slacks. He takes it out when he's in the office because it digs into his side when he's working at his desk, which has been more of a problem since he put on twenty pounds. The gun had been in its usual spot on top of the filing cabinet when Daubner came in to talk to Fran—again offering some totally worthless piece of "undercover" information. Fran had to run out of the office after one of his deputies used pepper spray on an unruly juvenile prisoner in the lobby. The boy was writhing on the floor of the lobby, crying and vomiting. His mother and stepfather got into a screaming match with the deputy, who then doused the stepfather with the pepper spray. It was a mess. By the time Fran got everything straightened up and went back to his office a half hour later, Rayce and the revolver were gone.

Daubner had started showing up and hanging around the office about a year before the revolver disappeared. After becoming sheriff, Fran had made it a point to stay away from his old buddies and teammates, particularly Rayce Daubner. The big scandal when we first moved to Jefferson County was that Daubner had set up Johnny Earl to take a fall for cocaine dealing. Then, the scumbag was suddenly spending a lot of time in Fran's office, hanging around, drinking coffee, acting like he owned the damn place.

"That guy is trouble. Why's he hanging around here?" I had asked.

"I'm using him for information."

"What kind of information? He has nothing to offer, and he creeps me out. Keep him out of your office."

But he didn't. Daubner kept coming around, leering and drinking our coffee. When the revolver was stolen, Fran had to report the loss to the State Bureau of Criminal Investigation, and it was a point of personal embarrassment. I had said to Fran, "You know he took it. Why don't you go squeeze his balls?" But he just shrugged and said there was no proof that he stole it. "The gun was in your office. Rayce was in your office. No one else was in your office. Rayce disappeared. Your revolver disappeared. I don't think it's going to take Sherlock Holmes to figure this one out." But he was not going to confront Rayce Daubner, and I dropped the subject.

Fran continued, "Daubner was a snitch for the feds. As soon as they find out that he was killed, they're going to be all over Jefferson County. And all over my ass. They sort of frown on people killing their informants. It's just another opportunity for them to come snooping around. Ever since Bonecutter screwed up, the federal prosecutor has had a hard-on for Jefferson County. He thinks everyone elected here is on the take or dirty."

"Fran, it's just a coincidence that he was shot with a thirty-eight."

"A coincidence is all the feds need to make my life a living hell." He took a breath and sat back in his chair. "There's another fly in the ointment. Daubner had been having an affair with Dena Marie Xenakis."

I nodded and said, "Well, isn't that interesting. She certainly makes the rounds, doesn't she?"

He got up and walked past me. "Don't wait up. I'll be late." Just before he left the room, Fran stopped, turned, and said, "And I *will* be working."

Things now were much more complicated. The feds would certainly investigate the death of one of their informants. Then they would make a potential link between the caliber of bullet used to kill Daubner and Fran's missing service revolver, which wouldn't be all that damning until they discovered that Fran and Daubner had both been sleeping with Dena Marie. God, what an incestuous little town this was. The papers would have a field day with this.

My plan had been going so well when suddenly there was a dead possum, bloated and ready to explode, right in the middle of my road to the governor's mansion.

CHAPTER SEVEN
SHERIFF FRANCIS ROBERSON

As my chief deputy, Toots is head of the detective bureau, which consists of him, Stan Borkowski, and Phillip Gearhard. When I became sheriff, I was experienced in investigating white-collar crimes, but I had virtually no experience in investigating burglaries, robberies, sex crimes, or murders. So Toots took me on dozens of investigations, patiently walking me through each step and repeating his mantra: "No one is immune from a moment of anger or a moment of stupidity." He repeated it over and over so that I would never overlook a potential suspect. If I ever make it to the governor's mansion, I'm going to appoint Toots as my chief of staff. I have never met anyone who is more meticulous and conscientious about his work.

A few hours after we had found Daubner dead, I was at my desk when Toots entered my office. I set my pen on the blotter and stretched. "Everything clear on the search warrant for Daubner's house?" I asked.

He gave me a barely perceptible nod. "Yup. It's good to go." He pushed the warrant across my desk.

Toots wasn't one to rattle easily, but he had been acting distracted the entire afternoon while we investigated Daubner's murder. "Toots, have you got something on your mind?" I asked.

"No."

"Really? Looks to me like maybe you do."

He shrugged. "Maybe a little something."

"Well, spit it out."

"Daubner was hanging around here an awful lot. When I asked you about it, you said you were using him as a source. Remember?"

I nodded. "I remember."

"Sheriff, that worthless excuse for a human being was hanging around here all the time, and I never saw one lick of information come across my desk. If he was giving us anything of value, wouldn't your chief of detectives know about it? So I've got to believe there was more to it than him supplying us with information, if that's what was really going on. Now, Sheriff, if I was a betting man, which I'm not—"

"One of the few vices you've managed to avoid," I interjected.

A tiny grin surfaced from beneath his salt-and-pepper moustache. "Right. But if I *was* a betting man, I'd bet he wasn't here giving you information. I'd bet that he was here squeezing your balls over that little fling you had with Dena Marie Xenakis."

He paused a moment to let the words settle in. I asked, "That's what you'd bet, huh?"

"Yep. That's my bet."

"How do you know that wasn't just a vicious rumor?"

"Because I'm the chief of your detective bureau, for one. I get paid to separate the bullshit from the facts. I've seen the way you look at her. Let's just assume I'm right. Up until you and Dena Marie started fooling around, she and Daubner were having a pretty torrid affair. She'd get off her shift at the grocery, then swing out to his place for a quick romp before the kids got home from school. I heard she cut him off about the same time she took up with you. I heard that Dena Marie was just looking for some action, but Daubner really liked her. If she dumped him for you, that couldn't have set well with him, and he wasn't the kind of guy to take an insult like that lying down. So, like I said, if I was a betting man, I'd bet he was threatening to drop the dime on you."

"How so?"

"Maybe he had pictures of you and her together. Maybe he was going to give them to the guy who ultimately runs against you for Congress."

"You've been giving this some thought, huh, Toots?"

"Look, boss, I'm not about to accuse you of killing Daubner; I like my job too much for that. But what I'm saying is this: If I was one of those federal investigators who are no doubt going to be in here looking at this mess, you'd be at the top of my list of suspects. You know people are going to tell them about you and Dena Marie—she was blabbing it all over town, and they're also going to find out that Daubner had been banging her. You say that your revolver was stolen and he was shot with a thirty-eight. Even those numb-nuts at the FBI can put two and two together. All one of those clowns has to do is tell some reporter that you're being questioned in connection with Daubner's murder and you're screwed, blued, and tattooed. Doesn't matter if it's true or not; your credibility will be in the toilet. Everyone will assume you killed him to shut him up, and before you know it you'll be down in Florida playing bingo with Beaumont T. Bonecutter."

Of course, I knew all this, though it sounded infinitely worse hearing it from Toots. "Toots, just so you know, I did screw Dena Marie, but I didn't kill Rayce Daubner."

"Good. I'll eliminate you from my suspect list. But just out of curiosity, if you don't mind me asking: if you had killed him, would you tell me?"

"I doubt I would offer it up without first consulting my attorney."

Toots smiled, just a bit, and said, "Okay, so who does that leave us with?"

"I've got to consider Johnny Earl a suspect."

"Uh-huh. A couple weeks ago, I was driving into the lot of the Town & Country Market on the other side of Wintersville and happened upon what appeared to be the tail end of an ass-whippin' that Johnny Earl was putting on Daubner."

"You're just telling me about this now?"

"It didn't seem like a big deal until Daubner got his ticket punched. I didn't actually see anything. I pulled into the lot, and Daubner was picking himself up off the asphalt. Johnny was standing there; he said Daubner fell, and Daubner didn't offer anything to the contrary. I told Johnny to mind his manners, and that was that."

"Christ Almighty," I groaned.

"Okay, so we round up Mr. Touchdown for questioning. Anyone else?"

"Did you hear anything about Daubner beating the tar out of Smoochie Xenakis a couple months ago?"

Toots nodded. "I heard Rayce had been harassing Dena Marie—making phone calls to the house and running his mouth to her at the A&P—calling her a slut and a whore. Smoochie supposedly confronted him, and Daubner broke his arm and nose."

"That part ought to be easy enough to check out. Even so, I don't think Smoochie Xenakis would have the heart to squash a bug, let alone shoot someone—even someone who was screwing his wife. However," I said, grinning, "a lawman whom I respect an awful lot told me on several occasions, 'No one is immune from a moment of anger or a moment of stupidity.'"

"Touché. I didn't think you were paying attention."

"I'll take Borkowski and go search Daubner's house. You take Gearhard and round up Johnny and Smoochie. Given the circumstances, I'd say that we better get Johnny under wraps. If it was him, he's the one most likely to bolt."

CHAPTER EIGHT
JOHNNY EARL

I'd hidden my drug money in Pittsburgh, on Mount Washington. On a bright Friday, I cruised the area and checked on the location. I needed to formulate a plan to get it and then get clear of Pittsburgh. On my way home, I stopped at the O.K. Carryout in Brilliant and bought a six-pack of Iron City, then picked up a couple of cheeseburgers and an order of French fries and gravy at Paddy's Diner in Mingo Junction.

I turned off Ohio Route 7 onto Washington Street for the drive to Pleasant Heights. I pulled my ball cap low on my brow in hopes of not being noticed. I stopped at the light at Fourth Street and looked around at the sad remains of my hometown.

Steubenville was once the steel center of the Ohio River Valley. We were home to a sprawling Wheeling-Pittsburgh Steel plant that was the linchpin of the local economy. The Steubenville of my youth—known to most as, simply, "the 'ville"—was a bustling city with a vibrant downtown of theaters, bakeries, shops, and five-and-dimes. The mob controlled the whorehouses on Water Street and two full-fledged casinos. Steelworkers loved vice of any kind, and that made the Ohio River Valley a very profitable area for the mob.

Steubenville has three favorite sons: Edwin Stanton, who was Abraham Lincoln's secretary of war; famed odds-maker Jimmy "The Greek" Snyder; and, of course, the greatest entertainer the world has ever known, Dean Martin. There is a statue of Stanton on the courthouse lawn, and there are probably a smattering of historians who could identify Steubenville as his hometown. And, there might be a few gamblers or bookies who remember Snyder. However, as soon as word got around the penitentiary that I was from Steubenville, Ohio, every mafioso from New York and Chicago tracked me down, pointed at me, and said, "Hey, Steubenville, Dean Martin." They all wanted to know if I'd ever seen his boyhood home.

"Of course," I said. "It's a shrine in Steubenville."

Neither of those things is true, but I thought it was smart to ingratiate myself with the mobsters. The fact that I had supposedly visited Martin's boyhood home wasn't going to make me a made man, but it might afford me some protection in a pinch.

I had always hoped to make it to the Baseball Hall of Fame and become Steubenville's fourth favorite son, maybe even knocking ol' Dino off the top pedestal. But obviously that didn't happen.

By the time I got back to the apartment and sat down on the mattress to eat, the food was cold, but I had gotten used to eating food that way in prison.

I turned on the television for the six o'clock news. The male anchor—looking very grave—opened the newscast by saying, "Tabitha Donley is live near Richmond tonight, where a man has been found shot to death at Jefferson Lake State Park."

I popped a few fries in my mouth and muttered, "That's not good."

Tabitha Donley was blond and attractive. She, too, was looking very serious, standing in front of yellow crime-scene tape. "I can tell you that a life has been cut short here in this western Jefferson County park. Investigators from the sheriff's department are on the scene, seeking clues into the apparent murder of a thirty-five-year-old man who Sheriff Francis Roberson has identified as Rayce Daubner of Steubenville."

Okay, I thought, *that is really not good*. Not good for him, and worse for me. Don't get me wrong, it tickled me beyond belief that Rayce Daubner was dead. I would have loved to have shot him for setting me up on the drug rap—and for being a miserable human being—but I didn't, and that's a fact. However, I was smart enough to know that there were men wearing badges who would think of me as the most logical suspect. Aloud, I said, "Johnny, my boy, it is time to get out of Dodge," and I leapt up from the mattress, ran to the bathroom, and scraped my toiletries off the vanity and into a leather shaving kit. I had a trunk and a few cardboard boxes full of personal items that my mother had packed away for me before they moved to Florida, an armload of blue jeans and shirts, and a suitcase of other clothes. The car was parked in the garage below my apartment. I grabbed the trunk and boxes and ran down the staircase at the back of my apartment. The first load filled up the trunk of the Camaro. I threw the clothing and suitcase into the backseat, then ran back upstairs for the foil-wrapped burgers. The mice could have the fries. I was dreadfully out of shape, sucking for air as I patted down my pockets, making sure I had my wallet and keys.

I unlatched the wooden garage door, slid it to the side, and found myself staring at the lacquered black finish of a Jefferson County Sheriff's Department cruiser. Deputy Phillip Gearhard was leaning against the front fender, his arms folded, smiling and working over a piece of gum. Deputy Majowski stood behind the open driver-side door. "Going somewhere in a hurry, Mr. Earl?" Gearhard asked.

I swallowed. "I'm just going down to the corner to get a newspaper."

He nodded toward the car. "You've got a lot of clothes there. Are you going to the dry cleaners, too?"

"Yeah, I thought I might."

"Maybe you should come with us," Majowski said.

"What for?"

"We need to chat."

"Really? What about?"

Gearhard took two steps toward me and said, "Oh, I don't know, maybe how the body of a former FBI informant, the same informant whose testimony sent you to prison, ended up out at Jefferson Lake State Park full of bullet holes."

"I wouldn't know anything about that."

"Oh, I'm sure you don't, but you'll be happy to tell us what you don't know, won't you?"

"I'm not sure I want to do that."

Majowski squeezed between Gearhard and the garage door jamb. "Given your current status with the US Department of Justice, I'm not sure you want to quibble over this one, Johnny."

"I'll close the garage door for you," Gearhard said, grinning at my frustration.

Aunt Connie came out the back door, a look of panic on her face. "Johnny, what's going on?"

"Nothing, Aunt Connie. I swear. I just need to talk to them about something. I'll be back in a little while. Please don't call my parents. It will just upset them."

I knew she was going to call them the minute she got in the house.

Majowski opened the back door to the cruiser. "Watch your head," he said as I slid inside.

"I know the drill," I replied.

It was less than a mile to the sheriff's department. We drove down the ramp to the parking garage and walked down the hallway that led to the jail. "Where are we going?"

"The sheriff wants to talk to you," Majowski said.

"Yeah, so why are we going to the jail?"

"Because he's not in his office at the moment."

"Okay, let me wait in his office."

"Can't do that. You need to wait in a holding cell."

I stopped. "Oh, Christ, no way. I'm not under arrest. I came down here voluntarily."

"You did, but you're being held for questioning on suspicion of murder. We can legally hold you for twenty-four hours."

I didn't argue further. If I could have run, I would have, but I was now trapped in the bowels of the jailhouse, walking between two rows of jail cells with two beefy law enforcement officers between me and the only door out. I stepped into the holding cell and waited for the familiar sound of the door clanging shut. When it did, Fritz Hirsch jumped off the bunk in the cell across from me, grabbed his imaginary microphone and said, "Well, ladies and gentlemen, this is an honor. We have a very special guest with us tonight. He is making his premiere appearance at the Jefferson County Jail. I give you the former star of the Steubenville Big Red—John-eeee Earlllll."

CHAPTER NINE
MATTHEW VINCENT "SMOOCHIE" XENAKIS

I have disproportionately large lips.

They're grotesque, and I'd consider them comical, were they not attached to my face. Because of my lips, no one in Steubenville knows me as anything but "Smoochie." I detest the nickname, but I will never escape or outgrow it. Most everyone around here has a nickname, and once you've been tagged, you're stuck. For a time in the eighth grade, I quit responding to anyone who called me "Smoochie." Unfortunately, not many people noticed my silent protest, and those who did simply quit talking to me altogether, so I ended the standoff and accepted the nickname.

When I die, my obituary will read: Matthew Vincent "Smoochie" Xenakis. If they omitted my nickname from the obit, I would no doubt go to my grave without anyone in town realizing that I was dead. Down at Erna's Coffee Shop, someone would read the morning paper and say to no one in particular, "Who is this Xenakis fella who died—Matthew?" And someone else would respond, "Beats me. The only Xenakis I know is Smoochie." As nicknames go, it isn't the worst in Steubenville—I knew a Dago, Gum-Nose, Polio, Tweet, Numbie, and Toad—but it's definitely in the top ten.

I was never popular in school, and my protruding lips made me an easy target for abuse. In the fifth grade, the high school music teacher said I had the perfect mouth structure for playing the trombone or the tuba. Not being an athlete or a particularly good student or the least bit popular, I believed this to be a tremendous compliment and my ticket to popularity. I bragged about it at school, which turned out to be a classic blunder. "Yeah, those lips are perfect for playing a musical instrument," said Rayce Daubner, one of my perpetual tormentors. "It's the perfect mouth for blowing on my skin flute." This brought a roar of laughter from my classmates.

The trombone became my only source of accomplishment, but it meant being branded as "a bandie." I was a trombone player in a community where football players, even bad ones, were treated as gods. You could play in the marching band and still preserve your heterosexual image, but only if you played basketball in the winter and baseball in the spring. Then you were considered multitalented. But if you were in the marching band in the fall, concert band in the winter, and chorus in the spring, like me, you were simply a faggot.

I did go out for the wrestling team my freshman and sophomore years and earned yet another humiliating nickname—Canvas Back—by getting pinned in every junior varsity match in which I wrestled. Seeing that my prospects were not likely to improve after roughly thirty straight defeats, I hung up my singlet to focus on the trombone.

However, I don't want to give the impression that my childhood and adolescence were terrible. Guys like Johnny Earl and Francis Roberson didn't harass me. Frankly, I doubt that Johnny Earl even knew who I was in high school. But guys like Rayce Daubner and the gang of mutants that he ran with were merciless, and for no good reason. I was the perfect target, because I was weak and didn't fight back. One reason I didn't fight back is that my dad was a Presbyterian minister. I had been raised in the way of the teachings of Jesus Christ and to turn the other cheek. The other reason I didn't fight back is that I am a coward. I remain one to this day. It pains me to admit that, but I am. I want to stand up to people, but I can't. I usually avoid confrontation at all costs. Rather than admit to my humiliating cowardice, I simply choose to blame it on Jesus.

There's a tradition in Steubenville in which incoming freshman boys are subjected to all types of verbal, mental, and physical harassment. This neatly falls into the category of "initiation," and it is therefore nodded and winked at by school officials. This includes any type of torment and torture that can be dreamed up by the upperclassmen. Nick Simkowski was captured by some seniors and put in a dress, high heels, and makeup and then pushed out of the car at the intersection of Fourth and Market without so much as a dime to call home. I spent the entire summer before my freshman year within a sprint of home because I was so afraid of getting initiated. Despite my best efforts to stay hidden, Carter Drake and Eugene Filopovich grabbed me after band practice one afternoon a week before school was to begin. They stripped me down to my undershorts, duct-taped my ankles and wrists together around the trunk of a small maple tree in front of the high school, then poured pancake syrup in my hair. They wouldn't let any of the other band members free me until Eugene ran to his house and got a camera so they could capture the moment for posterity.

Most of the upperclassmen eventually tired of harassing me, but Rayce made a career of it during all four years of high school. The Bible says that you should not hate, but I hated Rayce. The truth is—and this is not a Christian way to think—for years I fantasized about killing him. I used to dream about being a cop. In those dreams, I would pull over Rayce every chance I got, and when he got so fed up with the torment that he reached for the door handle, I would coolly unload my revolver, spattering his brains all over the passenger-side window. I lost sleep at night in high school because I would play this scene over and over in my head, each night killing Rayce with a bullet to the temple, or to the middle of the forehead, or into his mouth. I always shot him before he got out of the car, because even in my fantasies I was afraid of him.

It's terrible to go through life as a coward. You want people to think that you're not cowardly, but in your heart you know the truth. You will do things—anything—to avoid confrontation. It costs you your freedom. Many beautiful days of my childhood were lost, spent in my living room in front of the television because there were guys outside, somewhere, and I *might* get picked on. I wouldn't go anywhere. I wouldn't participate. I didn't live. Life starts to slip away because of fear. Sometimes, I was afraid and I didn't even know why. I would often tell myself that it was a fear of getting punched or picked on. But that wasn't it. It was the humiliation that came with getting picked on. At school, whenever I would get punched in the back or put in a headlock while one of my tormentors scraped my scalp raw with his knuckles, the other kids would watch from across the room, and I could see the pity in their eyes. They were silently pleading for me to fight back. *Do something*, they were telling me. *Stand up to them. Stand up for yourself.* But I couldn't.

Instead of standing up for myself, I looked for an escape. When I was in elementary school, I looked forward to junior high. I got to junior high, and it turned out to be the most brutal two years of my life. So I looked forward to high school, and that wasn't much better. I thought it would be better once I got out of high school. But nothing has really changed. I still don't have much backbone, and it has kept me down.

I'm the assistant social director at Ohio Valley Hospital, and I've been in the same job for ten years. My boss doesn't really like me; he knows I'm weak and he takes advantage of that. He dumps work on me, screams, and throws temper tantrums. When he gets upset, his face burns crimson. He pounds his fists on his desk and yells, "Xenakis, in here, now!" It's more degrading than getting shoved into a locker in junior high.

We have a real nice secretary in our office—Shirley McConaughey —and when he throws one of his fits, she looks at me with that same mournful look that I once saw in the eyes of my classmates. *Stand up to him; be a man*, her eyes seem to say. But I don't. I just continue to take it. I don't even have the confidence to go out and look for another job. I'm afraid he'll find out and I'll get fired. I create excuses and new reasons to worry.

After high school, I had very little contact with Rayce Daubner. That was, until I learned that he was having an affair with my wife. And, as I guess is the case in these sorts of things, I was apparently the last person in town to know, which added to my humiliation.

My brother Luke told me about it, and I imagine he took a degree of delight in doing so. Luke is one year my junior and the most brutally honest man I've ever met. I was the perfect preacher's son—quiet and obedient. By contrast, Luke came home drunk when he was fourteen. He wrecked three cars by the time he was seventeen. He played football and ran track and was as fearless as I was meek. When I was a senior and Luke was a junior, Audie Kimbel, a raw-boned senior who was a linebacker on the football team, decided it was funny to stop by my locker every morning and give me a headbutt. After about a week, Luke came out of nowhere, jammed a forearm under Audie's chin, and pinned him to the lockers. Audie couldn't get any air, and as his face turned purple, Luke said, "Everyone else may be afraid of you, Audie, but I'm not. So knock it off." My problems with Audie ended right there. Luke was loud and ornery and caused my parents many sleepless nights. However, you would be hard-pressed to find anyone in Steubenville who didn't like him, with the exception of my wife. He didn't like Dena Marie, either, and he made that clear from the day I announced that I was engaged to marry her.

"Why would you go and do a fool thing like that?" he asked.

"Because I love her."

He rolled his eyes. "She'll cheat on you."

"She will not."

"She cheated on her first husband."

"I'm not her first husband. She's changed."

"People don't change, brother."

"They can."

"She won't."

"You don't know that."

He shrugged and said, "It's your life."

After high school, Luke bought a small steel-processing business outside of town. Well, he said he bought it. I heard he won it in a poker game from Red Birnbaum. Actually, calling it a business was a bit of an exaggeration. It was a dump of a place in an aluminum pole barn, consisting of a steel cutter and a couple of benders. Birnbaum had cut steel for a locker manufacturer in Canton, but he was a horrific drunk and so noto-riously unreliable that the company quit buying from him and he closed it down. There were several coils of tin plate in the pole barn, which gave Luke some stock to begin working. He found a few customers and started working sixteen-hour days, seven days a week. He cut steel for a company that made safe-deposit boxes. Then the locker company hired him to cut and bend parts. He got a big contract to cut steel for a company that made fishing tackle boxes. Within a couple of years, he had thirty people working for him. He's a millionaire several times over, but you would never know it by the way he dresses or the battered pickup truck he drives.

Six months ago, he showed up at my office at the hospital. The door was open; he rapped twice on the jamb but never broke stride entering the office.

The only other time Luke had been in my office was the day he cut off his pinkie at the second knuckle. Instead of going straight to the emergency room, he showed up at my office with a dirty rag wrapped around the stub and carrying and the tip of the finger in a Dixie Cup with a couple of ice cubes. "You got anyone here who can help me out with this?" he asked, holding out the cup. We got an ambulance to take him to Allegheny Hospital in Pittsburgh, and they sewed it back on. It's about as good as new.

"So, to what do I owe this honor?" I asked. "All your digits seem to be attached."

He wiggled his fingers. "All accounted for." He closed the door behind him and sat down in the chair in front of my desk. "I have some-thing that I want to talk to you about, and I didn't think that your living room would be the best location."

"Okay. What's on your mind?"

"Remember that conversation we had the day you said that you were going to marry Dena Marie?"

"I remember."

"Well, it's happening. She's cheating on you."

I could feel burning pinpricks race up my neck. "No, she's not. She wouldn't do that."

"Big brother, what planet are you from? Of course she would. She's done it before, remember? She's meeting Rayce Daubner almost every afternoon after she gets off work at the A&P."

"I don't—"

"And don't say that you don't believe me," he said, cutting me off. "You may be a little naive, but you're smarter than that. She's playing you for a chump while you're busting your ass to pay off her credit-card debts and take care of her kids."

"They're my kids, too."

He nodded. "I understand that, but they're your kids because you wanted them. You adopted them. Otherwise, she'd be raising them herself, because that deadbeat who fathered them sure isn't pitching in. You work your ass off, you're a great father, and she repays you by jumping on Rayce Daubner every afternoon."

I sat in silence for a long time. Frankly, I had suspected something was going on, but I didn't know who she might be seeing. The fact that it was Rayce made the pill all the more bitter. "You're sure?" I asked after a few minutes.

"Want to go up on the property tomorrow and see for yourself?"

I did. Luke had bought ninety acres along a ridge south of Route 26 that had been the Demski and Berta farms. The old Berta home was on the edge of the property, and we entered through the front door and climbed the stairs to the back bedroom. With binoculars, we could clearly see Rayce's house. At twenty minutes after twelve, our van—my van, actually—pulled into his driveway, around the corner of the house and out of view from the road. At five after two, Dena Marie pulled out of the drive and headed for home.

Part of me, the part with the slightest bit of backbone, wanted to drive home and confront her that minute. But that part of me was over-ruled by the part that was afraid of how she might react. I feared that she would simply say that she no longer wanted to be married to me. I love her, and I adore the children. I'm not sure how I would react if she were to say, "You're right. I've been having an affair with Rayce and I'm leaving you for him, and I'm taking the kids." Maybe that says volumes about my character. This may sound odd to most people, but most people aren't the class dweeb who ends up married to the homecoming queen. When I was in high school, I never even spoke to Dena Marie Conchek. She was a goddess, the gorgeous homecoming queen who dated the star athlete. I was the pimply trombone player who got picked on every day. And yet, years later, she had been married and divorced and was troubled, the star athlete was in prison, and I was available. Deep inside, in an area of my heart so remote that I could barely admit it to myself, I knew that she would always love Johnny Earl. But I didn't care.

Dena Marie and I started talking one day after church. I do little magic tricks, something I use as an icebreaker with the kids I counsel, and I was making a fifty-cent piece disappear to the great amusement of Dena Marie's son and daughter. Dena Marie came up, and we casually spoke. She was incredibly beautiful in a white dress that probably revealed too much skin for most of the parishioners of the Steubenville First Presbyterian Church, but not for me. There happened to be a potluck that day after church, and I invited her to stay. The kids—Cody and Elizabeth—pleaded to stay for the dinner, and so she did. I had matured greatly after high school. I was never going to be mistaken for a movie star, but I am tall—about six foot two—and attractive. My head has grown to the point where my lips, though still large, are a little more proportional to my other features.

After the potluck, Dena Marie said, "The kids really like you. Why don't you come over for dinner some night?"

"I'd like that," I said. "I'd like that very much."

In all my life, I could not have imagined that Dena Marie Conchek would have been interested in me, but she was. We didn't have a passionate relationship, but she seemed very content. After her stormy relationship with Johnny Earl and her divorce from Jack Androski, I think she was looking for stability and someone who would support her and the children. I fit that bill. Along with my job at the hospital, I work two evenings a week and one weekend a month on the Steubenville emergency squad. I'm responsible. I own my own house and have no debt except for my mortgage. For a divorcée with two kids in Steubenville, Ohio, I was a catch, except for the terrible nickname and big lips.

We began dating, and two weeks into the relationship we had sex. I forgot all of my father's sermons about the sins of having sex out of wedlock. We were in her bed, and as she took my erection in her hand and slid it between her legs, all I could think was, *Oh, my God, I'm having sex with the homecoming queen—me, Smoochie Xenakis.* We were engaged six months after our first date.

As a social worker, I work with troubled human beings every day of my life. And I can say, without question, that Dena Marie is the most spectacularly troubled woman I have ever met. She is a pathological liar. She will lie when it's easier to tell the truth. She will lie over the most insignificant things. If she had oatmeal for breakfast, she'll tell you she had bacon and eggs. She says she abhors smoking, yet slips to the basement at night and sneaks cigarettes, using Mason jars for ashtrays that she tries to hide until she can sneak them to the trash. She's afraid of growing old. She craves attention and will act out at any cost to get it. She's a compulsive spender and, unless I miss my guess, has battled bulimia several times. And, of course, there are fidelity issues and the ugliness with Rayce Daubner.

When I suspected that she was suffering from bulimia, I insisted that she get some professional help. Surprisingly, she agreed. We met together for a consultation with a psychiatrist. He agreed to take on Dena Marie as a patient, and I agreed to pay for twelve sessions and then we would reassess her condition. I think she went to one session. The other times, she took the money and pretended like she was going to the sessions, but I'm certain that she just went shopping.

One night, six weeks after I watched her drive into Rayce's driveway, I checked to make sure the kids were asleep, then walked over by the couch where she was curled up watching television, and I said, "I don't want you to ever see Rayce Daubner again." She frowned and started to protest, but I held up a hand and shook my head. "Don't speak, because, if you speak, a lie is going to come out of your mouth, and I don't want to hear any lies. What's done is done. Don't do it again." And I went to bed.

I sensed that Dena Marie was embarrassed that I had confronted her about the affair, but we didn't speak another word about it. To the best of my knowledge, I don't think she ever saw him again. I had Luke do a little spying for me, which he was only too happy to do, and he reported that she was heading home right after work. Some time later, I did receive an anonymous phone call from a male who muttered, "Your wife is screwing Sheriff Roberson," then hung up. I dismissed the notion as preposterous. Although I had no doubt that Dena Marie could stray again, I knew Francis Roberson. He's our sheriff, a good family man, and a good Christian. He has too much integrity to engage in such behavior.

A few months later, the phone began ringing at night—after I had gone to bed, but while Dena Marie was still up watching television. Not every night, but once or twice a week. I picked up the receiver in our bedroom one night and listened. It was Rayce, pleading to see her again. He was drunk and slurring his words.

"I can't," she said.

"Just once," he said. "Just one more time. I need to see you."

"No. I can't," she whispered. "Rayce, it's over. You have to quit calling."

I could hear commotion and the crack of pool balls in the background. I assumed that he was calling from the Starlighter Bar, which was where he hung out. "You know what? Now that I think about it, I don't want to see you anyway, you fuckin' whore! I'm tired of your sorry pussy anyway, you fuckin' cunt!" She hung up. He was still screaming when I hung up.

The next afternoon, I left work early and drove to Rayce's house. He came out when he saw the van. He was wearing a navy T-shirt with white sweat rings fanning out from the armpits, and he was smiling until he realized that it was me driving and not Dena Marie. I walked up to him, my guts on fire, my mouth parched, terrified. In my opinion, it is impossible to look intimidating with bulbous, protruding lips.

"What do you want, *Smoochie*?" he sneered.

"I want you to stay away from my wife and quit calling my house."

"Really?" He looked at me with a smile that was part amused, part menacing. He walked around me, smiling all the way, cutting me off from the van. "And, uh, what if I refuse, *Smoochie*? What if I decide that I like fucking your wife?" The smile was gone. His eyes were dark and angry. "What are you going to do then, *Smoochie*?" He started walking toward me, and I began moving backward. "Huh? What are you going to do about it?" He reached out and slapped me across the face. "What are you going to do then, Smoochie? Tell me. What?" He slapped me with his other hand. "Want me to tell you? Nothing." Another slap. My face stung and burned. I could feel the tears welling in my eyes. "You must not be much of a man, or she wouldn't have come up here begging me to screw her." He slapped me again, this time following up with a backhand. Blood trickled from the corner of my mouth. "You've got a lot of fuckin' nerve, junior, coming up here and thinking that you're going to tell me what to do." He slapped and backhanded me five or six times. I was crying and wishing that I had the nerve to swing at him. "I fucked your wife because she wanted me to. If you took care of things at home, she wouldn't have been knockin' on my door." He reached out and grabbed my nose between two fingers and twisted until blood gushed from my nostrils, covering the front of my shirt. He laughed. It was more embarrassing than painful. I felt helpless against him, and I could not escape. Blood ran from my nose; tears ran from my eyes. He took another step toward me, and I instinctively stepped back, stepping off the sidewalk and turning my ankle. My right arm twisted under my hip as I fell. I heard it snap, and pain seared through my arm. My forearm looked like a "V." Rayce reached down, grabbed my dress shirt under my chin and effortlessly pulled me to my feet. He released my shirt and grabbed my belt in the back of my pants and walked me to the van, pinching my balls, forcing me to walk on tiptoe. "Don't ever come around here again, Smoochie. The next time, it'll be a lot worse." The tears were so thick that I could hardly see. I took a step toward the open door of the van and lost my footing in the gravel. My forehead hit the edge of the door and I pitched backward into the ditch. A gash opened up along my hairline and blood poured down my face. "Christ,

Smoochie . . ." He picked me up and set me in the driver's seat. "Get the hell out of here before you bleed to death."

I pulled out my handkerchief and tried to stanch the bleeding from my forehead and nose. I fumbled to get the key in the ignition. When I got the van in gear, Rayce was standing directly in front of my grill, a hateful smirk on his lips. I toyed with the idea of running him over, but I didn't even have the guts to do that.

When I walked through the door at home, blood covered my face and shirt. Elizabeth didn't recognize me under the blood; she screamed and ran off. Dena Marie, too, screamed. "Oh my God, sit down. Elizabeth, get me some wet towels."

"It's not as bad as it looks," I said. "Put some pressure on the head wound. I'll hold my nose. I've got to get to the hospital. My arm is broken."

"I'm going to call the emergency squad," she said.

"No. Don't. I'll be okay. Help me get cleaned up, and drive me to the hospital."

"What happened?" she asked.

Elizabeth had gone to her room. I turned and said, "Your boyfriend beat the hell out of me."

I must admit that I felt a degree of satisfaction in having confronted Rayce. The results were disastrous; most of the damage was self-inflicted. But it was by far the most courageous thing I had ever done. As she drove, I cradled my broken right arm in my left, while trying to keep pressure on the gash in my forehead, making the trip with my head down.

"I can't believe you went up to his house and confronted him. I just can't believe you would do that," she said.

"Why is that so hard to believe?"

"Why would you do that? I haven't seen him in months. It's over."

"I picked up the telephone last night and heard the things he said to you. Do you think I'm going to let him talk to you like that?"

"I just can't believe you went up there. What were you thinking?"

For all her dalliances, romances, boyfriends, and husbands, Dena

Marie had never had anyone defend her honor, and now her eyes betrayed her. She could pretend to be angry or upset, but I could see the love in her eyes. As we sat in the emergency room, waiting for the doctors to set my arm and stitch my head, she sat on one of the folding chairs in the corner. Her eyes were red-rimmed, and she looked at me with more passion in her eyes than I could ever remember. I was her Lancelot, and at that moment I felt fortunate to have this woman in my life.

It didn't take long for the rumors to start. One had Rayce propping my arm on a porch step and breaking it with the heel of his work boot. I supposedly got the gash in my head when he put me in a headlock and rammed me into the grill of the van. Of course, even if that was true, it wouldn't have earned Rayce any status. People would have just said, "Well, who couldn't beat up Smoochie Xenakis? He's nothing but a little band geek." Rayce hadn't wanted to really hurt me. His objective had been simply to humiliate me. He could get a lot of mileage out of that story down at the Starlighter. I knew how he would begin. He would say, "Guess what I did to ol' blubber lips?" Then all the mill rats would lean forward on the bar and listen and roar with laughter when he told them how he slapped my face and how it made me cry. They would snort when he told them how I became so flustered that I fell and broke my own arm and how I became so disoriented by tears and blood that I nearly knocked myself unconscious trying to get into the van. Yes, they would all have a grand laugh.

He didn't call the house again, as far as I know. Much to my good fortune, two months after our encounter, he was found shot to death in Jefferson Lake State Park.

CHAPTER TEN
SHERIFF FRANCIS ROBERSON

When Toots and Gearhard left to round up Johnny Earl and Smoochie Xenakis for questioning, Borkowski and I drove out to Daubner's house, which was a couple miles outside the city limits on Route 26, between Cross Creek Road and Fernwood State Forest. When we arrived, Deputy Kirk Wagner was sitting in his car in the driveway. He got out of his car and walked up to mine.

"Evening, boss," he said.

"How ya doin', Kirk? Holding down the fort?"

He nodded. "Yes, sir. It's been quiet."

"Is the place secure?"

"The doors are locked. I checked all the windows; none of them appear to have been tampered with."

"Good work. You eaten yet?"

"No, sir."

"Well, why don't you go grab yourself some dinner. We'll be here for a while."

"Yes, sir."

Daubner's house was a two-story frame that had been covered with white aluminum siding while his parents were still living. He had done little besides live in the house, and it was in disrepair. The front porch roof sagged, and several floorboards were missing. The door looked like it hadn't been used in years. "Let's go around the back," I said, leading Borkowski to a small stoop protecting the back door. I got out the ring of keys that had been retrieved from Daubner's pocket and gained entry to the kitchen. Borkowski and I circled through the downstairs, from the kitchen to a pantry and hall that led to the front foyer, left into the living room and through a wide opening to the dining room and back to the kitchen. The drapes were faded and tired, and they were coated with a patina of dust. The carpet was threadbare on the path leading to the kitchen. Nothing had been replaced or cleaned for years. "How do you live like this?" Borkowski asked.

"He rarely took a bath, for Christ's sake," I said. "Does it really surprise you that his house is a pigsty?"

Borkowski followed me through the upstairs and then into the basement, which was dominated by the hulk of a coal-burning furnace that had been retired years earlier and replaced with a smaller gas furnace. A dilapidated coal bin had been built into one corner; the washer and dryer stood against a whitewashed wall across from the coal bin.

"You take the living room, dining room, cellar, and garage," I said. "I'll check the kitchen, pantry, and upstairs."

"What am I looking for?" he asked.

"Drugs, cash, photographs, written records, weapons—anything that might give us a clue as to who wanted him dead. You'll recognize it when you see it."

"There won't be any shortage of suspects, Sheriff. Nobody liked the son of a bitch."

I started in the kitchen, first checking out the refrigerator and freezer. Borkowski gave the dining and living rooms cursory looks, then disappeared into the basement. He was back upstairs before I closed the refrigerator door. "I didn't find anything," he said.

"Did you check the heating ducts?"

"No."

"Did you check inside the old coal furnace?"

"No."

"Did you take the back off the washer and dryer?"

"No."

I could feel the heat creeping up the back of my neck. "Stanley, you're supposed to be an investigator, for God's sake. Once the feds learn that one of their favorite snitches was murdered, they're going to be crawling all over this county. If they come up here and find something that we should have found, I'm going to be very, very angry. Get your ass downstairs, and I want every inch of that basement searched. The same goes for the living room, dining room, and garage." I could tell he wanted to say something. His jawbone was twitching, and I knew he had a smart-ass remark that he was dying to unload, but he wisely returned to the basement without comment.

We were in the house for the better part of three hours. I found a video camera and an orange crate full of unmarked videotapes, which I took out and tossed in the trunk of the cruiser while Borkowski was busy in the garage. When he emerged, I waved him over to the car. "Find anything?" I asked.

"No, sir. Nothing of interest."

I shook my head. "I would have bet my bottom dollar that we would have found drugs and a stash of cash."

As we drove off the property, Deputy Wagner was back at his post. I rolled down the window of my cruiser and said to Wagner, "Fairbanks is guarding the property overnight. You tell him that under no circumstances do I want him to leave his post."

"Yes, sir."

"You tell him that's a direct order from me."

"Yes, sir."

When we got back to the department, it was nearly midnight. Toots was standing at the copy machine while it spit out copies of a summary of his interview with Smoochie. "How'd it go?" he asked.

I shook my head. "Nothing. He was smart enough not to leave anything lying around the house. How about tomorrow morning we go out there together and give it another look? You have a good eye; maybe you'll see something that I didn't."

Toots nodded. "Sure."

"How did it go with Smoochie?"

"Not much of an alibi. He confirmed that Daubner broke his arm, but he says it was an accident and he certainly didn't kill him."

"What do you think?"

Toots shrugged. "He's got motive—Daubner beat the living hell out of him. And, it was the perfect time to kill him because everyone would naturally look at Johnny Earl as the primary suspect. Smoochie said he knew Daubner and Dena Marie were having an affair. That's why he confronted Daubner."

"How about Johnny?"

Toots pointed his pen in the direction of the jail. "He's in cell number two, and he is *not* a happy camper."

"Have you talked to him?"

"Not really. I listened to him piss and moan on the ride in. He's worried that he's going to get sent back to the pen."

"He ought to be worried. Do you want to tag-team him tonight?"

"Sheriff, I'm whipped. How about we do it in the morning after we get back from looking over Daubner's place?"

I nodded. "Works for me. Of course, that means Johnny gets to spend the night in the Hotel Jefferson."

"Tough break. You want me to tell him that he's going to be an overnight guest?"

"No, I'll tell him."

It had been fifteen years since I had even laid eyes on Johnny Earl. The last time we hooked up was during Christmas break my junior year in college. By the time I took over as sheriff, Johnny was already in the federal penitentiary.

I unlocked the main security door and walked down the brick corridor to the cells. On this night, only Johnny and Fritz "The Masturbator" Hirsch were in the jail. Fritz had been convicted of exposing himself and masturbating in public. It was his third time through the system, and he was awaiting a mental evaluation and a trip to a state mental facility. Johnny must have heard me coming down the steps, because when I walked down the row he was leaning against the bars. He gave me a look of disgust, like when one of my errant passes skipped three feet in front of him. "Fran, what the hell is going on?" he asked impatiently. "Get me out of here."

I walked over to the cell and grinned. "When did you go bald?"

He rolled his eyes. "A while back. That's not really the issue right now."

"Sorry. But you were always so damn vain about your hair. It's sort of funny."

"Yeah, it's fuckin' hilarious, Frannie, and it's good to see you again, too, pal. Now get me the hell out of here."

"I can't do that just yet, Johnny. You and Rayce Daubner had a little scrap at the grocery parking lot the other day, and now he's dead. Given your history with him, that makes you a prime suspect."

He moaned and let his chin drop. "Goddamn it, Fran, they'll send me back to the pen. I didn't kill that asshole. I'm glad as hell he's dead, but I didn't do it. Besides, there must be two dozen people who had motive to kill him. Why are you jamming me up?"

"I hope to God you didn't, Johnny, but you know how the game is played. I've got to keep you in here until you've been questioned."

"Okay, fine, when do we get started?"

"Tomorrow morning."

"What?" he yelled. "Aw, Fran, no way. Tonight! Get me the hell out of here tonight. I didn't do anything, and you've got me stuck down here with a guy who does nothing but pull his pork all night. He's beat off three times since Toots put me in here."

Fritz looked up from his bunk and smiled, revealing teeth that were disappearing from soda rot.

"We're going to search Daubner's place again first thing in the morning. Then we'll get things rolling."

"This is a fuckin' nightmare." He went back to his bunk, rolled onto his back and covered his eyes with his pillow.

There was nothing left to say. *It's funny*, I thought, *how things have changed*. For years, I was just an extra in the Johnny Earl Show. He owned Steubenville High School during our days there. I had been an all-conference quarterback, not because I deserved it, but because

I quarterbacked the team that had Johnny Earl in the backfield. Our football, baseball, and basketball teams won ten conference championships when I played, and I got a plaque and a chenille patch for each. I got those awards because I had the good fortune to play with Johnny. He knew this. He had been worshipped like a god. Now, he was sitting in my jail, and I had control of his life. He had fallen out of a tree eight years earlier, hit every branch on the way down, and was now shocked that he had yet to hit bottom.

I stopped by the radio room and instructed Sergeant Bobby Armor to tell Deputy Fairbanks not to leave that driveway. Armor smiled. Fairbanks was a whiner and not one of Armor's favorites. "Will do," he said.

"How's Johnny doing?" Toots asked as I was heading out the door.

"Not two weeks ago he walked out of the federal penitentiary and probably thought there was a tiny bit of light at the end of the tunnel..."

"And now he thinks it's an oncoming train," Toots said.

"Yep."

CHAPTER ELEVEN
MATTHEW VINCENT
"SMOOCHIE" XENAKIS

There was no short list of people who would have liked to see Rayce Daubner dead. Or, more precisely, there was no short list of people who would have liked to have taken a bat and beaten him until his mother couldn't recognize him, beaten him until Jesus Christ himself leaned down from the heavens, tapped the beater on the shoulder and said, "Hey, pal, he's had enough." This, Jesus would do so the batter didn't jeopardize his or her chances of getting into heaven for too thoroughly enjoying extracting the life from Rayce Daubner. It would have nothing to do with a concern for the deceased, since, based on my beliefs, he was getting nowhere near heaven. In spite of the considerable list of people who hated Daubner, I knew my name would be somewhere near the top.

Thus, it came as no great surprise when Chief Deputy Sheriff Lawrence Majowski—his nickname is "Toots," which I consider to be worse than Smoochie—and a scrub-faced deputy named Phillip Gearhard knocked on my door at nine fifteen on the night that Daubner's body was found. My wife answered the door. I heard her ask, "What's going on?"

"We need to speak to your husband," said Chief Deputy Majowski.

"What about?" she asked.

I walked in from the kitchen, and when neither deputy would tell her, I said, "They want to question me about the murder of Rayce Daubner."

Her eyes darted between me and the deputies. "Is this true?" she asked, backing away toward the staircase, the tips of both hands covering her open mouth. I felt sorry for her. She stood there, frozen.

"Come on out in the kitchen and sit down," I said to the officers.

"We'd rather you come down to the station and talk," Majowski said.

My son ran out of the living room and into his mother's arms. She crossed her arms over his chest and pulled him against her legs. I walked over to them and held both hands out in front of me to be cuffed. Majowski looked at me quizzically for a moment, then said, "That won't be necessary, Mr. Xenakis. You're not under arrest. We just want to ask you a few questions."

As we rode to the jailhouse, I recalled the times I had fantasized about murdering Rayce Daubner and thought that perhaps this was not the best time to bring that up.

I had watched a lot of cop shows on television. When you serve as a punching bag for kids who don't have big lips and bad acne, you tend to spend a lot of time watching television. I loved the detective shows and knew cop jargon and how they squeezed confessions out of people. I was expecting to be put into a little room with a table, a chair, and a two-way mirror. The detectives would pace the room, shining the light in my eyes, while the sheriff and the prosecuting attorney watched from behind the mirror. Consequently, I was more than a little disappointed when they led me into the lunchroom. There were two empty soda cans on a food-stained table and a paper cup half filled with coffee, in which floated half a dozen cigarette butts, the filters smeared with lipstick. The room smelled of stale smoke and burnt coffee. The carpeting was worn and in bad need of shampooing. A refrigerator hummed and rattled in the corner.

"I saw you and the kids fishing out at the quarry the other day," Chief Deputy Majowski said, getting himself situated in a chair. "Catch anything?"

"Bluegill and a bunch of smallmouth," I said. "Little ones. We let them go. They were hitting the line about as fast as we could put them in the water. The kids got a kick out of it."

"It's good to take kids fishing."

I assumed that one of the officers would be the good cop, the other the bad cop. This was a tactic used by television detectives all the time.

But, to my surprise, they both seemed to be playing the good cop. "Can I get you a soda or a cup of coffee, Smoochie?" Deputy Gearhard asked.

"No. I'm fine. Thanks."

On one hand, I was relieved. On the other, I was a little insulted. They didn't really think I was capable of murder, which should have pleased me. I'm a good Christian man, or I try to be, and I had never wanted to be considered a murderer, but even a good Christian hates being looked at as a weakling. They were simply going through the paces. They had heard about my altercation with Rayce, and this was the obligatory interview. They didn't seriously think I could have killed him. After all, I was little Smoochie Xenakis. Harmless little Smoochie. Did they think I was capable of killing anyone? No. They knew I didn't have the guts. This was more humiliating than being duct-taped to the maple tree.

Gearhard had turned a chair backward and was straddling the seat; Majowski was resting his forearms on the table, scribbling down something on lined notebook paper. "Based on the comments you made to your wife, you obviously know why we're here," Majowski began, looking up from his pad. "Rayce Daubner was found murdered this afternoon. The reason we want to talk to you, Smoochie, is because we heard that you and Daubner had a little go-round a while back."

"A go-round?" I asked.

"A fight. We heard you and Rayce had a fight."

I shook my head. "It wasn't a fight."

"I see. Well, if it wasn't a fight, how would you characterize it?"

"I wouldn't characterize it at all. I just went out to his place to talk to him."

"I see."

"What did you want to talk to him about?" Gearhard asked.

"I'd rather not say. It was a personal matter and not germane to anything we're talking about here."

"Smoochie, this is a murder investigation," Majowski said, a sharper tone to his voice. "I'll determine what's germane to the investigation. And right now you're in the middle of it. So telling us that you'd 'rather not say' is akin to telling me that you'd rather not cooperate."

I looked at him but did not respond.

"If it wasn't a fight, then how did you end up with a broken arm and that gash over your eye?" Gearhard asked.

"I fell."

"You fell?"

I nodded. "Yes. I fell."

He smiled and looked over at Majowski. "How many times?"

"Twice. I fell and broke my arm, then I fell and hit my head."

"Really? That isn't what I heard. I heard that Rayce Daubner propped your arm on a step and stomped on it."

I shook my head. "No, as I told you, I just fell on it."

The two law enforcement officers looked at each other, both of them smiling. They thought I was lying. I didn't blame them. I had been a social worker for years. During that time, I had interviewed dozens of women who obviously had been knocked around and punched. In some instances, I had been on the emergency squad run that brought them into the hospital. In the squad, they would tell me that their husband had struck them. But when they appeared in my office the next week, they would simply say, "I was mistaken. He didn't hit me. I just fell down the stairs." This was no different, except that I was telling the truth. However, the truth simply wasn't as plausible as the rumors that had circulated around Steubenville.

"So, Smoochie, did Rayce Daubner punch you when you went up to talk to him?" Chief Deputy Majowski asked.

"No, not really."

"What does 'not really' mean?"

"He slapped me a couple of times, but he really didn't hit me."

"He did strike you, though."

"Slapped. He wasn't really trying to hurt me, I don't think."

"Uh-huh. You went up there to talk to him, and he hit you."

"Yeah, I guess."

"But he didn't break your arm."

"No. I told you, I fell."

"Did you fall because he slapped you?"

"No. I fell because I tripped."

"How did you get those stitches in your head?"

"I fell against the door of my van."

"Because he slapped you?"

"No. I was trying to leave, and I fell against the door. He wasn't anywhere near me."

"Bullshit," Gearhard said, his voice climbing. "You expect us to believe that you went up there, he knocked you around, and yet none of your injuries were the result of the confrontation?"

"That's right."

"Here's what I think happened," said Gearhard. "I think that you found out that Daubner had been giving it to your old lady." He made a phallic symbol with his forearm and fist and made one, sharp upward motion. "You went out to Daubner's place to defend her honor, and he beat the living shit out of you. He obviously wasn't trying seriously to hurt you, because if he was, he could have killed you. I'm betting that he slapped you around, like a cat toying with a mouse, until he got tired of playing. He busted you in the face and you went down, maybe smacking your head on a step or the sidewalk. And while you were on the ground, he stomped on your arm and snapped it." His eyebrows arched, and he awaited a response.

"I told you what happened," I said. "I fell. Twice."

They left the room for a few minutes, then came back in and repeated the questioning process. They asked the same questions, and I gave the same responses. Gearhard's frustration seemed to grow. Majowski appeared unaffected. After several rounds of questioning, Majowski said, "Smoochie, I don't really believe you. I think it's obvious that Deputy Gearhard doesn't either. I find it wildly improbable that you sustained your injuries from simply falling."

They asked for a detailed accounting of my whereabouts for the previous twenty-four hours. I gave it to them, along with a list of people who could verify that I had been nowhere near Jefferson Lake State Park. "We don't have any more questions right now," Majowski said. "But we're going to want to talk to you some more as our investigation progresses. You're free to leave, sir."

They had been glad to give me a ride to the sheriff's department for questioning, but I was on my own to get home. Fortunately, I lived only about twelve blocks away, so I just walked. The downstairs was dark when I got home. A light burned in our bedroom. When I unlocked the door and pushed, I heard Dena Marie moving upstairs. By the time I had removed the key and locked the door from the inside, she was standing on the landing of our staircase. She looked at me and began to weep. She must have been distraught. I assumed the reality of the situation had been overwhelming and had given her cause to think. Tears began rolling down her cheeks. I walked up the steps to where she was standing, her hips leaning against the banister. I moved behind her and gently wrapped my hands around her. I hugged her, then moved my hands upward until they covered her breasts. I kissed her neck and held her close. "Don't worry, my darling, everything will be all right."

I led her back to our room. I brushed away her tears, and we made beautiful love together. I love her deeply, and I believe, truly believe, that she loves me with all her heart. Her eyes give her away. She has been hardened by years of confusion, and though she puts up a harsh and hardened front, her eyes betray her. They are beacons that reveal how deeply and completely she loves me.

CHAPTER TWELVE
DENA MARIE CONCHEK ANDROSKI XENAKIS

I hate my husband's living guts.

I hate him with the searing white heat of Main Street in hell. If water were hate, I'd be the Pacific Ocean. If granules of sand were hate, I'd be the Sahara fucking Desert.

He's the kindest, most thoughtful, most decent, gentle, caring man I have ever met. He buys me cards and writes me love notes and hides little gifts around the house for me to find. There is hardly a month that goes by that I don't get flowers. He absolutely adores me. He worships me. I've never been treated so well in my life.

And I am so consumed with hate for him that my stomach churns, acid boils in my throat, and my bowels clench up.

He's a good Christian and a deacon in the church. He is careful with money, and he built us a house that is nicer than any place I have ever lived. He adopted my two children from a previous marriage and is a wonderful father. He takes them camping and fishing, and they adore him. I've never seen him drink anything harder than a beer. He doesn't smoke or gamble or swear. He would die before ever raising a hand at me. He works around the house, cooks, does dishes, and helps the children with their homework. He has more patience than anyone else alive. He calls me "sweetheart" and, without question, the thought of being unfaithful to me has never crossed his mind.

And, God help me, if sacrificing his soul to burn in hell for all eternity would get me out of this marriage, I wouldn't think twice.

He is the worst lover I have ever had. Being kissed by him is like going nose-to-nose with a giant Ohio River carp. Those baggy lips are suffocating. He refuses to go down on me, and I love having men go down on me. He'll touch me, but he won't taste me. He says it's not Christian-like. "Show me in the Bible where it says a man cannot perform oral sex on his wife," I have protested on many occasions. He tried it once and gagged. Gagged! Now he won't even consider it, which is fine, because I don't need to be cleaning vomit out of my clit. He's also a premature ejaculator. On those rare nights when I do consent to having sex with him, it is a very brief affair.

It's just another line on the list of things I hate about him. I hate his perfection. I hate the way he pronounces each word with great distinction, and watching those lips roll around every syllable is worse than a yeast infection. I hate it that he constantly corrects my grammar. He's the most fastidious, hygienically conscious person I've ever met. He brushes his teeth *one . . . tooth . . . at . . . a . . . time*. Then he flosses, flicking little bits of food and teeth boogers on the mirror. Then he gargles with mouthwash, swishes, spits, and repeats. Twice a day. Every day. His dental hygiene routine alone takes a full fifteen minutes. Before coming to bed, he hangs up his bathrobe and places his slippers in precisely the same location under the bed. He wears pajamas—tops and bottoms. He works two jobs and drives a sensible car—beige, four doors, cloth seats—because he wants to save money for the kids for college.

He makes me crazy. I wish he would die. I wish that it had been him and not Rayce who had been shot to death in the park. Rayce was a miserable human being. He was rough in bed and smelled like soured milk and testosterone, but he had a cock like a donkey and was an incredible fuck. He could go for hours, and he never needed prodding. When I walked in the back door of his house, I could see the hard-on already pushing against his jeans. Every time we were together, he would eat my pussy and ride me until I could barely walk out to the car. He liked to bend me over his dresser, grab my hair, shove my face into the wood, and drive into me from behind. He did it hard, and there were times when I knew he was trying to hurt me. It made me cry, which he liked, and his lack of compassion made me feel like the slut I have become. And the next day, I'd be back at his door.

I'm embarrassed that I, Dena Marie Conchek, the homecoming queen and the most popular girl at Steubenville High School, ended up married, somehow, to pimple-faced, baggy-lipped Smoochie Xenakis. What in the hell was I thinking? Obviously, I wasn't. I know all my friends are looking at me, laughing behind my back, and saying, "Oh . . . my . . . God! She married Smoochie." My mother says I should be grateful that I have a husband who is loyal and kind and has a good career. She says, "Sure, look at all your friends from high school. Their jock husbands all turned out to be adulterers, bums who won't get off the couch and get a job, or wife beaters. You've got a good man who will work for you. You should count your blessings." She's right, of course, but I still hate him, and frankly, I'd rather take a good beating from any of a dozen men I know than listen to Smoochie gargle one more time.

I often wonder how different things would be if that dipstick Johnny Earl had stayed with me. I was absolutely committed to him, but he broke up with me our senior year after he signed a contract to play professional baseball. I was crushed. We had been named Mr. and Miss Steubenville High School. The vote tally came in after he had been drafted by the Orioles. I was a mess. I couldn't quit crying because I knew he was leaving. Still, we had to get photographed for the yearbook. We met at the photo studio, and he was in his football jersey and varsity jacket and I was wearing my cheerleading uniform. It took us two hours to get the damn photo because I couldn't stop crying and the mascara kept streaming down my face. I looked like some kind of evil clown, and I had to keep going to the restroom to reapply my makeup. It was a disaster.

It pains me to say this, but it was my fault. I allowed myself to crumble after Johnny broke up with me. For years, the only thing I had wanted to be after graduation was Mrs. Johnny Earl, and my parents were okay with that. They didn't think I needed an education beyond high school. My older brother, they preached to him about the importance of an education. He went to the University of Wisconsin and studied economics and now works for a brokerage firm in Philadelphia. I used to say, "What about me?" And my dad would respond, "Honey, you're pretty." My brother was smart. I was pretty. I thought that was important. With that as a foundation, I've been able to secure a fine career as a twenty-hour-a-week cashier at the A&P grocery store. I shouldn't blame my parents. I've never been a model of ambition. I was okay with the prospects of being a mother and obedient wife, as long as I was being obedient to Johnny Earl.

We were sexually active in high school. My parents used to go visit my grandmother at the nursing home on Sunday afternoons, and I think they did that so I could have some time alone with Johnny. I used to give him head while he drank my dad's beer and watched the Steelers games on television. Dad was a loyal Steubenville Big Red athletic booster and openly disappointed that my brother had been gifted with brains and not great athletic ability. However, if his daughter were to marry the greatest athlete in the history of the high school, that would be redemption for the shame of having fathered a mathematics genius. And if his little girl had to give a little head in the process, so be it.

When Johnny went off to play baseball, I embarked on a series of bad choices. I first married Jack Androski, which was a colossal mistake. Jack was a nice guy, but he was a farmer and the most boring human being I have ever known. He wanted me to help raise chickens, for God's sake. At the time, I had no better prospects, and I married him in a moment of absolute weakness. My marriage to Jack broke up after I had an affair with Alan Vetcher, who in high school was known as "Vetcher the Lecher," because of his huge pornography collection. I was never really interested in Alan, and I think I had the affair so I would get caught. Jack was a proud man, and I knew he would never tolerate me having an affair.

After I married Smoochie, Rayce started coming into the grocery store and flirting, and then he started calling me. He asked if I wanted to go out with a real man. I hung up on him, but he kept calling back. All I could really remember about him in high school was that he went easy on the deodorant. He persisted, and eventually I agreed to let him stop by one night when Smoochie was out of town camping with the kids. I swear I wasn't planning to sleep with him, even though I was horny as hell. We were talking in the living room and he threw a boner that was pushing up above his belt. I had never seen anything like it. God, what a cock. He pulled me onto him and fucked me on the couch in the living room.

Someday, just out of sheer meanness, I plan to tell Johnny Earl that Rayce's dick was the biggest and hardest I've ever had. It'll make Johnny crazy to think that there was something in the world that Rayce had bested him at. And with Rayce being dead, he retired the champion.

I liked having sex with Rayce because it was dirty and hot and fun, and when it was over I would leave. He wanted me to leave Smoochie and marry him, but in a lifetime of making hideously bad decisions concerning men and my love life, that is one I avoided. I was just using Rayce for the sex.

I never stopped loving Johnny. After he hurt his leg and all that silliness about a professional baseball career was over, I assumed that we would pick up right where we left off before he left for the minor leagues. He wasn't interested. He pretended like he was, for a while, but he was just using me to get his nuts out of hock. I went off the pill in hopes of getting pregnant, but it didn't take. He ended up moving to Pittsburgh and then got sent to prison on a trumped-up drug charge. Rayce set him up, I think. Rayce said Johnny was a drug dealer, but I never believed that. Rayce set him up because he had always been jealous of Johnny. When Johnny got sent to prison, I wanted to kill myself. Even though he hadn't been interested when he came home after baseball, I always figured that he would come to his senses and change his mind. He was never going to find anyone who loved him like I did, and in my heart I always thought that we would be together. I guess you can make yourself believe anything.

I was a twenty-six-year-old divorcée, a former homecoming queen with a bad reputation, when I met Smoochie Xenakis. Actually, we had gone to high school together, but I have only a vague memory of him. He was a bandie with a bad complexion who was always getting stuffed into the lockers.

I started talking to Smoochie one day after church. I was not a regular churchgoer, but I had heard that Chip Bromfield and his wife were having problems and I knew that he went to the First Presbyterian Church. Chip had been a couple years ahead of me in school and was a state wrestling champion. He had a body to die for. I hoped Chip would see me in my little white dress, which was probably too slinky for the Presbyterians, and it might spark some interest. Unfortunately, he and his wife had patched things up. On that same Sunday, Smoochie was standing outside the church and showed my kids some lame trick with a fifty-cent piece that losers learn while sitting in their house instead of having a real life. After that, the kids loved him and wanted to go to church every Sunday to "see Mr. Smoochie," which I have to admit I thought was cute.

A couple of my friends said, "Oh, he is so nice. You should totally marry him." Right. They just wanted me to marry him so they could all laugh behind my back. I should have told them, "Yeah, well, if you like him so much, you marry him." But I didn't. I made yet another bad decision and married him. I started going to church to align myself with a state wrestling champion, and I ended up married to Mr. Blubber Lips. That was God getting back at me for trolling his church for a married man.

I can't imagine why Smoochie wants to stay married to me. I've been unfaithful to him. I treat him like dirt. During one particularly trying time, he insisted that I go see a psychiatrist. I agreed to do it. I actually thought it might do me some good. He agreed to pay and not interfere. I went to the first session, and that fucking quack said that I was insecure. Me! Dena Marie Conchek, insecure. Can you believe it? I asked, "What do I have to be insecure about? I was the most popular girl in school. I was the homecoming queen. The Steubenville Winter Festival queen. The Valentine's Day dance queen and the prom queen. I was Miss Steubenville High School, for Christ's sake."

He said, "The mere fact that at age thirty those accomplishments are still important is a sign that you are insecure."

I wanted to slap his chubby face. I never went back. Instead, I left the house like I was going to my session and went shopping. Smoochie was never the wiser.

Now I've gotten myself in a rotten position. He's adopted my kids. He loves them, and they love him. While I hate to admit this, he is a stabilizing force in their lives. I hate to think that I'm the kind of mother who would sacrifice the happiness and security of her children simply because I'm embarrassed about being married to him, but that pretty much sums it up.

He's never going to give me any reason to leave him. Even after he found out I was screwing Rayce, he stayed with me. For Christ's sake, he even went out and tried to defend my honor. I appreciate the effort, but he was lucky that Rayce didn't kill him. He came home covered with blood and looking like he had been in a car accident. When we were sitting in the emergency room, he was cradling his arm and looking like a whipped puppy, and I was thinking, *You are such a dipshit.* I was going to tell him, too, but he was feeling so damn gallant about confronting Rayce and defending my honor that I didn't want to break his heart.

I don't know how he found out about me and Rayce, but I'll bet it was that prick of a brother of his. I hate him almost as much as I hate my husband.

When that fat sheriff's deputy showed up at the house and hauled Smoochie's sorry ass out of there, I was so excited that I couldn't speak. I had to fight to control my elation. I tingled from my crotch to my ears thinking that he might be going to prison, maybe even the electric chair, and I would be done with his sorry ass. I could divorce him without guilt. I put the kids to bed and danced by myself in my bedroom. I was so excited that I spread out on the bed and masturbated twice. He was going to be charged with killing Rayce to defend my honor. Oh, how precious. Of course, to think that my husband was capable of murdering someone is laughable. That didn't matter. The thought of someone killing another man to defend my honor was exciting. Even if they just charged him with the murder, I could file for divorce, claiming I was doing it for the safety of my children. It was so, so delicious. I was in my room daydreaming of all the mileage I would get out of this—a lot of sympathy and attention. I probably would get asked to be on television.

And then . . .

A few hours later, I heard the deadbolt on the front door slide open, and that mousy little son of a bitch walked back into my life. When I saw him standing in the foyer, I was so upset I started to bawl. I was crushed. I had envisioned him on the witness stand trying to deny everything while I sat in the gallery, pretending to be the loyal wife in total anguish, while I sent telepathic messages to the jury. *He's guilty, you idiots. Guilty! Guilty! Guilty! Convict him.*

Here's how sad things can get sometimes. I was standing on the landing, crying because he wasn't in jail. Without a doubt, he thought I was crying for joy because he had returned. It would have been laughable if it hadn't been so tragic. He wrapped his arms around me, and I shuddered. We went upstairs and, after he brushed and flossed and gargled, he pulled his hard little pecker out of his pajamas. I was so upset I consented. I just endured it and cried about my terrible luck. As usual, he came in about twelve seconds and then fell asleep, drooling on my shoulder. I stared at the ceiling for hours. This was not an acceptable outcome. As slobber rolled over his fat lower lip, I plotted to get rid of him. I had to come up with a plan. I couldn't allow this opportunity to be wasted.

It comes down to the fact that I really only care about one thing in life. I still want to be Mrs. Johnny Earl. Despite everything that's happened, if he would have me, I would go to him in a heartbeat. I know that is the only thing in life that is going to make me happy and settle down and act like a decent human being. I don't even care that he's bald. I don't care that he didn't become a famous major leaguer. I don't care that he's a convicted drug dealer.

I want to be Mrs. Johnny Earl.

CHAPTER THIRTEEN
SHERIFF FRANCIS ROBERSON

When the phone rang at 6:30 a.m., I'd been in bed about forty minutes. I hadn't slept. A combination of adrenaline and an inability to shut down my brain kept my eyes focused on the sunburst design of the ceiling plaster. I had been up much of the night watching the videotapes that I had confiscated from Rayce Daubner's house.

It is astonishing what goes on in a little town like Steubenville. Daubner had set up a small pornography studio in his bedroom. The tapes were grainy and of poor quality, but all featured Daubner servicing numerous women, several of whom I recognized, including Dena Marie. Why he felt compelled to record all these is beyond me. I will say this: the guy was hung like a bear. Unfortunately, none of the tapes revealed any clues as to who might have been his killer. I destroyed the tape with Dena Marie. Cops have gone to jail for destroying evidence, but I was going to copy the tapes and send them to the sheriff's offices in neighboring counties for assistance in identifying the women, and I didn't want them watching Rayce bending her over his dresser.

The lack of sleep was giving me a headache by the time I turned off the television and the tape player and climbed the creaking, curved staircase to the bedroom. The faintest hint of sunrise was already creeping over the West Virginia hills when I crawled into bed. "You stink," Allison said after I had settled into my side of the bed. "You've been smoking again."

"I get fidgety when there's a big case; you know that."

"You promised the kids that you'd never put another cigarette in your mouth."

"So did you," I whispered. I had showered, but the acrid odor of the smoke lingered on my clothes, which were in a heap on the cedar chest at the foot of the bed. I should have put them in the washing machine. Allison fell back asleep; my mind continued to race with thoughts of the dilemma that Daubner's death was creating for me.

When the phone rang, I bolted upright and answered it before the second ring.

"You awake?" Toots asked.

"I'm vertical," I said.

"Well, Sheriff, your day's about to get off to a bad start. Look out your front window."

I slipped my fingers between the drapes and parted them just wide enough to see High Street below. "The Kimbler kid is delivering the *Intelligencer* to the Farmwalds," I said flatly.

"Not that. Look up," he said.

If you walked out my front door and went straight across High Street, though the Farmwalds' yard, across Delphos Road and Sunshine Park Road, across the old Adena and Ohio Valley Railroad tracks, then up the hillside until you were just outside of the city limits, you would have traversed, as the crow flies, about a mile, and it would put you right at the back door of Rayce Daubner's house. From that very spot billowed towers of gray and black smoke. I stared at the mushrooming clouds for a few seconds before I finally said, "Don't tell me."

"Oh, yeah. The Daubner mansion," Toots said. "It's a torch."

"Shit!" I yelled.

"What?" Allison asked.

"Daubner's house is on fire." She gave me a blank look, but I didn't see the need to explain further. I grabbed a clean pair of blue jeans from the dresser and pulled them on as I hopped toward the door. A navy T-shirt with a silk-screened sheriff's badge over the breast rested atop a stack of clean clothes. I pulled it over my head and covered my uncombed hair with a black cap with "Sheriff's Department" in yellow stitching on the front.

By the time I pulled off the road, a hundred feet past the driveway to Daubner's house, the roof had already caved in, sending the second and first floors crashing into the basement. The Daubner place was several blocks from the nearest fire hydrant. The fire department had emptied the pumper on the blaze, but it was already out of control. By the time I walked up the driveway, all the firefighters could do was watch the flames as the walls collapsed.

Toots was waiting for me at the top of the driveway. "This is great. Just great," I told Toots through clenched teeth. "The feds will be in my shorts, for sure."

I scanned the chaotic scene for Deputy Leonard Fairbanks.

I spied him skulking around his cruiser, desperately trying to look busy and avoid my glare. "Sergeant Armor, did you assign Deputy Fairbanks to watch the house as I requested?" I asked between clenched teeth.

"Yes, sir," he said.

I nodded and motioned for Toots to follow me down the gravel drive. "Good morning, Deputy," I said to Fairbanks.

"Good morning, Sheriff," he responded, continuing to inspect the gravel drive. Leonard Quincy "J.C." Fairbanks was a fifty-three-year-old, thrice-divorced career deputy with a gut like an overstuffed pillow that protruded both above and below his gun belt. He was not an unlikable guy, but I marveled at his ability to screw up every task to which he was assigned. He was a model of consistency in that regard. He had earned the nickname "J.C.," which stands for Jesus Christ, because supervisors so frequently began bitching at him by saying, "Jesus Christ, Fairbanks . . ."

I took a breath and said in a calm, even tone, "Sergeant Armor said he assigned you to watch this property last night. Is that so?"

He nodded, faintly, and said, "Yes, sir."

"When you relieved Deputy Wagner, did he reinforce that order?"

"Yes, sir."

"Did he tell you it was a direct order from me?"

"Yes, sir, he did."

"Did you do as you were ordered?"

"I did."

"At any point during the night did you leave your post?"

"Well, yes, sir, I ran down to the diner for a couple of minutes—twenty, tops—to grab a sandwich and—"

I slammed my fist down on the hood of his cruiser. "And that's when someone torched the house!" I screamed. "That is why you were given a direct order not to leave the area, so no one would disturb the house of a murdered federal informant!"

I am not generally a yeller or screamer. I've never seen the value in it. But now my voice rang out over the roar of the blaze, and firefighters turned to witness my meltdown.

"But, Sheriff—"

"No buts!" As I yelled, flecks of spittle flew from my mouth. "You disobeyed a direct order, and someone burned down the house while you were out playing grab-ass with one of your ex-wives! Deputy, you had better pray to Jesus in heaven that the arson investigators tell me this was spontaneous fucking combustion, or whoever did this didn't get out alive and we find his charred remains at the bottom of this mess. Otherwise, your ass is mine. The FBI's going to be all over me, and when they ask me who I think killed Rayce Daubner, I'm going to tell them it was *you*." I was getting light-headed and had to step back and take a breath. In a calmer voice, I said, "Now, as of this moment—this instant—you are suspended. Take the cruiser back to the department, and I want to see your badge, revolver, and keys on my desk when I get back."

Fairbanks had tears in his eyes as he climbed into the cruiser and backed it out of the driveway. Toots walked over to me, crossed his arms, and said, "Well, I think that went well. How about you?"

I shook my head and said, "I'll hang that lard-ass."

"Hey, remember who you're talking to," he said, rubbing his hand over the basketball-sized mound of his stomach.

"You look like a Russian weightlifter. You could probably stop a bullet with your gut," I said.

Toots grinned. "On the outside chance that was a compliment, thanks." He turned serious again. "I don't think I've ever seen you quite that upset."

I leaned against the passenger-side door of the fire chief's car, pressing the heels of my hands into my eyes. When I removed my hands, my eyes adjusted just in time to see the last remaining wall crumble into the basement and a wide spray of orange sparks erupt from the hole. The pumper truck pulled up with another tank of water and began pouring it onto the smoldering pile; it was an exercise in futility. It was two hours before I left. By the time I got back to the office, the little headache I had been fighting that morning had morphed into a thumper directly behind my right eye.

There was only one cure for such a headache—caffeine, sugar, and aspirin. I fetched my favorite mug from my office and filled it from the coffee urn in the reception area, grabbed two doughnuts from the box— Allison always bought doughnuts at the Downtown Bakery on Saturdays—and retired to my office. I poured the last three aspirin from the jar in my desk drawer into my hand and washed them down with too-hot coffee. The donuts were gone in a couple of bites. I had Johnny Earl in a jail cell and had to address that issue, but I couldn't even think about it until the pain in my head subsided. It was at that moment that my Saturday morning went from bad to worse with the piercing squeal of the voice that in all the world I least wanted to hear. She barged into my office, her wooden heels pounding out a staccato rhythm on the marble floor, and said, "Francis! I can't believe you let him go."

"Good morning, Dena Marie. What in the hell are you talking about?"

"You let him go. How could you do that?"

"Dena Marie, I'm dealing with an unsolved homicide and a horrendous headache. At this moment, you're keeping me from one and contributing to the other. Let who go? Smoochie?"

"Yes, Smoochie."

"Why exactly would I keep him in custody?"

"Why? Because he killed Rayce Daubner, that's why."

I rubbed my eyes. "You expect me to believe that Smoochie killed Rayce Daubner?"

"Yes. I can't believe you didn't figure that out."

"Dena Marie, last week I saw Smoochie in the hardware store, and he was buying one of those catch-and-release mousetraps. You're telling me that the same guy who can't bring himself to kill a mouse shot a human being in cold blood?"

"It's an act. It's all a big act. You don't know what he's really like."

"I've known Smoochie since I was six years old. His dad was our preacher. I went to school with him. I've got a pretty good idea what he's like, and the guy doesn't have a mean bone in his body."

She laughed and rolled her eyes. "Oh, you are such a fool. I can't believe you're falling for that act. He's vicious."

"Vicious?"

"Very. He's violent. He beats me."

"Smoochie beats you?"

"All the time, especially when he drinks."

"Really? I didn't know Smoochie drank."

"Oh, my God, he drinks all the time. He's a mean drunk."

"And then he beats you?"

"Yes. So why didn't you arrest him?"

"Dena Marie, I have a lot of things on my to-do list today, not the least of which is interviewing your former boyfriend, Johnny Earl, who is very anxious to get out of my jail. Let's cut to the chase. Why would you think that your husband killed Rayce?"

"He said he wanted to."

"He did?"

"After Rayce beat him up a couple of months ago, he said if he'd had a gun he would have killed him; he would have shot him dead."

"Okay."

"Well, how much more evidence do you need? Arrest him."

I folded my arms and leaned back in my chair. "I know what you're thinking. You want me to help get you out of your marriage to Smoochie. It's a good plan. I arrest Smoochie; he goes to prison. Bingo, you're a free woman. But I'm not going to send a man to prison just so you can clean up another one of your mistakes."

"He's a killer."

"He wouldn't hurt a fly."

"He said if he'd had a gun, he would have shot him. He said that. I'll testify to that."

"Anyone who took a beating like Smoochie took from Daubner would say something like that. I'll grant you that it's motive, but you can't indict and convict someone on motive. Otherwise, there are probably fifty people in Jefferson County who could be suspects. Nobody liked the son of a bitch, including Johnny Earl, who, if you'll excuse me, I need to go interview."

At that moment, my wife appeared outside the door, looked at Dena Marie, mouthed, "You miserable son of a bitch," and disappeared down the hall. The little vein on the side of my head began to thump with my heart.

"You have to investigate Smoochie some more. You need to bring him down for more questioning. Squeeze him. He'll crack."

This woman was trouble. She was one of those individuals whose life was always in a deep state of chaos, as were the lives of those with whom she had even the slightest contact. She could create a situation in paradise. My dad had said she was poison, and he was right. Despite this, I wanted to pull her across the desk, rip off her jeans, splay her legs across my hips and have my way with her. She was braless under a blue stretch top, her nipples erect and practically winking at me. I was starting to jump in my loins. My wife was pissed, I had a headache that was causing my vision to blur, the FBI would soon be swarming over my county, my career was teetering on a precipice, and still I couldn't not think of taking Dena Marie on my desk.

This, of course, is exactly what she wanted me to think. She wanted me to believe that as soon as Smoochie was tucked away in prison, it would open a wonderful opportunity for the two of us to be together. In reality, it was simply an opportunity for me to completely ruin my marriage and all my political aspirations. Fifteen minutes after the judge gave Smoochie the death penalty, she would be pantiless and charging through Johnny Earl's front door.

Still, beneath my desk my erection grew. "I am a troubled man," I muttered.

"What?"

"Nothing. Okay, I'll talk to him again. But I don't believe for one second that he did it, and I think you know that, too. You just want me to do your dirty work."

She tilted her head to one side and offered a slight grin. "Squeeze him hard. He's weak."

"I thought you said he was vicious."

"Maybe he'll confess."

"To a crime that he didn't commit? I doubt it."

Dena Marie used the polished nail on a pinkie to brush a strand of hair away from her eye. The tip of her tongue brushed her lips. "You never know, Francis. Maybe we'll both get lucky."

CHAPTER FOURTEEN
JOHNNY EARL

I have really screwed up my life. Have I mentioned that yet? I've been home from the federal penitentiary for two weeks, and I am now a prisoner in the Jefferson County Jail, where I'm being held on suspicion of murder. Despite the fact that it's a totally bogus charge, it might be enough to cause the feds to revoke my parole.

Making things worse, if that's possible, is the fact that there is only one other prisoner on the floor—Fritz "The Masturbator" Hirsch. The loony bastard is also known as "the announcer," because he never carries on a normal conversation, but rather walks through life announcing the events around him as though he was a sportscaster. At first, it's funny, though it doesn't take long before you want to punch him in the face. He walks down the street, talking into his right fist, which is wrapped around an imaginary microphone, broadcasting anything he sees.

"Oh, there's Mrs. Eleanor Donaldson, mother of the luscious Kelli Ann Donaldson, Steubenville Catholic Central High School class of 1976. You all remember Kelli Ann, she was a little Catholic hottie, folks—runner-up homecoming queen, as I recall. Mrs. Donaldson is now frantically digging into her purse for her keys. She appears to have been doing some grocery shopping at Schumacher's Grocery and Meats. That's Schumacher's Grocery and Meats in downtown Steubenville, Ohio, your number one supplier of fresh meats and poultry since 1936. When you want it fresh, you want it from Schumacher's. Yes, sir, picking up some groceries and a twelve-pack of Iron City Beer for Mr. Donaldson. Iron City—the beer drinker's beer. When you're really ready to pour it on, pour on the Iron. Oh, and now Mrs. Donaldson is practically sprinting to her Oldsmobile Cutlass, which she purchased at Orion Oldsmobile in Steubenville. Yes, that's Orion Oldsmobile, a dealer you can trust, located on Sunset Boulevard in Steubenville. She's getting in the car now for the short drive to the Belmont Street home that was the recent recipient of a fresh paint job by Hap Strausbaugh. As most everyone in town knows, Hap is a latent homosexual and possesses the finest collection of dildos in town."

When Deputy Majowski had left after locking me in my cell, Fritz, in the cell right across from me, immediately went into his routine. "Oh, can you believe our luck, ladies and gentlemen? It's Steubenville's most famous jailbird, former star of the Steubenville Big Red, Johnny Earl. Johnny, Johnny, over here, Johnny, could we have a few words with you, please?" he said, extending his arm and the imaginary microphone outside the cell. "Johnny, what are you doing back in jail? Really, your adoring fans want to know."

This monologue went on nearly all night. He talked incessantly, broadcasting any appearance by the deputies, giving me a play-by-play of eating his dinner. "The star of tonight's dinner is meatloaf, and Fritz is a huge fan of jailhouse meatloaf. Oh, and they brought succotash tonight, always a crowd favorite . . ."

The events of the evening had put my bowels in an uproar. Some people get nervous and eat. I get nervous and shit. I was on the toilet before every game I ever played. Also, I detest an audience when I'm using the john. As you might imagine, this created a bit of a problem in prison. There was a single toilet in my prison cell—the throne—but I only used it under the most dire of circumstances. I worked in the prison library primarily because it had a restroom that offered at least a modicum of privacy. So I sat on my bunk in misery, my bowels rattling like castanets, dreading a potential play-by-play of a trip to the toilet.

The single light that burned in each cell was turned off at 10 p.m. The fluorescent lights in the corridor between cells burned all night. I stretched out on the cot and fought off the urge to go until two in the morning. By then, the pressure was nearly unbearable, and I was confident that Fritz was asleep. I silently eased myself off the cot and onto the toilet.

No sooner had I started my business than Fritz leapt off his cot and began talking into his hand. "Ladies and gentlemen, we're back live from the Jefferson County Jail where former all-state star Johnny Earl has just hopped on the crapper for a late-night dump, and let me tell you, sports fans, there's been a major eruption in cell number two. It sounds like a flock of sparrows taking off. Johnny, what did you eat today to cause such a spectacular release?"

He was still standing at the bars of his cell, grinning, when I crawled back in my cot and draped my right arm over my eyes. I fell asleep, awoke briefly when the overhead light in my cell went on at six, then dozed again until I was jolted awake by a booming, familiar voice. "Earl! On your feet, soldier."

I bolted out of my cot, and had anything been left in my bowels, I would have lost it. "General Himmler! What are you doing here?"

He stood erect, hands clasped behind his back, jaw tight, staring hard at me. He was in camouflage fatigues, shiny black boots, and a green beret pulled down on his brow. The little weasel of a preacher, Reverend Wilfred A. Lewis, poked his head out from around the general. He was in an ill-fitting, double-breasted green suit with braided gold epaulets and brass buttons the size of quarters. He looked like a hotel doorman. "Salute your general," the preacher said.

I did. He returned the salute and said, "At ease, soldier."

"General, I didn't think you were getting out for another month."

"The important thing is, I'm here." He smiled; the preacher looked at me in disgust, as though I was unfit to be in the mere presence of the general.

I was pretty certain why he had lied about his release date. He suspected my lack of commitment to the cause and had allowed me to believe I had a bit of a buffer to get my money and leave town. I had been outsmarted by a man with a unibrow who couldn't tell German from Yiddish.

"So, tell me, Colonel, how did you manage to get yourself back in jail so soon?" the general asked.

I shook my head. "It's no big deal. How did you know I was here?"

"I stopped by your aunt's house. She said two deputies showed up at the house last night and hauled you off." The disgust on the preacher's face melted into a smirk. The little weasel had pried into my release papers for my aunt's address.

"When are you getting out?"

"I don't know."

"That's right, he don't know," announced Fritz, up against the bars of his cell and again talking into his hand. "Suspicion of murder. Could be in here for a long time, folks. But wait—what's this? Suddenly, Johnny Earl, the great Earl of Steubenville, gets two mysterious visitors, and one is called 'the general.' Let's see . . ."

The general turned to face Fritz, who glanced up at him and immediately dropped the imaginary microphone and backed away from the bars. It was the first time I had ever seen Fritz intimidated into shutting his mouth. The general turned back to me and said, "That isn't the answer I was hoping to hear. You see, that creates a problem. We need to get started. The republic needs us. In order to expedite our operation, just tell me where you hid the money, we'll get it, and you can catch up with us when you get out of jail."

"What if I don't get out of jail?"

"Then you won't need the money."

The preacher cackled. I shook my head. "I don't like that. Besides, you couldn't find it without me."

"You see, General, I told you he wasn't committed to the cause," the preacher said. "He was going to take the money and run."

"This is very disturbing, Colonel, and after I put so much trust in you. I feel the reverend is right. Your lack of faith in our cause is troubling."

"General, I think I'm insulted that you would say such a thing," I said, stalling for a way out. "I'm as committed to the cause as ever. I can't believe you would question my commitment." In reality, I was thinking that with a five-minute head start and a half-tank of gas I would be a vapor trail.

"You say you're committed, yet you refuse to tell me where you've hidden the money," the general said.

"I'm not refusing; I can't. I buried it, and you'd never find it. It's probably going to take *me* a while to find once I get back up there."

"Where is it?"

"It's up on Mount Washington. That's a section of Pittsburgh. It's in a wooded area, not too far from the incline. It's buried deep, though. It's near a culvert. And if you stand where I buried it, you can see a house with green shutters. Well, it had green shutters eight years ago."

The general's brow bulged and the little preacher said, "Horseshit."

"Nice language, Reverend," I said.

The frown slowly disappeared from the general's face, and a smile creased his lips. "Okay," he said. "We'll wait. When you get out, we'll all go together."

"General, I can't wait to serve the Aryan Republic of New Germania."

They left, and I dropped back to my cot, draping my right arm over my eyes to block out the light. Then I uttered a phrase that will never again cross my lips. I said, "Mother of Christ, my life can't possibly get any more screwed up."

"Johnny. Johnny, get up," Dena Marie said in a tone not much above a whisper.

I lifted my arm, blinked her into focus, and asked, "Dena Marie, what in hell are you doing here?"

She had both hands wrapped around the bars of my cell. "Come over here. We need to talk."

"Oh-oh, what do we have here, folks? It looks like the former homecoming queen has stopped by to visit her old flame, Johnny Earl." Fritz was up and broadcasting. "You've got to ask yourself this question, sports fans. Does her husband know she's here?"

Dena Marie whirled and started marching toward Fritz's cell, her right index finger counting down with each step. "I am in no mood for your bullshit, Fritz," she said. "So sit the fuck down and shut the fuck up." He did, and she returned to my cell. I was up and standing near the bars. "Don't worry. It's going to be all right. I'm going to get you out of here."

"How, pray tell?"

"Because I'm going to get Smoochie arrested for Rayce's murder."

"Smoochie? Your husband, Smoochie?" I laughed. "Dena Marie, you don't expect me to believe that Smoochie killed Rayce, do you?"

"He's all but confessed. They're going to interrogate him again tonight. He'll crack and spill his guts."

"Why are you telling me all this?"

"Because I don't want to see you in jail."

"What's the real reason?"

She pressed her forehead closer into the open space of the bars and licked her lips, which I hate to admit caused a tingle in my loins. "He'll be out of the way."

Although I knew full well what she meant, I still felt compelled to ask, "Out of the way for what, Dena Marie? Please don't tell me that you're still harboring hopes that you and I will be together."

"That's the way it was meant to be, Johnny. You and me, together forever."

"Dena Marie, go home."

"Don't admit to anything," she said.

"I don't have anything to admit to."

She winked and gave me the slightest of nods. "Okay," she whispered.

"I don't, goddammit."

She pressed the index and middle finger on her right hand to her pouty lips and gently blew. "Until we meet again, my love."

"I am not your love," I said in a strained whisper.

She left, and I wanted to vomit. I wasn't sure which was worse: having a massive white supremacist waiting to take my money and whisk me off to marry multiple wives of his arranging in God-knows-where, or having Dena Marie attempting to save me from the death penalty. Frankly, at this point in the morning, a trip to the electric chair didn't seem like a bad option.

"Hey, Mr. Earl." I looked up. It was Fritz, standing at the front of his cell, his hands in his front pockets. It was the only time in my life that I could remember him speaking in a normal voice and not pretending to broadcast the scene around him. "If I get out of here and they don't send me to the loony bin out in Columbus, can I go with you?"

"Go with me where?"

"To that New Germania place."

"Fritz, I . . ." I paused and nodded. "Yeah. Sure, you can go. Why not?"

I eased myself back onto the cot, now thoroughly exhausted. I hadn't closed my eyes for five minutes when I heard footsteps and the jangle of keys. I opened my eyes as the jailer, Reed Nevel, was opening the door to my cell. Deputy Majowski was leaning against the side of the door. "Up and at 'em, sunshine," he said. "The sheriff wants to talk to you."

"About goddamn time," I said.

"Stick out your arms," he said, pulling his handcuffs off his belt.

"I'm not under arrest. Why do I need cuffs?"

"Standard jail procedures."

Another man might have been humiliated. At that point in my life, I was beyond that. Majowski walked me up the steps, a thick hand wrapped around my left triceps. "Is that really necessary?" I asked. He didn't answer. "Smells like the steel mill in here," I said when we reached the sheriff's office. "What's burning?"

"It's my clothes," Fran said, getting up from behind his desk and walking to a conference table in the corner of the room. He sat at the head of the table and gestured for me to sit on his left. "Rayce Daubner's house burned down last night. I've been out there all morning."

"His house burned? I'm sorry to hear that."

"Why would you be sorry about that?" Majowski asked.

"Okay, I'm not sorry it burned. I'm just sorry that Rayce wasn't still alive to die a fiery, painful death, is all."

Fran pinched the bridge of his nose. "Just as a note of reference, it would be good if you didn't say things like that during a police interrogation. It doesn't help us eliminate you as a suspect. Where were you Thursday night?"

"Thursday night?" I repeated, thoughtfully massaging my chin. "Let's see. Thursday night. Oh, yeah, I was sitting at home, watching television, trying not to violate my parole."

"Did you kill Rayce Daubner?"

"Why are you asking me that?"

"That's why we're here. We're investigating a murder, remember?"

"I know that, Fran, but I thought you already knew who killed Rayce." He frowned. Try as I might, I couldn't not smile. "I heard Smoochie Xenakis killed him."

"You've been talking to Dena Marie, I presume?"

"She stopped by for a little chat."

"Let me ask you again. Did you kill Rayce Daubner?"

"Oh, how I wish that I had."

"But you didn't, right?"

"At the very least, I would have liked to have watched. It wouldn't have been as satisfying as actually wrapping my hands around his throat and squeezing his eyeballs out of their sockets, but it wouldn't have been bad."

"You're not answering my question."

"If you do find out who killed that loathsome bastard, let me know, because I'll give him a big kiss—right on the lips."

"Johnny, you don't seem too upset over this."

"Imagine that. The guy who set me up so that I spent seven years of my life in prison is found shot to death, and you're surprised that I'm not upset."

Fran turned to Majowski and asked, "Do you have any questions for our friend?" Majowski slowly shook his head. Fran turned back to me and said, "Don't be leaving town. I might have follow-up questions."

I swallowed. The reality of my situation came into clear focus. Somewhere, probably just outside the jail, a hulking white supremacist was waiting for me. "You're not cutting me loose, are you?"

"Yeah, you're free to go."

Considering my prospects, I was suddenly very content being an incarcerated murder suspect. "I can't leave."

"What do you mean, you can't leave?"

"I can't go out there. There are people waiting for me that I don't want to see."

"Who?"

"Some guys from prison who want to have a little reunion."

"I don't know what you've gotten yourself into, but that's not my problem." He turned to Majowski. "Cut him loose."

"No, wait. Maybe you should keep me locked up for a couple more days until you've verified my alibi."

"Are you nuts? I don't think you did it anyway. I just brought you in here to cover my ass when the feds show up."

"Aren't you worried that someone might say you let me go out of favoritism because we're old friends?"

Fran yawned as he stood, keeping his knuckles pressed to the corners of the glass-topped table. He said, "Sorry, pal, but I've got nothing to hold you on. Get out of here."

I can't say that I gave my next move a lot of thought, because if I had, I wouldn't have done it. But in that instant, it seemed like a good idea. My hands were cuffed, so I stood, reared back, and gave Francis the most vicious headbutt I could muster. It caught him square on the nose. Blood splattered all over his face as he flew back, landing on his back and yelping like a little girl. I hit him so hard it made me a little woozy. "There, now you've got something to hold me on. You're a lousy sheriff, and you were an even worse quarterback. The worst I've ever seen. If it hadn't been for me, you would have been lucky to make junior varsity." Majowski was already up; he locked his arms around me and pinned me against the wall. I danced around a little bit, but I didn't make any serious attempt to get loose. Fran crawled to his knees and cupped his hands over the gnarled cartilage. "It's a good thing you had me cuffed, or I would have whipped the shit out of you, Roberson."

"Goddamn you, Johnny," he moaned, blood running through this fingers. Then, to Majowski: "Lock his ass up."

CHAPTER FIFTEEN
SHERIFF FRANCIS ROBERSON

The one good thing about getting head-butted in the nose was that it made me quit thinking about my headache, which paled in comparison to the throbbing pain emanating from the middle of my face. Johnny knows I'm a bleeder. In high school, I would sneeze and get a nosebleed. Every time I bumped my nose, it would bleed. I ruined a dozen shirts a year. And that son of a bitch rammed his forehead square in the middle of my face. I hope he goes back to prison.

Doc Baughman, our jailhouse physician, stopped by and chuckled as I told him the story. He set a piece of tape gently over the bridge of my nose, which extended out in comic proportions beneath a pair of blackening eyes. "We won't be able to do anything about it until the swelling goes down," Doc said. "Might be an improvement, anyway."

I ignored his attempt at humor. I was thinking about handcuffing Johnny and letting Toots put the boots to him.

Doc was finishing up when Allison appeared in the doorway. "Phone on line one."

"Who is it?"

She had disappeared before I finished the question. She was still steamed about Dena Marie's surprise attack that morning. I had no control over the visit, but given my recent dalliance with the former homecoming queen, I can't say that I blame her. "Well, let's see what fresh hell this will bring." I pushed the flashing button on my phone. "Sheriff Roberson."

"Sheriff, Marshall Hood over at the *Wheeling Intelligencer*."

Marshall was the bureau chief for the *Intelligencer's* Steubenville bureau. He was a very good reporter.

"Hi, Marshall. Did you get all the information you needed on the fire?"

"Everything but who or what caused it."

"That's still the million-dollar question."

"Any suspects?"

"Oh, I've got a couple people in mind."

"Anyone you'd care to name?"

I laughed. We both knew the answer to that question. "No, I don't believe I would. If we charge someone, you'll be the first person I call. Take it easy, Marshall."

"Wait! That's not the reason I'm calling." I hated hearing that. "I was told that you've questioned two suspects in Rayce Daubner's murder."

"Marshall, you know I can't comment on suspects in an ongoing investigation."

"I realize that, but I wanted to give you a chance to comment. I'm writing a story for Monday morning's paper that says that you questioned Matthew Vincent Xenakis and Johnny Earl in connection with the murder. I also heard that Mr. Earl spent the night in your jail on suspicion of murder and is now being held on an assault charge for striking you earlier today."

I could feel the heat creeping up around my ears. "Who told you that?"

"Come on, Sheriff, you know me better than that. I'm not going to reveal my source, but I can tell you that it's extremely reliable."

"I can't comment."

"Understood, but I'm still running with the story. I was told that Daubner assaulted Xenakis a while back—busted him up pretty good. There's motive. Also, I was told that Daubner was the guy who set up Earl on the drug bust that sent him to prison. Excellent motive, wouldn't you say?"

"I wouldn't say anything. Do you have any more questions that I might actually comment on?"

"Sheriff, that FBI training to never comment on anything is not helping you as an Ohio sheriff."

I hung up and yelled, "Goddammit!" which made my nose hurt even worse. I stormed out into the hall. Toots was standing in front of Allison's desk; I interrupted their conversation. She looked away and began brushing her hair behind her ears the way she did when she was nervous. "I just got off the phone with Marshall Hood at the *Intelligencer*. He knows we questioned Johnny and Smoochie; he knew Daubner had kicked the shit out of Smoochie; he even knew Johnny gave me a headbutt to the nose. How in the hell did he find out?" I focused in on Allison and said, "You're looking awful damn guilty about something."

"Excuse me?" she said. "You have the nerve to say that *I* look guilty?" Red splotches were popping up on her neck. I didn't know if they were from nerves or anger, but I knew I had crossed the line. She had the enameled compact mirror I had given her for her birthday in her hand and appeared ready to launch it at me. "You are treading on such thin ice it's unbelievable."

"*Someone* called him!" I yelled, looking at Toots.

"I certainly hope that you don't think it was me," he said.

I knew it wasn't Toots, but no one was above suspicion. "Then who the hell was it?"

Toots shrugged. "Fairbanks? He had motive after this morning."

I shook my head. "He couldn't have known about my nose." Toots grinned. "What?"

"Sorry to tell you this, Sheriff, but it's all over Steubenville. I went down to the diner for lunch, and everyone at the counter was already talking about it."

"Jesus Christ! This place is an information sieve."

"It's no big deal, boss. I wouldn't lose any sleep over it."

"I don't need this, Toots. Christ, I want to run for Congress. I don't need this kind of ink."

"You said just the other night that any interview with the press was a public-relations opportunity."

"This isn't what I meant. I was talking about judging the pie contest at the fair or teaching bicycle safety at the elementary school, not answering questions about a murdered federal informant and getting whacked in the nose by a suspect in the case, who was supposed to be a friend of mine, and who called me a lousy quarterback."

"He said you were a lousy *sheriff*. He said you were a worse quarterback."

My teeth sounded like a grinding transmission in my head. "Are you done?"

Toots laughed. "Okay, just so we're clear, you're saying this isn't a public-relations opportunity?"

"It's a fuckin' nightmare, that's what it is! If I find the cocksucker who called that reporter, I swear to Jesus, I'll string him up by his balls."

CHAPTER SIXTEEN
ALLISON ROBERSON

First of all, I have no balls by which he could string me up. And, second, I haven't been a cocksucker since I learned of his tryst with Dena Marie Xenakis. From the good sheriff's perspective, it has been a particularly agonizing punishment, as he is very fond of oral sex, and I happen to be an exquisite provider. But he should have thought of that before he slithered between the sheets with that little tramp.

Yes, I called the reporter. That nitwit husband of mine needs the attention. I swear to Jesus I don't know how someone could be so smart and so naive at the same time. This *is* a public-relations opportunity. If he seriously wants to make a run for Congress, then he needs this kind of attention. Judging pie contests at the fair? Give me a break. This is an opportunity to demonstrate that he's a strong lawman.

My call to the reporter is causing nine shades of hell at the department, and Frannie is probably so mad that boiling mounds of white spittle are collecting in the corners of his mouth. He's no doubt roaming the halls, questioning and accusing all who cross his path. I don't feel the least bit guilty. Frannie's the one who backed me into this corner.

Tonight, he'll be pacing the floor and chugging antacid right from the bottle. He'll pace, mutter a few profanities, then take a pull on the pink fluid. Good. Serves him right. There's no use in trying to explain why I did it, because he just wouldn't understand. He thinks all he has to do to get elected to Congress is show up, smile, tell people that he was in the FBI and that he played in the same backfield as Johnny Earl, and everyone will vote for him. I've explained to him on numerous occasions that winning an election to Congress is going to take hard work, but he just smiles and says, "You worry too much."

You're goddamn right I worry too much. I'm living in a dying little hellhole in eastern Ohio. I have reason to worry. He would sit back and do nothing more to get elected to Congress than toss bubble gum from his cruiser during the Fourth of July parade. Getting elected sheriff was easy. Hell, he could probably win two terms after he was dead. But that's not the plan! The plan is to run for Congress, and then the governor's office, and he doesn't get it.

Well, I get it. I get it just fine. I know exactly what it's going to take to get his ass sitting in a leather chair in Columbus. That's why I've appointed myself his unofficial director of media relations, and I'm going to keep calling that reporter.

While it's true that I want to get out of Steubenville, I'm also doing this for Frannie. I do love him. He's a good man, and I believe that his fling with Dena Marie was an error in judgment and it won't happen again, though I believe he still lusts for her. He can lust all he wants, but he better keep that tool in his pants.

After learning of the fling, I ordered him never, under any circumstances, to speak to Dena Marie again. I told him, "If you find that bitch standing in an alley with a bloody knife in her hand and a mutilated body at her feet, you goddamn better well call Toots to the scene to order her to drop the weapon."

About five minutes after Dena Marie left the office this morning—about the time required to do some push-ups and work off the semi he was no doubt sporting under the desk—he came out and said, "Allie, she just charged into my office and started talking. It wasn't my fault. She ambushed me."

"I made fresh coffee," I said, as though I hadn't heard his explanation.

He skulked back into his office. I'm going to lighten up on him pretty soon. I don't want him to be worrying about our relationship when he should be concentrating on becoming a United States congressman.

CHAPTER SEVENTEEN
MATTHEW VINCENT
"SMOOCHIE" XENAKIS

Every Monday morning began with what my boss called a one-on-one meeting. I called it a flogging session. It was his way of jump-starting the week—berating me for thirty minutes. During these meetings, we reviewed everything I had done the previous week and everything I hoped to accomplish in the coming week. The flogging sessions took place before another weekly meeting with the hospital's chief executive and his staff. This gave my boss fodder to make jokes at my expense and take credit for my accomplishments. He did it right in front of me, and I never once had the guts to call him on it.

He liked to summon me into his office. He would call me on the phone and say, "Let's go." If I showed up uninvited at his office door, his brow would furrow and he would say, "Give me five minutes. I'll call." He liked the control. Thus, despite the fact that we had a standing meeting at nine each Monday, I waited in my office to be summoned.

I was especially not looking forward to his meeting today. The previous Friday, while I was at lunch, he placed a manila envelope with my annual performance review on my chair, then left for the day. It was scathing. He marked me deficient in nearly every category and placed me on probation. I was crushed. I'm not one to brag, but I work hard at this job, and it was a totally unfair evaluation. It would seem that he's starting a documentation trail in order to fire me. I'm just sick about it, and I know that I won't have the guts to stand up to him. On top of that, someone rifled through my desk over the weekend. I assume that it was one of the cleaning people looking for money, because it's not the first time that it has occurred. They tried to cover it up, but I could tell that they had rummaged through it because my pencils were all askew. I'm very anal about my pencils and line them up neatly in my drawer, then slowly close it so they don't roll around. They were scattered everywhere when I opened my drawer this morning.

At nine fifteen, however, I still hadn't gotten the call. I collected my pens and portfolio and walked across the hall. The door was open, but he wasn't in the office. "Have you seen Mr. Oswald?" I asked his secretary, Shirley.

She swallowed, looked at me with wide eyes, and shook her head. She acted as though she was scared to answer me. *She knows*, I thought. *She saw the evaluation and figured I'm a dead man walking.* "No," she finally blurted. "He left a while ago. I don't know where he went. He didn't say. Honest to God."

"'Honest to God'?" I said. "I believe you."

"Okay, good, because he didn't tell me. Really."

"I believe you, Shirley," I repeated. I checked my watch. "Is he coming back before our ten o'clock with the executive staff?"

"I don't know, Mr. Xenakis. He didn't say. Really."

Mr. Xenakis? I couldn't ever remember Shirley ever calling me "Mr. Xenakis." All of a sudden, she had taken a very formal approach to our relationship. This was not good.

The phone was ringing as I walked back into my office. It was my brother, Luke. "Did you do it?" he asked.

"Did I do what?"

"Did you kill Rayce Daubner?"

"Don't be absurd. Of course I didn't kill Rayce Daubner."

He laughed. "I didn't think so, either. I never thought you had it in ya, but it's kind of exciting having a brother who's suspected of murder."

"I'm not a murder suspect. Who told you that?"

Several seconds of silence passed. "You haven't seen the morning *Intelligencer*, have you?"

"No."

"Well, big brother, I suggest you get a copy. You're all over the front page."

"Hold on," I said. I set the receiver down on the desk and walked out to the lobby. There was a newspaper rack between the elevators. In the upper left corner of the front page was a two-deck headline that spanned three columns.

Detectives Question Former Star Athlete,
Social Worker in Steubenville Slaying

I slipped a quarter into the steel box and bought a copy, reading it as I walked back to my office. "You still there?" I asked, picking up the phone.

"Yep. Get one?"

"This is terrible. This reporter names me as a suspect in the murder."

"This comes as a surprise to you? They did haul you in for questioning, didn't they?"

"Yes, but they don't really think I did it. They said it was just a cursory thing."

I could hear my brother exhale. "Matthew, if they call you in for questioning, you're a suspect. Period. You've watched enough television to know better. They probably told you that so that you'd relax, maybe slip up and say something to implicate yourself."

"But they can't seriously think that I killed Rayce."

"That has nothing to do with anything. Right now, you've got a sheriff with political aspirations investigating the murder of an FBI informant. He's going to want to get it cleaned up to keep the feds off his ass, and he doesn't want a high-profile murder to go unsolved while he's getting ready to make a run for Congress."

"He's going to run for Congress?"

"It's not official, but his dad has been all over the county for the past year trying to raise money and grease the skids."

"Are you saying that he would arrest someone for murder just to make himself look good in front of the voters?"

"I think that's one reason he might do it."

He was, I knew, implying that the good sheriff might be interested in my wife. "I don't think I have anything to worry about."

"I'd like to know how many disasters throughout history have been preceded by that statement. Look, if they called you in for questioning, you're a suspect and you should talk to an attorney."

I groaned. "I don't know."

"Daniel Sabatino—200 South Fourth Street. He's the guy who does all my business work. Does some criminal defense work, too. Good guy and tough as nails. He'll give you good advice. I'll call him and tell him that you're going to stop on your way home."

It made sense. "I'll do it. Thanks. I've got to go to a meeting."

"Okay, killer, have a good day."

The executive staff meetings are more of a lesson in humiliation than the morning floggings with Mr. Oswald. The hospital's president sits at the head of a huge boardroom table with his direct reports seated on either side. I never sit at the table; I have to sit along the wall with the secretaries. Behind my back they call me "Mr. Oswald's bitch." They think I don't know about that, but I do. There's no logical reason for me to be at the meeting, except it gives Mr. Oswald someone to whom he can pass directives.

I arrived early for the meeting and found Mr. Oswald in conversation with the president. They both looked startled when I walked into the room. "Was there anything you wanted to talk to me about before the meeting?" I asked my boss. He shook his head, keeping his eyes on the notepad in front of him. "Weren't we supposed to meet at nine?" I asked.

"Yes, we were, but I got busy. I apologize for not telling you I couldn't make it this morning."

This was very bad. First, Shirley had called me "Mr. Xenakis," now Mr. Oswald had apologized. In the ten years that I had worked for him, not once had the words "I apologize" crossed his lips. Phrases such as "I apologize," "I'm sorry," "Excuse me," and "Pardon me" were simply not part of his vocabulary, at least when he was dealing with me. He was being polite to the condemned. He was the brutal prison guard who started treating the prisoner with kindness the day before he went to the electric chair. I was going to be fired; it was just a question of when.

The meeting was uneventful in that not once did Mr. Oswald give me a directive. When the meeting was over, he almost sprinted out of the room. I walked back to his office. It was empty, and the light was off. "Did Mr. Oswald come back here?" I asked Shirley.

"Just for a minute. He ran into his office, then dashed out the door."

"Did he say when he would be back?"

"No."

"I have some work to do. Would you let me know when he gets back?"

"I'd be happy to, Mr. Xenakis."

Again with the *Mr. Xenakis*. What was up with her? What was up with Mr. Oswald? It was all very strange. I had to talk to him. I would be straightforward. If he was trying to get rid of me by giving me undeserved evaluations, he needn't bother. I would start looking for another job and leave as soon as possible. I would rather leave on my terms than get fired.

Mr. Oswald did not return to the office that day. At four thirty and tired of waiting, I left for my meeting with attorney Daniel Sabatino. When I walked into his office, he was standing behind his receptionist, pointing at a document on her desk and telling her what changes to make. He looked up, nodded, and asked, "Are you Xenakis?"

"Yes, sir."

"Be with you in a minute." He was wearing a tailored pair of gray slacks and a white shirt with French cuffs and cufflinks made from Mercury head dimes. His tie was red and navy striped. Not a hair was out of place. After another minute of instruction, he motioned me to the back. His desk was a beaten-up oak piece that looked like it should belong to a first-grade teacher. The office was somewhat spartan—a contrast, I thought, to his dress. He pushed the door closed behind us and started talking before he had planted himself behind the desk. "You're the murder suspect, huh?"

"That's what the paper said."

"Did the cops ask you to come in and talk?"

I nodded.

"Then you're a suspect. Would you like me to be your legal counsel?"

"What's it going to cost me?"

"That's not a problem. It's been taken care of."

"My brother?"

"Yes. He thinks your wife will try to set you up to take the fall."

"He told you that?"

"Yep."

"What else did he say?"

"The truth?"

I nodded.

"He said that she's a heartless bitch."

"They're not what you would call close."

"Apparently not. Do you want me to help you out?"

"Sure."

Sabatino slid a document and a pen across the table. "Sign and date that. It's a simple contract stating that I am representing you as legal counsel in this case." When I did, he said, "Good. You understand that this is all confidential. As your lawyer, nothing leaves this room. Understand?"

"I do."

"Good. Now, are there any surprises out there that I need to be prepared for?"

"No, I didn't kill him."

"I'm sure you didn't. I'll ask you again. Any surprises?"

"No. I really didn't kill him."

He chuckled to himself. "As I said, I'm sure you didn't. I just don't want to be surprised, that's all."

"You won't be."

"Okay. Good. Here are my instructions—"

"Do I need to write this down?"

"I think you'll be able to remember."

"Go ahead."

"If someone comes up to you and asks about the newspaper story, you ask them, 'Do you think it will ever rain?' If someone asks you if you killed Rayce Daubner, you say, 'Christ Almighty, can you believe this heat?' If the cops call and want to ask you more questions, you say, 'This heat gives me a rash on my balls.' Then . . ." He pulled a business card out of the holder on his desk and flipped it across the desk to me. "You tell them to call me. You are not to answer one more question. Not one. Understand?"

I smiled. I liked this guy; I liked being represented by a hard-ass lawyer. "I give them the weather report and that's it."

"I like to keep it simple."

"I really didn't kill him, you know?"

"Then you have nothing to contribute and no reason to talk to them, do you?"

CHAPTER EIGHTEEN
JOHNNY EARL

The Common Pleas Court judge in charge of my arraignment was the Honorable Lester Theodous Pappas—"Lester the Molester." He was tall—about six foot five—and soft, virtually devoid of muscle tone. He smiled without parting his lips, hiding the grandest set of horse teeth ever seen on a human. Judge Pappas was reputed to have a fondness for young boys, which he sated on his regular vacations to the Caribbean. I don't know if that was true, but he was a member of the Steubenville Big Red Athletic Boosters and was always in the locker room after the games, passing out Coca-Colas, congratulations, and pats on the back that seemed a little too affectionate.

I was the only one on the docket that morning. Photographers from the *Herald-Star* and the *Intelligencer* were there to take my photo as I was arraigned. In the corner sat the general and the preacher. I gave the general a curt nod as I entered the courtroom, but he didn't acknowledge me. He had traded in the camouflage outfit for a pair of jeans and a worn blue work shirt. The preacher was still dressed like a movie usher. Fran and Deputy Majowski stood on the spectator side of the courtroom, talking across the railing to the prosecutor, Edward Temple, who had been two years ahead of me in school and a catcher on the baseball team. Fran had a piece of white tape across the bridge of his nose, and his face was a blooming arrangement of black, blue, and purple. I had to avert my eyes to keep from laughing.

My court-appointed defense attorney introduced himself as Marion VanderFust. He had braces on his teeth and looked all of four-teen years old. His suit was too big for his little frame, and I could have shoved my arm in the gap between his collar and pigeon neck. We sat at a table as he scanned over the incident report. After a few minutes, he whispered, "This isn't good, considering you're on parole, but I think they were out of line to keep you overnight. They've charged you with aggravated assault, which is a little much. We'll plead not guilty and try to get them to drop it to simple assault. I'm sure I can get you out of jail today on your own recognizance."

Under the table, I grabbed his right leg behind the knee, squeezing the tender sides until he nearly came out of the chair. "You'll do no such thing," I whispered. "When the prosecutor requests bond, I don't care how high, you agree to it. Under no circumstances do you get me out of jail. Understand?"

He winced and tried to struggle loose, but I had him locked tight. "Are you crazy? Why do you want to stay in jail?"

"That isn't your concern, Counselor. You just make sure I stay there. Got it?"

"Yes," he whined, and I released my grip just as the bailiff stood and said, "All rise. The Common Pleas Court of Jefferson County, Ohio, is now in session, the Honorable Lester T. Pappas presiding." After a few minutes of legal blather, the judge asked my attorney, "How does your client plead?"

"Not guilty, your honor."

After a few more minutes of discussion and filing of documents, the judge looked at the prosecutor and asked, "Bond?"

Edward Temple stood, cleared his throat, and said, "Your honor, considering Mr. Earl's past criminal record, the fact that he is currently on parole from his previous federal charge, and that, unprovoked, he struck an officer of the law, we recommend a one-million-dollar bond."

The judge's brows arched as he looked at my attorney, who swallowed and said, "That seems fair, Your Honor."

The judge frowned and looked back at Edward Temple. "Is it necessary to have such a high bond? I mean, after all, it's just Johnny. He's not going anywhere."

Uh-oh. Lester the Molester was attempting to do a good turn for the former star of the Steubenville Big Red. Edward shook his head and said, "Your honor, in light of Mr. Earl's history—"

"What Mr. Earl? It's Johnny," the judge said. "You've known him all your life. You were his catcher, for God's sake. He's not going anywhere." He turned to me. "You won't leave Jefferson County, will you, Johnny?"

I put both hands on the table and slowly lifted myself from the chair. "You bet your sweet ass I'm going to leave Jefferson County. As soon as I get out of here, I'm renouncing my US citizenship and immediately moving to the Aryan Republic of New Germania."

My response took Lester completely off guard, and he asked, "Where?"

"I am a legal citizen of the Aryan Republic of New Germania, and you have no jurisdictional right to hold me. In fact, I am a colonel in the army of that country, and I have diplomatic immunity. Your laws don't apply to me, and I demand to be set free immediately."

"What?" If I had been speaking Arabic, he couldn't have been any more confused. "New Germany?"

"New Germania, you horse's ass. Now, I demand to be set free this instant." I slammed my fist down on the table. "You have no right to hold me." I turned to the general, stomped twice on the hardwood floor, and gave him the Nazi salute. "Tell him, my gen-er-all!" I yelled. "Tell him I'm a colonel in your army and their rules don't pertain to me!" I turned back to the judge. "We have no extradition treaty with your fascist, oppressive government. Once I am across the border, I won't come back until the day that we invade your country and overthrow your bourgeois government. I am a prisoner of war. I have rights under the Geneva Convention. I demand to see a representative from the Red Cross. I will report you all to the United Nations."

"The United Nations? What the—"

"This is an act of war! Tell them, General, tell them they have no right to hold me!"

The general was stoic, glancing at me out of the corner of his eye.

"Get him out of here!" Lester yelled.

"Your ass will be sorry. When we attack your country, you'll be the first one we come after, you homo!"

Lester was beating his gavel so hard he knocked a glass of water to the floor. "Get him the hell out of my courtroom. Set bond at one million dollars." He again slammed his gavel, and it splintered into three pieces.

The flashes from the news photographers' cameras went off in rapid succession. Two deputies had my arms and were trying to drag me out. I grabbed the defense table and held on. "This is bullshit. You have no right. I demand to speak to my spiritual adviser, the right Reverend Wilfred Lewis, chaplain of the state for the Aryan Republic of New Germania. Pray, reverend, pray very hard. Ask God to smite down these heathen bastards. Tell him to kill 'em all. While you're at it, tell him to send the Jews and niggers and faggots to hell, too, just like you said."

Two more deputies came from down the hall to help out, but by this time the fight was nearly over. "General, help me! Oh, dear God, don't let them take me back to the torture chambers, I beg of you!" They dragged me out to the hall. As they did, the general and the preacher, their heads down, headed out of the courtroom; Lester was whipping his desk with what was left of his gavel handle; Fran was slouched in his chair, his thumbs hooked in his gun belt, looking dumbfounded behind his swollen nose and Technicolor face. The deputies dragged me down the steps to the jail. I kept kicking and yelling, all for show, but one of the deputies didn't see the humor and gave me a good dousing of pepper spray. Then I went peaceably.

CHAPTER NINETEEN
SHERIFF FRANCIS ROBERSON

"That was quite a performance up there," I said calmly, waiting for Johnny to get off the cot. Then I yelled, "What in God's name is wrong with you? Have you completely wigged out?" I turned and pointed an index finger toward Fritz, who was getting off his cot. "Broadcast one word, Fritz, one fuckin' word, and I swear to Jesus I'll wash your face in that toilet and you won't get another cupcake the entire time you're in my jail." Fritz skulked back to his cot, and I turned to Johnny. "What was that all about?"

"I've been trying to tell you, Fran, I can't leave the jail. Did you see that beast sitting in the back of the courtroom?"

"He was a little hard to miss."

"He was my cellmate in prison. His name is Alaric Himmler, and he's a lunatic of the first degree. He wants to drag my ass to Idaho or Utah or Montana, somewhere out there, to join his new country."

"He has a country but he doesn't know where it is?"

"It's sort of a floating target. Reality is not this guy's first language. He's not real strong on the details. He's apparently got a few wives lined up for me and a commission in his pretend country's army. I didn't think he was getting out of prison for another couple of weeks, and by that time I'd planned to be long gone. Now, I'm hosed. Not only will everyone think I'm crazy, but a Nazi to boot."

"Don't forget suspected murderer," I said.

"You're hilarious, Fran."

"Why don't you just tell Mr. Himmler that you don't want to go?"

"That won't work. He doesn't respond well to words like 'no.' Besides, he really wants my money."

"You have money?"

"Oh, yeah. A boatload. Left over from my drug-dealing days. I hid it and the feds never found it—four hundred and seventy-two thousand dollars."

I put my hands over my ears. "Christ, Johnny, I'm the sheriff. Don't be telling me that."

"You've got to help me out, Fran. Keep me in here until I figure out how to get out of town."

"You pretty much took care of that with your antics upstairs. Johnny, I've got to ask you, did you really mean what you said yesterday?"

He shook his head. "Hell no, you're a good sheriff."

"I don't mean that. I mean about being the worst quarterback you've ever seen."

"What? Of course not. I was just trying to get under your skin."

"I played four years of football at Bethany and was the starter for two, you know?"

"It was just something to get you riled. That's all."

I nodded. "Okay. I'll get the prosecutor to ask Judge Pappas to give you a mental evaluation. Given your antics in court today, I'm sure he won't question that request. That should keep you locked up for a while. But I know the judge, and he's not going to let you stay here forever. He'll cool off eventually, and you'll have to go."

CHAPTER TWENTY
MATTHEW VINCENT
"SMOOCHIE" XENAKIS

For the next three days, Mr. Oswald didn't come in to his office. Shirley continued to call me "Mr. Xenakis" and said his absence was due to a heavy schedule of off-site meetings. "I really need to talk to him," I said.

"I'll be sure to pass your message along, Mr. Xenakis."

She was treating me like I was a salesman trying to schedule an appointment. "Shirley, is there something wrong?"

She struggled to swallow and shook her head. "No, sir. Everything is fine."

On my way home that night, I was passing through town when I saw my brother, Luke, getting out of his car in front of the Starlighter Bar. He spotted my car and waved for me to stop. He pushed his head into the open passenger-side window and said, "Hey, killer."

"That's not funny, Luke."

He winked. "Sure it is. Come on in, and I'll buy you a beer."

"I don't know, Luke, I need to get home."

He rolled his eyes. "One beer. Come on."

I pulled my car to the curb and followed him inside. The day-shift workers from the steel mill were lined up at the bar. When we entered, people's heads turned, and I felt the gaze of a dozen steelworkers. When we sat down, Luke said, "You're a celebrity."

"What do you mean?"

"Did you see the way everyone was looking at you?"

I shrugged. "I don't come in the Star that often."

He grinned. "That has nothing to do with it, big brother. You're the talk of Steubenville. Everyone thinks you killed Rayce Daubner." He caught the attention of the waitress and held up two fingers. "Rolling Rocks."

"No one believes that I killed Rayce. They know I'm not capable of something like that."

"Don't fool yourself. Everyone's wondering if they misjudged you. No one thinks it was Johnny; it would be too obvious. They think *you* killed him. Look around the bar. Everyone in here is looking at you and whispering. It's all about *you*, bro." He was right. When I looked up and made eye contact, their eyes dipped back to their drinks. Luke took a hit of his Rolling Rock and grinned. "Turns out, everyone thinks you're a very dangerous man."

Even I had to smile at the very thought. "You know, the secretary keeps calling me 'Mr. Xenakis,' and my boss hasn't been in the office for three days. I'd swear he's ducking me."

"He probably is. All this time he's been beating up on you, and now you're a suspected murderer. That would make *my* ass pucker." He leaned across the table and lowered his voice. "Matthew, this is a great opportunity for you. You've been presented a chance to change your life. The best thing that can happen here is that no one is ever charged with Rayce Daubner's murder. You'll always be the suspect. You'll be the guy who killed him and got away with it. Everyone will always wonder if you'll snap again. It's perfect. Take advantage of this. Play the cards you've been dealt. Let everyone think you're a very dangerous man."

I love model trains, and I have a big setup in our basement. As a kid who was prone to abuse from nearly every other kid in town, I spent a lot of time in my room with my trains and train magazines. I have continued the hobby and have made by hand a detailed, scale model of the steel mills and the railroads that service them. The *Herald-Star* did a feature story on it a few years ago, and they took a photo of me standing in front of the display and wearing an engineer's cap, which Dena Marie said made me look mentally retarded. I'm now working on a model of the railroad trestle that spans the Dillonvale Gorge east of Adena, Ohio. Dena Marie doesn't mind my hobby, and I sometimes think it's because it keeps me in the basement and away from her.

After dinner, I went downstairs to work on the trestle, but I couldn't focus on it. I couldn't stop thinking about the looks I had received in the Starlighter Bar and my brother's words: "Everyone thinks you're a very dangerous man." I've read stories about men and women who after years of abuse become violent. They just snap. That certainly isn't me, but I guess no one else knows that. In turn, my brother's other words kept popping into my head: "Take advantage of this."

I put down my paintbrush and walked to the half-bath we had in the basement. There's a small mirror above the sink, and I stared hard into my reflection, then started to laugh. As I mentioned, it's difficult to look intimidating with bulbous lips. I pressed my lips together and tried to roll them under, squeezing the excess flesh between my teeth. I noticed for the first time in my life that when I frown, my right eyebrow dips lower than the left. Holding the pose, I leaned toward the mirror and in a barely audible tone said, "Call me 'Matthew.'" It didn't sound right. I tried again: "Call me 'Matt.'" Not intimidating enough. Again, I rolled my lips and held my frown, and in a low, slow voice tried my middle name. "Call me 'Vincent.'"

That was it. For twenty minutes, I practiced the pose, working to keep my lips tight and my eyes steady. "Call me 'Vincent.'" I wet down my hair and rubbed in some of Dena's hair gel that was sitting on the back of the toilet. It gave me a harder edge and made my eyebrows more pronounced. Suddenly, there was nothing funny about what I was doing. "Call me 'Vincent.'" Perhaps Luke was right. This was an opportunity. I postured in the mirror for another hour, practicing sneers and holding stare-downs with my reflection. The corners of my mouth, I learned, would turn down slightly when I frowned. "Call me 'Vincent.'"

I gripped the edge of the sink and was staring hard into the mirror when Dena Marie yelled down the stairs. "Smoochie, are you going to help the kids with their homework or play with your trains all night?"

I walked to the bottom of the steps and looked up, my face frozen in the stony expression I had practiced. She swallowed, the look of disgust on her face melting away. I waited a moment. Then I said, "I'm not 'Smoochie' anymore. Call me 'Vincent.'"

Carmel's Clothiers, on Market Street, is the only men's clothing store in Jefferson County. At one time, when the steel mills and coal mines were booming, Carmel's did a handsome business. But the demand for fine suits tumbled with the mills. Carmel's was sold several times and now carries a scaled-down line of clothing.

The Beckett kid—the one they called "Hootie," who was always talking through a mouth full of saliva—had worked at Carmel's since graduating from high school a few years earlier. He's lazy and a wise guy. He stands out in front of the store, rocking from heel to toe, hands stuffed in his pockets, always wearing a garish polyester shirt with the top three buttons undone, pants that look like they belong on a disco floor, and shoes that need polishing. He laughs after every comment with a nervous, snorting laugh as he sucks air into his spit-filled mouth.

When I walked into Carmel's the morning after meeting Luke at Starlighter, Hootie was dressed in a bright-purple shirt and pale-yellow pants.

"I need a suit and I need it today," I said.

"We got a lot of suits. What kind?"

I fingered a few of the dark suits on a rack against the wall. "I want a suit that will help me make a statement."

He laughed, and little flecks of saliva spewed onto his chin. "You? What kind of statement would that be?"

"A statement that doesn't say I'm a reject from the disco era." I cupped my hands and slapped his ears the way Rayce Daubner had done to me every morning in high school.

"Mother fuck, Smoochie, what's wrong with you?!"

I grabbed his ears, twisted them, and pulled him close. I had seen that in a movie. "My name isn't Smoochie. My name is Vincent Xenakis. You, you little punk, can call me 'Mr. Xenakis.' Got it?"

The boy's eyes widened, and a stunned look consumed his face. "Yes, sir."

"Good. Now listen carefully. I want a suit that conveys the message that I'm not someone to be toyed with." I fished the newspaper from my hip pocket and dropped it on the counter, making sure the story of my suspicion of murder was faceup. His eyes went to the paper, then back to me. "I'm a 40 long. What do you have in my size?"

He practically sprinted to the rack of suits ahead of me. He parted the suits, exposing a dozen or so in my size. The first one was summerweight wool—charcoal with light gray and white pinstripes. I plucked it from the rack and took it to the dressing room without comment. When I returned, Hootie was waiting with his tape measure and tailor's soap. He marked the cuffs on the sleeves and pants. It was good around the waist.

"You can pick it up next Tuesday, Mr. Xenakis."

"We seem to be having a problem communicating, Hootie. I hear the sewing machine in the back, so I'm guessing that Mrs. Sadowski is back there. I'm going down the street to get a haircut, maybe a shave. When I come back, I better be able to wear that suit out of the store. I don't care if you've got to hem it yourself, it better be done. Now I need to use your phone."

"No one's allowed to use it except employees."

I picked up the handset and started dialing. As the phone on the other end of my call began to ring, I looked at Hootie and asked, "Did you say something?"

"No."

"Good. Is my suit done yet?"

Hootie swiped at some stray saliva with the back of his hand. Then he turned and walked to the back room. Shirley answered the phone, "Social Services."

I waited until she had repeated herself before responding. "Shirley, this is Vincent. I won't be in today."

It took a moment for her to realize who it was. "Oh, Mr. Xenakis. Okay, ah, is there a reason why you won't be in?"

"Of course," I said.

She waited for an additional explanation, which didn't come. "F-fine," she stammered. "I'll tell Mr. Oswald. Will you be in tomorrow?"

"I don't know. It's still today." I hung up.

I went down to the Ideal Barber Shop. Frankie Faust, who had cut my hair since I was a kid, was in the barber chair, reading the sports page. Okie Piergowski was loafing in a chair, working the crossword puzzle. "Morning, Smoochie," Frankie said.

"My name's Vincent," I said, sliding into the chair that he had vacated.

"Okay . . . Vincent," he said. "What's new?"

"I saw you reading the paper, Frank. I'm sure you know what's new. The cops think I might have murdered Rayce Daubner." I looked at him and winked. "But we all know that I'm not capable of something like that, don't we?"

"Sure. You wouldn't do something like that," he said, struggling to swallow. "Ah, you want the usual?"

"No. Just trim it up on the sides. I want to wear it slicked back."

"Smoochie—I mean, Vincent—it'll be hard to keep your hair in place like that. I'll have to use a gallon of gel." He forced a laugh.

"Then use a gallon of gel," I said without the slightest hint of humor. "And give me a shave, too."

I walked out of the barber shop thirty minutes later, smelling of talc and hair gel and bay rum. I wanted to make sure that I gave Hootie enough time to get the suit altered, so I stopped by the diner for breakfast. "Coffee, wheat toast, and two eggs, scrambled," I told the waitress. "And I don't want the eggs runny."

She was cracking her gum as she nodded. "You got it, sweetie," she said.

I really didn't care if the eggs were a little runny, but I liked my newfound assertiveness. I was looking for opportunities to give orders. The tab was $2.50. I made a bit of a show of dropping a ten-dollar bill on the table as I left for Carmel's. Hootie was standing out in front of the store; he saw me coming and ducked inside. He was holding the suit by the hanger when I walked in.

"You're a good boy, Hootie," I said, snagging the hanger as I walked by and went into the dressing room. It was a perfect fit.

I bought a white shirt and the brightest red tie they had. After I paid for them, I tucked a ten-dollar bill into the breast pocket of Hootie's purple shirt. "Here. Go buy yourself another ugly shirt."

I liked the way the suit fit; Mrs. Sadowski had done a nice job. The tie and a highly buffed pair of black loafers set off the suit. When I left Carmel's and walked back to my car, I could feel eyes on me from within the bank and stores along Market Street.

And I liked it.

Fifteen minutes after leaving Carmel's, I walked into my brother's steel-fabricating plant. As I made my way through the middle of the shop toward my brother's office, one of his employees, Dwight Yakovac, said, "Hey, look who's here. It's John Wilkes Xenakis. Smoochie, you shoot anyone today?"

Everyone in the area laughed.

I stopped and turned to face him. "No, Dwight, I haven't," I said, giving him a quick wink. "But the day is young, isn't it? Anything could happen." I watched him swallow hard and continued on. As I grabbed hold of the door knob to my brother's office, I turned and said, "By the way, my name is Vincent."

I closed the door and stared out at Dwight through the open blinds in the door window. Without blinking, I slowly twisted the lever until the blinds closed. "Oh, my God, this is so much fun," I said, pulling up a chair from the corner of Luke's office.

"What's fun?" Luke asked.

"Being a tough guy—a badass. I know I'm just pretending, but it's a blast."

"Where in God's name did you get that suit? You look like Al Capone."

I pumped my fists in front of my chest like a boxer, throwing jab after jab. "Perfect. That's just the look I was going for. No kidding. This is the best. All of a sudden, everyone's afraid of me. Dena Marie, I think she is flat-out convinced that I killed Rayce."

"Good."

"I know!" I scooted closer to his desk and hunkered forward so I didn't have to talk too loud. "You know that feeling you get when you're walking down the street and all of a sudden there's a stray dog standing in front of you and he's growling and showing his teeth and you have to catch yourself or you'll piss your pants? I can tell from Dena Marie's eyes that she's that kind of scared. She looks at me like she really thinks I did it, and maybe that I would do it again."

Luke tilted his head back and laughed. "This is excellent. You're in control of the marriage for a change."

"She's terrified of me. Maybe that's not right."

"Oh, please. Considering everything she's done to you, you've been a saint. Was it right for her to shack up with Rayce Daubner?"

I was smiling. "I'm going to try this on my boss, too."

"Oswald?"

I nodded. "Sometimes, brother, the world can be a beautiful place."

CHAPTER TWENTY-ONE
SHERIFF FRANCIS ROBERSON

It was like a toothache. Not the sharp, stabbing jolt that feels like the pulp of the tooth has turned to molten steel, but that dull throb that never quite goes away. Anchored somewhere deep in my skull, it pulsated with each beat of my heart, reverberating inside my ears. There were times when, for a few minutes, I could ignore it, but it was always there, gnawing away.

I pondered the train wreck that had become my life. And as I hid in the solitude of my office—elbows on my desk, palms pressed to my temples—I wondered how such a smooth-running machine could have gone so far south so quickly. Its genesis, I'm sure, was the tiny leap in my loins the day I stopped by the grocery to buy a pack of gum and Dena Marie was behind the counter in a white blouse that revealed her cleavage and the lacy top of her bra. I could have easily survived the indiscretion that followed. But then that goddamn Rayce Daubner had to go and get himself murdered. It was hard to believe that the death of someone as loathsome as Rayce Daubner could cause me so much grief. For the most part, nobody cared that Daubner was dead. But it was already causing me problems from which my career might never recover. The feds would certainly investigate the death of one of their informants. The man who at one time had been my best friend was locked in my jail, my nose was the size of a lemon, my wife was barely speaking to me, and I had a neo-Nazi running around town trying to kidnap the suspect in a murder case.

As my father likes to say, "Other than that, Mrs. Lincoln, how was the play?"

I'll tell you what I needed. I needed Allison to come in the office, crawl under my desk, and relieve a little of my stress. Once, sometimes twice a week, she would come in, lock the door, and give me head. That hadn't happened since I screwed Dena Marie, and I doubted it would happen any time soon. If I wanted relief, I was forced to employ the solo technique of my adolescent years.

Because the door that separated the sheriff's office from the main hallway of the courthouse building was warped, it skidded on the floor whenever it was pushed open, causing the frosted glass in the top of the door to vibrate in its molding. This effectively alerted us to visitors. At the FBI, we had a camera in the lobby; at the Jefferson County Sheriff's Department, we had a warped door with loose glass.

When the door skidded at about nine o'clock on this morning, the air was pierced by the squeal of my wife, who in a dancing, high-pitched voice said, "Oh, my God, I can't believe it. Oh, my God, what are you doing here? Fran will be so happy to see you."

She was wrong. I knew she was wrong because at that moment there was no one I wanted to see. I had no clue as to the identity of the visitor as I listened to the footfalls approach my office.

Whenever I'm ambushed—say, my wife walks into my office and asks whether I've been having an affair with Dena Marie Xenakis—a wave of heat races up my neck, I blink rapidly, and I nervously swallow. That was the reaction that came over me the instant Alfred Vincenzio walked through my door.

"Hey, Francis," he said, extending his hand before I could get out of my chair. "Great to see you again."

The saliva frothed in my mouth, and a scalding rash erupted under my collar and ripped up the back of my head, causing each follicle to scream and stand erect. The pounding in my head was deafening. Alfred Rockford Vincenzio—my nemesis at the FBI Academy and the man from whom I had stolen my wife—was standing there wearing a tailored suit and a phony grin.

"Al, Christ Almighty, what a surprise," I managed. "What brings you down here?" I had to swallow again before I could return a phony smile. He didn't respond. We both knew what had brought him to Steubenville—the corpse of Rayce Daubner. Not only was the bureau investigating his death, it was doing so with the one person in the world I least wanted to see snooping around Jefferson County. We shook hands, and Alfred squeezed too hard, still trying to impress.

"What the hell happened to your nose?" he asked.

"An unfortunate encounter with one of our jail residents," I said.

"Looks like it was very unfortunate." He gestured toward his partner, whom I hadn't even noticed. He was a squat black man with a furrowed brow. "Francis, this is Agent Elvis Norwine."

I extended my hand toward Norwine. His brows converged upon one another as he pumped my hand once. "Francis? That your name, Francis? You got a girl's name?"

"Names can be funny. How many black guys do you run into named Elvis?" I shot back.

"You got a problem with that?" he asked.

I shrugged. "Just making an observation, that's all."

They both took uninvited seats in front of my desk. Norwine was a bullish man with thick hands and fingers. His thinning stubs of hair were flecked with gray, and he had the nose of a former boxer. Vincenzio was his usual fastidious self, not a hair out of place, everything about him neat. "Francis and I were classmates at the academy," he explained to Norwine, who was now boring in on me with a pair of dark eyes. "Francis was a rising star in white-collar crime with the bureau in Minneapolis until he resigned to become sheriff of Jefferson County."

Norwine looked around the room and gave a little laugh of surprise. "You gave up a bureau assignment to work in this shithole of a town?"

"This is where I grew up."

"I'm sorry for your luck."

"He did it for political reasons," Vincenzio said. "Francis is using this as a stepping-stone. Unless I miss my guess, he still wants to be president of the United States."

Norwine laughed. "Yeah, and I want to pitch for the New York Yankees."

"Better start working on your curveball," I offered.

"I haven't thrown a baseball since my senior year in high school, but I've got a better chance of standing on the mound in Yankee Stadium than you do of getting to the White House."

"So, Alfred, did you and Elvis come down here to insult me, or is there a reason for this call?"

"It's not a social call, Francis."

"Really? I'm shocked."

"We're investigating the death of Rayce Daubner."

"That's interesting. Why would the death of a two-bit thug like Rayce Daubner be of interest to the Federal Bureau of Investigation?"

"He was a federal informant."

I tried to sound surprised. "Get out! Rayce Daubner? A snitch for the feds?" They knew I knew. It was part of the game. "Things must be getting tough at the bureau if you're forced to use the likes of Rayce Daubner as a snitch."

"We prefer the term 'informant.'"

"I'm sure you do."

"He was actually a very good informant."

"Is that a fact?"

Norwine said, "He told us that you were banging some little tart down at the grocery store." His cramped little mouth turned up at the corners.

The heat was burning through my collar. "You can't believe everything you hear. Maybe he wasn't as good a snitch—excuse me, *informant*—as you thought. Besides, since when did the bureau turn into the morality police?"

"We're not, but we take very seriously the death of an informant," Norwine said.

"Look, Alfred, let's put our cards on the table, shall we? I'm not so naive to believe that anyone at the Federal Bureau of Investigation gives a good rat's ass about Rayce Daubner. The only reason you're here is that you're hoping to jam it up my ass sideways. Wouldn't that be a nice trophy for your wall—local sheriff, former agent, and the guy who stole your girl." This brought a smile to Norwine's face. "Even so, the bureau wouldn't let you waste your time like this, so what's up?"

"The bureau has been interested in Jefferson County for quite some time. That probably doesn't come as a big surprise to you, given the county's history of corruption. We were using Daubner for inside information, and he was doing quite well. He said he was close to dropping the package on a high-ranking elected official in Jefferson County."

"Really?"

He laughed. "No, I'm just fucking with you. He never said it was a high-ranking official. I made that up. What he actually said was he was getting ready to drop the package on *you.*"

I fought the urge to swallow. "He must have been on cocaine when he made that one up."

"No idea what he was talking about, Francis?"

"He was delusional."

"He said he was working closely with you on some projects. He said he might be getting close to some very embarrassing information on you. Are you sure you don't know what he was talking about?"

"Rayce Daubner was a pathological liar, on top of his many other redeeming qualities. What were you paying him for this inside work?"

Norwine ignored my question and asked, "Who torched his house?"

"What makes you think it was torched?"

"Looks like a cover-up job to me."

"That's an interesting theory."

"Was it?" Vincenzio asked.

"I don't know. The fire chief hasn't gotten back to me."

Vincenzio frowned and nodded slowly. "Now, Francis, don't you think it's interesting that someone with arson training, such as yourself, and the chief law enforcement officer in the county, isn't doing the investigation?"

"Why is that interesting? It's not my jurisdiction."

He shrugged. "You're obviously the most experienced arson investigator in the county. I know Ohio law. The sheriff can take over any investigation within his jurisdiction. Why would you let some backwoods fire chief conduct the investigation?"

"Just because they're not from Pittsburgh doesn't mean they aren't qualified investigators."

"Maybe you don't want the real cause found," Norwine offered.

"I don't care for the implication."

Norwine puckered his lips and twice kissed the air.

"We'd like to see the investigative file on Daubner's murder," Vincenzio said.

"Not without a court order, you won't."

Now the red was creeping up around Vincenzio's neck. "Sharing information is generally considered common courtesy among law enforcement agencies."

"Is that so? When you come in here and tell me that one of your informants was trying to drop a package on me, that doesn't make me feel particularly courteous. And I doubt my mood is going to swing any time soon."

"I don't think you realize who you're screwin' with," Norwine said.

"Don't flatter yourself. I spent more than ten years in the bureau, and I'm not intimidated. You want to go ask questions, be my guest, but don't fuck up my investigation."

Vincenzio stood to leave. "Francis, I was really hoping this wouldn't get ugly."

"I don't believe that for one minute, Alfred. I think you'd like to make it as ugly as possible."

He smiled. "Allison is still a beautiful woman."

"Why wouldn't she be?"

"I don't know. Living in a place like this can wear on a person. What did she say when she found out you were screwing the little tramp down the street?"

He was trying to rile me, hoping I would lash out. "I've got a lot of work to do, boys." I walked around the desk and opened the door. "See you around."

"Count on it," Norwine said.

When they were gone, I flipped the deadbolt on my door. I went behind my desk, dropped to one knee, and threw up in the wastebasket.

I tied up the plastic liner of the wastebasket, trying to stem the stench of a regurgitated ham-and-cheese omelet. When my head quit spinning, I stood, steadying myself with a hand on the corner of the desk, walked across the room, and opened a window.

After releasing the deadbolt on the door, I walked back behind my desk and eased into my chair. No sooner had I closed my eyes than my dad walked into my office unannounced, with the same entitlement with which he had entered my bedroom when I was twelve. He had taken just two steps into the office when he curled up his nose and said, "Phew, it smells like vomit in here."

"There's a good reason for that," I replied.

"Sick?"

"Nah, my stomach's just a little jumpy. I've got a lot on my mind. It got the best of me."

"Little Miss Sugar Britches causing you problems? I hear she's been visiting you lately."

"Good Lord, do you have this place bugged? How do you hear this stuff?"

"I hear things, that's all."

"You've got some mole planted here, is what you've got."

"Well, it's true, isn't it?"

"Yes, she's been around, but it doesn't have anything to do with—"

"Your romp at the no-tell mo-tel?"

"That's right," I said.

He poured himself a cup of coffee and slipped into one of the chairs in front of my desk. "What's up, then?"

"Dena Marie says Smoochie killed Rayce Daubner."

He nearly snorted coffee out his nose. "Smoochie Xenakis! Christ Almighty, I'll bet he's never even held a gun. She just wants to get him out of the picture."

"I know."

"Not because she's interested in you, you understand?"

"I know that, too, Dad."

He waved at the air. "If I were you, I wouldn't bust my ass trying to solve that murder."

I pulled a piece of gum from my top drawer and shoved it in my mouth. "That sounds a little odd coming from you. I figured you might see some political advantages for me if I solved it. Besides, you and Petey Daubner were pretty good friends."

"Petey Daubner was a terrific guy. He'd do anything for anyone. He gave that boy everything. Worshipped him. And when Petey was lying in that bed down at the hospital, eaten up with cancer, do you think Rayce would go up and visit? No. Not once." He sipped his coffee. "Rayce was nothing but a bully and a punk. His mom and dad are dead, so I guarantee there is not a person in this county who gives a rat's ass that he's dead. In fact, most of 'em are probably glad. Just let the investigation die. Tell the reporters that you're working hard but there aren't many clues. In a week or so, someone else will get caught screwing someone they shouldn't, and everyone will forget about Rayce Daubner. You're not going to win any votes solving the murder of someone most people in Steubenville considered a lower life-form."

"I tend to agree, but I've got more problems. Daubner was a snitch for the FBI, so they're in town sniffing around."

"I wouldn't think they'd be that interested."

"Well, the truth is, it looks like they were trying to set up a sting operation here in the county."

"Who were they after?"

I just looked at him.

"Jesus Christ. That's what he was doing up here in your office all the time—trying to set you up. I told you to quit letting him hang around here."

"I was trying to use him for some information."

"That's what you thought. He was trying to drop the dime on you. Do those FBI agents think you got rid of him to kill their investigation?"

"I don't know what they think, Dad. But the guy who's heading the investigation, he was Allison's old boyfriend before I stole her from him."

"Oh, that's jim-dandy. So he's had a hard-on for you, anyway. Christ. Every problem you have revolves around your inability to keep your dick in your pants. This guy's trying to set up a sting to nail your balls to the wall for stealing his girl, and his main snitch gets whacked. That's great, just great." He ran his hands over his face. "Well, that would make me puke, too." He stared into his coffee and then into space. Several moments passed.

"You okay, Dad?"

"I'm fine. I was just thinking about the FBI snooping around. That's bad. That would be very bad publicity, particularly if they somehow intimated that they had to come in because you were either incompetent or involved in the murder."

"I had nothing to do with the murder."

"Doesn't matter. If this guy's carrying a boner for you, all he has to do is make people think you do."

"He couldn't do that with any credibility."

"Don't be so naive. It doesn't matter. A guy who's running for Congress can't have that cloud over his head." He chewed his lower lip for a minute. "Do you think there's anything to Dena Marie's claims?"

"About Smoochie?"

Dad nodded.

"Absolutely not."

"Sometimes it's the quiet ones that surprise you. I'm thinking that there could be some good publicity in this. Plant a story about how this investigation is personal, that you're trying to solve the death of your boyhood friend. Make up some bullshit story about how he helped win some football game and you've never forgotten it. Then, you arrest the husband of a woman involved in a love triangle with the deceased. Rayce beat the hell out of Smoochie a while back, didn't he? There's motive. Oh, that's beautiful. Once you charge someone with the crime, what's left for the FBI to investigate? Nothing. It gets them off your back."

"You're starting to sound like Dena Marie. You want me to convict an innocent man in order to make my life easier?"

He waved at the air, annoyed. "How do you know he didn't do it, goddammit?"

"Dad, two minutes ago you laughed at the idea that Smoochie Xenakis would kill someone. Then you told me to call off the dogs and let it die. Now you're telling me to arrest Smoochie." He looked at me in silence, as though I wasn't there, his gaze cutting through me. "You're acting a little distracted," I finally said.

He got up and started toward the door. "Just give it some thought," he said. "It might ultimately help pave your way to the Oval Office."

CHAPTER TWENTY-TWO
ALLISON ROBERSON

W hen Alfred Vincenzio walked through the doorway of the sheriff's office, I had actually been happy to see him. It hadn't dawned on me that he was in town in hopes of finding incriminating evidence to make my husband's life a living hell. If he was successful, God knows how long I would be stuck in Steubenville. Fran and I were suddenly allies again with a common enemy.

In reality, none of this was about Fran. It was about me. Alfred is a vindictive prick, and this was his effort to make my life miserable.

I met Alfred at the FBI Academy, just like Fran. He was very good-looking in an almost pretty sort of way. Some might describe it as effeminate, particularly with the buffed fingernails. "Prissy" was what my dad called him the first time they met. He was impeccably neat and had the most perfectly coifed hair I had ever seen. It couldn't be messed up. I would run my fingers through his hair, and it would fall right back into place. He also smelled good. It's stupid, I know, but I've always had a weakness for cologne.

Alfred—he insisted on Alfred, not Al—was too fussy for his own good in the academy. They like neatness and promptness and Boy Scout–like qualities, but they would pounce on any sign of weakness. Alfred was taking a class on forensics, and the instructor ordered him to move the arm of a corpse; he reached for the corpse's arm but then pulled back his hand. "Grab it, Susie, it's not going to bite," the instructor said.

From that point on, they called him "Susie," which he hated.

Our first date was dinner at Dehar's Italian Restaurante. Alfred was charming, and I did sleep with him that night. It was a mistake that I regretted almost from the instant of coupling. I had a mirror on my dresser, and I caught him looking at it while we were making love. He wasn't looking at us; he was looking at himself. He turned out to be the vainest man I had ever met. He would feed me cheesy lines that sounded like they came out of some bad movie. "Oh, baby, you are going to be in ecstasy tonight" was his favorite. "I'm going to take you to places you never dreamed of." He would promise me a night of ecstasy, but it was never more than a single, brief romp. He could never rally the troops for an encore performance.

When he was finished—for the record, I *never* finished—he always asked, "Was that the best you've ever had?" The last night we slept together, he asked me how it was and I said, "Oh, darling, it was the most incredible eighteen seconds of my life." He got up, dressed, and left without saying a word.

I was planning on breaking it off when I met Fran. Alfred thinks Fran split us up. So does Fran, and he's quite proud of it. But the truth is I was simply tiring of Alfred, and Fran's timing was good.

So in the summer of 1989, I was angry with myself for not immediately figuring out why Alfred was in town. What a lovely trophy that would be if he could somehow link Fran to the murder of Rayce Daubner and indict a former agent. I was sure that's what Fran was thinking, but I know Alfred, and I knew that wasn't his primary motivation. This wasn't about Fran. This was about getting even with me. I had crushed his Italian pride, and he wanted to get back at me by burying my husband.

CHAPTER TWENTY-THREE
VINCENT XENAKIS

After leaving my brother's office that afternoon, I called Shirley and reported off work for the following day. Then, the next morning, I went into work at six and sat quietly in my office, with the lights off and the door shut. I was planning an ambush.

The manila envelope with a copy of my scathing evaluation rested on the edge of the desk. I couldn't help but think about the chain of events that had caused my name to be plastered across the front page of the *Herald-Star* and the *Intelligencer*. Dena Marie had been unfaithful with Rayce, which for the first time in my life prompted me to show some backbone and confront him, which had ended with me bloodied and broken in the emergency room. But word of the thrashing he gave me had gotten around and made me a suspect in his murder, which caused the detectives to question me, which ended with my name in the paper and, ultimately, me scaring my boss witless.

It's funny how things work out.

I opened my desk drawer for no particular reason and looked at the neat order of my pens and pencils. It made me smile, because at that moment I realized how much I was in control of the situation. It hadn't been a janitor looking for change who had rummaged through my desk; it had been Douglas Oswald. He had gone through it in search of my review after reading the newspaper story that named me as a murder suspect. He was afraid.

I opened the envelope, removed the performance review, and reread the damning words. When I was a freshman in high school, there was one particular time when I was getting picked on in the locker room. Some guys were pinching my nipples; others were cracking towels at my privates. I was dancing around, trying to avoid the attacks, when someone took a tongue depressor with a glob of orange muscle balm and swiped it up between my legs, smearing my anus and testicles with the burning goo. It was the only time in my life that I could remember not being afraid. I lashed out, punching several boys in the face. I screamed and cried and flailed, and they ran from the showers. It was humiliating, but I felt good about myself. For once, I had stood up for myself. For once, I hadn't been afraid. Again, that same swelling entered my chest. My face burned. Not on the surface, but from within. The rage erupted, and I craved a confrontation with Douglas Oswald.

At a few minutes before eight, I heard Shirley come into the office and begin making coffee. A few minutes later, Oswald entered. They spoke briefly, and I listened as the latch on his door opened. For several minutes, I stared at my own reflection in the window, rolling my lips under, watching my eyebrow dip. With my countenance set, I left my office. Shirley looked up from her desk, and her mouth dropped. I never broke stride, opening the door to Mr. Oswald's office and walking in. When he looked up, the blood drained from his face.

"Xenakis, uh, I thought you were off today. I'm really busy right now, so . . ."

I pulled the door closed and tossed the envelope on his desktop; it slid to a stop on his blotter. "Not too busy, I hope, to talk about *this*."

"Is this your performance review?" he asked, quickly undoing the red thread that held down the envelope's flap. He pulled it out, noticed that it was a photocopy, and asked, "Where's the original?"

"Why do you want to know?"

He struggled to swallow. "I need you to sign the original so—"

I placed my palms flat on his desk, leaned forward, and said, "Shut . . . the fuck . . . up. I'll do the talking." He looked as though he was trying to swallow a tennis ball. "You leave here every day at two thirty and expect me to cover for you. You take credit for my ideas. You make fun of me in front of senior management. You treat me like dirt. I do enough work for three people, and yet you give me an evaluation like that and have the audacity to put me on probation?"

"I, uh, I just think that recently you've—"

"Didn't I tell you to shut your mouth?" Oswald's eyes fluttered, and he shook his head. Maybe we are more primal than we like to think. When I looked into Oswald's eyes and saw fear, adrenaline surged through my body. The fear in his eyes empowered me. "Now, Oswald, here's what we're going to do. I'm going to pretend like you haven't given me my performance review. When I come in here tomorrow, I expect there to be another evaluation on my desk. And it had goddamn better well reflect the contributions I make around here. Do you understand me?" He nodded, little beads of perspiration beginning to bubble on his forehead and upper lip. "Good, because if it doesn't . . . well, if it doesn't, things could get ugly." I winked and walked to the door. I opened it about six inches, as though leaving, then closed it again and turned back toward my pasty boss. "By the way—funny thing—when you went to that hospital social worker convention in Saint Louis last year, a friend of mine saw you there with a woman who did not look like Mrs. Oswald. In fact, he said it looked a lot like Patricia Felco, the emergency-room nurse." I gave him a mocking smile. "That's just another one of the little secrets I've been keeping to myself. See you in the morning, Dougie."

As I was leaving the hospital, my briefcase in hand, I walked past the coffee shop and overheard two nurses talking. One said, "He's such a nice, quiet man. I don't think he's capable of murder."

I went back to their table and said, "It's the quiet ones you have to look out for," then continued out of the hospital.

CHAPTER TWENTY-FOUR
DENA MARIE CONCHEK
ANDROSKI XENAKIS

Chief Deputy Majowski had called that afternoon and asked me to have Smoochie call him when he got home. I said that of course I would. I would be delighted. Nothing short of seeing that baggy-lipped bastard hauled away in handcuffs could have made me happier. There was an article on the front page of the morning paper the other day naming him as a suspect in the murder. I reasoned that even if he was never charged with murder, but remained a suspect, it would justify my leaving. After all, I had children to protect.

When he walked in about four—extraordinarily early for him—I said, "Deputy Majowski called. He wants you to call him." He didn't say anything. He just sat down at the kitchen table and looked at me like I was speaking another language. "Did you hear what I said?"

"I'm not deaf, am I?"

His response startled me. In all the time I had known Smoochie, he had never once used a harsh tone. "No, but I—"

"I heard you fine." For a long moment, he stared at me, and I swear it was the same look that Rayce would give me when he got disgusted with me, like after we'd had sex.

"Well, aren't you going to call him?"

"I got nothin' to say to the cops."

"But they want to talk . . ."

"I don't give a damn, Dena Marie. See if you can get that through that thick skull of yours. I talked to them the other night. Those detective wannabes can go bark up some other tree."

"Look, Smoochie—"

"What did you call me?"

"Sorry, sorry, sorry. Vincent..." I don't know what brought that on, either. He had been "Smoochie" all his life. Now, he was demanding to be called "Vincent." "You have to call him. How will it look if you don't talk to them? I think if they want to talk to you that you should..." I trailed off because he was giving me the meanest look I've ever seen. His jaw tightened and his face turned scarlet. I thought for a minute that he was going to jump up and hit me. "Fine, whatever you want," I said. I picked up a stack of folded bath towels and went upstairs. I used the bedroom phone and called the sheriff's office. "Deputy Majowski, please," I whispered. It seemed like it took him forever to pick up the phone.

"Majowski here."

"Mr. Majowski, this is Dena Marie Xenakis. My husband is here, but I don't think he's going to call. You might want to call back in a few minutes." I hung up and went downstairs. Smoochie was still at the kitchen table, going through his mail. When the phone rang, I picked it up. It was Majowski asking for Smoochie. "It's for you," I said, handing him the receiver.

He took the receiver and said, "Yeah." He was quiet for a full minute as he listened to the chief deputy, then, as God is my witness, he asked, "Hey, isn't this weather a motherfucker?" Never in my life had I heard him use that word. He listened for a moment, then said, "The weather. The heat. Don't you hate it? I do. It's one of only two things that chafe my ass, and talkin' to you is the other. That's why I'm not wasting any more of my time. If you have any further questions, you can direct them to my lawyer. His name is Daniel Sabatino. He's in the book. Feel free to give him a call. I'm sure he would be delighted to hear from you." He held the phone out to me. When I didn't take it right away he said, "Take the damn phone, Dena Marie." After I hung it up, he said, in a very soft and agitated tone, "Come here."

"What do you want?"

He smiled through clenched teeth and slowly uttered, "I said, 'Come here,'" and he pointed to a spot right in front of where he was sitting. I did as I was told, and when I got near him, he reached up, grabbed a handful of my hair, and pulled me down until my face was only inches from his. I was more scared than hurt, and I fought back tears. Still speaking in a soft tone, he asked, "Dena Marie, did you go upstairs and call the sheriff's office?"

"No, I—" He yanked harder on my hair, and I cried out. "Stop it! You're hurting me."

"I'm going to give you a reason to cry in a minute. Now, I'm going to give you one more chance to tell me the truth. Did you go upstairs and call Majowski?"

"Yes. I was worried that you'd get in trouble if you didn't talk to him."

"I don't need you to stick your nose in my business. You're my wife. We're supposed to be on the same side. Don't ever do anything like that again. Do you understand?" I shook my head. I had never seen him act this way before. He was terrifying me. "Now, fix me some supper. And that doesn't mean throw one of those goddamn frozen dinners in the oven. Fix me a real meal."

CHAPTER TWENTY-FIVE
SHERIFF FRANCIS ROBERSON

I hadn't even finished my first cup of coffee when I heard the familiar clacking of high heels across the marble lobby. At 7:25 a.m., Dena Marie Xenakis was again in my office. "You've got to arrest him, Francis. He really killed Rayce. I mean, really killed him."

"That's what you told me last week, Dena Marie."

"I know, but I was just making that up so you would get him out of my hair, just like you said I was doing. But this time it's for sure. He killed Rayce. I know he did because . . ." Her voice trailed off and she squinted hard at my face, which was still a magnificent array of purple and blue and yellow. My eye sockets were rimmed in black, and the eyeballs were full of bright blood, seepage from the little blood vessels that had ruptured when Johnny head-butted me. "What happened to you?"

"Your old boyfriend rammed his forehead into my nose."

"Johnny did that? You had a fight? Why? You've always been friends."

"Yeah, well, that's what I thought, too."

"Was it over me?"

I massaged my temples. "Dena Marie, you really need to get over yourself. No, it most certainly wasn't about you."

"It really looks bad."

"Really? I thought maybe it was a good look for a lawman."

"It isn't," she said, completely missing my attempt at humor. "When are you going to arrest him? He really did it."

"Dena Marie, what do you want me to do? I can't just run out and arrest Smoochie because you think, for real this time, that he killed Rayce Daubner."

"He did. You should see how he's acting. It's like he's in the Mafia or something. I thought he was going to kill me last night, and you should have heard how he talked to Mr. Majowski. He's got a lawyer and everything. It's scary."

"You know it's against the law to set someone up for an arrest, like you were trying to do to Smoochie. You could be arrested for that."

She licked her lips, leaned over my desk, and whispered, "I've seen the way you look at me, Francis, and I know you still want me. You could never arrest me."

She was right, dammit. "Maybe not, but I'm also not going to arrest your husband on some trumped-up charge."

"It's not a trumped-up charge now. Okay, it was last week, but now I'm sure he did it. You should see the change in him. I'm telling you, he did it." She stood there for a moment, tapping one toe on the floor. "Well?"

"I'll talk to the investigators, Dena Marie. But you have nothing more than a hunch, and you can't send a man to prison for that."

"Look, I know what I saw last night. I heard him talk. He did it. Trust me."

CHAPTER TWENTY-SIX
JOHNNY EARL

"**H**e's not as stupid as you think."

Even in the haze of my sleep, I recognized the voice of the Reverend Wilfred A. Lewis. I sat up on the edge of my jailhouse cot and rubbed my eyes. "What?" I asked.

"You think General Himmler is stupid, and there are times when I'll admit that he's not the sharpest knife in the drawer, but he's smart enough to know what you're up to."

"I have no clue what you're talking about."

"Sure you do. All those theatrics in the courtroom. You're not fooling anyone. You're trying to stay in jail. He knows that. He knows you're not dedicated to the cause. You're trying to stay in jail and hide so you don't have to give up your money."

"Let's reiterate that last point. It is *my* money."

He shrugged. "If you didn't want to give it to the cause, you shouldn't have told him about it."

I jumped off the cot, and the preacher moved quickly away from the bars. "Let's review. I didn't tell him. You did. Remember, padre?"

He smirked. "Oh, yeah. That's right." He looked around the cell. "You can't stay in here forever."

"How in the hell did you get in here, anyway? The sheriff said I'm not supposed to have any visitors."

"He can't keep me out. Law says even the most despicable prisoners are entitled to meet with their spiritual adviser. That's me, remember?

You said so yourself in the courtroom the other day." He smiled wide. "Tell me, how can I be of assistance, my son?"

"Step a little closer, father. Let me whisper it in your ear so everyone in the jail doesn't hear."

"Go fuck yourself, my son. I'm not getting any closer than I am right now."

Fritz Hirsch came out of the utility closet, pushing a stainless steel bucket on casters across the floor with the mop inside the bucket. His daily job was to mop the floor, which he did while broadcasting into the mop handle.

"Not much of a spiritual adviser, are you?" I asked the preacher.

"What I came down here to advise you of is that your ass is grass. Right now, the general is upstairs talking to the judge, trying to have you released on your own recognizance."

"He won't do that."

"Don't bet on that. The general is telling him that was all a big show up there in the courtroom. He's telling the judge that you owe him money and you staged that act so you could hide in jail. The judge thought he was punishing you by keeping you locked up. He'll take one look at the general, and he'll realize that the best way to punish you is to let you go. With any luck, it will be into the protective custody of your spiritual adviser." His lips pursed in an evil smile.

"Oh my, sounds like the man of the cloth is really a scam in the cloth," Fritz broadcasted loudly, standing right behind the Reverend Lewis. The broadcast startled the preacher, and he leapt away from Fritz. When he did, I thrust my left arm out of the cell and grabbed the reverend by the front of his black shirt and pulled him forward. He was off-balance and wide-eyed, his face wedged hard between two bars, and I buried my right fist in his nose. Blood squirted down his face and onto my left hand.

"You motherfu—" I hit him again. "You wait until the general hears about this," he sputtered through the blood. I hit him again. "He'll beat your ass, you damn river rat."

I hit him a fourth time—this time in the mouth. And again and again. "He might beat my ass, but he can't watch me forever," I hissed. "The first time he turns his back, your ass is mine." One of the sheriff's deputies was running down the hall, keys jangling, when I released the little preacher and he slumped to the floor, leaving bloody streaks on the bars of the cell.

Fritz was broadcasting. "You can't believe the excitement here, ladies and gentlemen—what a fight, what a fight! Touchdown Johnny Earl, the defending Jefferson County Jail heavyweight champion, has landed a right, and another right, and another. Down goes the preacher. Down goes the preacher. Down goes the preacher."

The deputy was Reed Nevel. His nostrils were flaring like an angry bull's as he ran down the corridor. "Goddammit, Johnny, you're going to get my ass in trouble for this," he growled, snatching up the barely conscious preacher with one huge hand and pulling him down the hall.

Fritz continued, "One, two, three . . . the referee has stopped the fight! It's over, it's over! Johnny Earl successfully defends his title! The crowd is going wild!"

CHAPTER TWENTY-SEVEN
SHERIFF FRANCIS ROBERSON

I had just stretched out on the leather couch in my office to take a nap. The headache that had lodged behind my right eye since the day the corpse of Rayce Daubner was found at Jefferson Lake State Park had refused to subside. My stomach was in knots, too, partly from the ulcer that Alfred Vincenzio was giving me, and partly from the aspirin that I'd been munching like after-dinner mints.

I was awake, but my eyes were still closed when the skidding of the lobby door brought me to attention. I could hear Allison talking to someone. A minute later, footfalls closed in on my door. Allison peeked in, then pushed the door open for Buzzy Crowley, a volunteer fireman who was wearing his rubber boots and tracking ash and dirt across my office floor. "Sheriff, Battalion Chief Fair sent me down here to get you. We've got a situation over at the Daubner place."

Why doesn't that surprise me? I thought. "What is it?"

"There are these two guys who say they're FBI agents, one black guy, one white, and they're over there bossing around the chief and trying to take over the investigation."

Buzzy was still talking when I ran past him and out of the office. I jumped into my car and headed toward the Daubner place, arriving no more than ten minutes from the time Buzzy walked into my office. When I pulled up, the chief and a few other firemen were sifting through ashes. There was no sign of Alfred Vincenzio and Elvis Norwine.

"Where are they?" I asked.

He shrugged. "Left. They told me I better not miss anything or screw anything up or they'll bring me up on conspiracy charges. And they said I had to tell them about anything I found before I told you."

My face started to burn. "Chief, the only person you talk to about this case is me. Period. Are we clear?"

"I understand, but I don't like having them feds out here. J. Edgar's boys make me nervous."

"J. Edgar Hoover died during the Nixon administration."

"Maybe so, but them federal boys got some power, that's for dang sure."

My jaw tightened, and I started to grind my teeth. "Chief Fair, in Jefferson County, Ohio, there is no more powerful law enforcement officer than the one you're talking to right now."

"Well, they're up here barkin' orders and tellin' me what to do and threatening to throw me in jail. What am I supposed to do?"

"Just do your job. No one is going to put you in jail, except *me* if you find anything of substance and don't contact me immediately."

"But they're the feds, Sheriff."

"And I'm the law in Jefferson County. When they cart their sorry asses back to Pittsburgh, I'm still going to be here. Remember that."

"All right. Just keep 'em off my butt."

I didn't respond. By the time I had walked the few steps to my cruiser, the stomach acid was gurgling in the back of my throat. I radioed Allison. "Is Toots back?"

"He just walked in."

"Ask him to meet me at the diner."

"Ten-four."

Toots loved the diner. He usually ordered the kielbasa, which came with sauerkraut, sliced tomatoes, and a heaping mound of fried potatoes. "I can hear your arteries clogging up as you're eating," I would tell him. He rarely responded. Once a plate of food was placed in front of Toots, his knife and fork didn't stop moving until the plate was clean. He would cram food into his cheek until it looked like he was working over a quid of tobacco, all the while continuing to talk, chew, gesture with his utensils, and reload. If I made it to the governor's office and brought Toots along, I would have to get him etiquette lessons.

I slid into the booth across from Toots. "Let's squeeze Smoochie Xenakis," I said.

He looked up from his plate, a slice of tomato dangling on his fork an inch from his lips. "You're kidding, right?" he offered. "What for?"

"I think he might be our guy. He's smart enough to know that no one thinks he's capable. He knew he could kill Rayce, then act pathetic, act innocent . . ."

"Hide in plain sight?" Toots offered, grinding on his kielbasa.

"Exactly," I said. "That's exactly what I think he might be doing."

Toots stopped shoveling in the food and pointed at my face with his fork. "You know what I think?"

"No, but I feel confident that you're going to tell me."

"I think those FBI boys got you pissin' down your leg, and you're thinking that if you go after Smoochie it'll draw the attention away from you."

"I hate you."

"Sorry. I'm a cop. I'm trained to look for ulterior motives." He grinned and went back to stabbing at his potatoes. "That's my job. That, and making sure you don't make any career-ending mistakes. Like, for example, arresting Smoochie Xenakis for murder."

"I still want to talk to him. Let's call him in for more questioning."

"I already tried. I called him the other night. He doesn't want to play ball."

"What does that mean?"

"He said I had to talk to his lawyer."

"That's interesting."

Toots nodded, stabbing at the last morsels of kraut and potatoes. "He was talking like a wiseguy—said his lawyer had advised him not to speak further."

"Jesus, there must be something there. Why else would he get a lawyer?"

"Because he's enjoying the negative attention."

"Explain."

"Smoochie Xenakis has been kicked around his entire life, and now he's got a chance to make people think he killed someone—make 'em think he's dangerous. Maybe he wants his wife to think he's dangerous, too. He's just having some fun playing a role. He went to Carmel's the other day and bought a new black pinstriped suit. I just saw him; he's hanging out at Dago Sam's—new suit, sunglasses, chewing on a toothpick, hair slicked back."

Dago Sam was Samuel Di LaGreca, who owned the bait and magazine shop on Railroad Street near the marina. He sold night crawlers, minnows, newspapers, and smut magazines. He also kept a sports book for the Antonelli crime family of Pittsburgh. Sam had been running a small-time gambling operation for decades—the numbers, late-night poker games, horses, and ball games. He didn't try to keep it a secret. He lived in a magnificent home a mile outside of town that everyone knew he couldn't have afforded just by selling bait and magazines. In his shop, the weekly sports spot sheets were right on the counter, next to the stacks of newspapers. They were marked "For Entertainment Purposes Only."

"Smoochie Xenakis is hanging out at Dago Sam's?" I asked. Toots nodded. "My world is spinning off its axis. Now I've got a social worker who thinks he's a member of the Gambino crime family. Well, give him a call. Let's see when he and his attorney can grace us with their presence."

The following afternoon, Smoochie followed attorney Daniel Sabatino into my office. The attorney was dressed in a navy suit and a gold patterned tie; Smoochie was wearing a shiny red nylon sweat suit, a thick gold chain, and reflective sunglasses, all while working over a piece of gum with exaggerated motion. "I'm bringing my client in for questioning against my better judgment," Sabatino offered, setting a briefcase on the conference table and deliberately avoiding eye contact with Toots and me. "However, he insisted on clearing his good name."

I said, "If he has nothing to hide, then—"

"Spare me the cop jargon, Sheriff," Sabatino said. "If you have questions to ask, ask them."

Toots looked up from his notepad, and for a moment I feared he would plant one of his massive fists square in the middle of Sabatino's face. He began drumming his fingers on the table, a sign that his patience was wearing thin. I began, "Smoochie—"

"Excuse me," Smoochie said, leaning forward and propping both elbows on the table. "My name is Vincent Xenakis. In these proceedings, I would prefer to be called 'Mr. Xenakis.'"

"I see," I said. Now I was the one straining to keep my temper in check. "Very well. Mr. Xenakis, the last time we spoke, we established the fact that you and the deceased, Mr. Daubner, had been in an altercation. Was that your last contact with Mr. Daubner?"

Smoochie leaned toward his attorney, who whispered in his ear. Smoochie nodded, then leaned back in his chair and said, "Under the advice of counsel, I respectfully decline to answer the question."

"What? Why?" I asked Sabatino. "That's a simple question."

"Sheriff, I'm sure you're familiar with the Fifth Amendment, which protects suspects against self-incrimination."

I turned back to Smoochie. "Mr. Xenakis, do you own a thirty-eight-caliber handgun?"

Again, he leaned toward his attorney, received his instructions, and said, "Under the advice of counsel, I respectfully decline to answer the question."

And so it went. For the next fifteen minutes, we repeated the routine of me asking the questions, Smoochie and Sabatino whispering back and forth, and Smoochie "respectfully" declining to answer each question. Finally, I asked, "Did you kill Rayce Daubner?"

"You're way out of line, Sheriff," Sabatino said. "And my client is finished answering questions."

"He hasn't answered a single question. I thought he wanted to clear his good name."

Sabatino stood and led Smoochie toward the door. "If you have any additional questions, contact me. I don't want you talking to my client again."

Alfred Vincenzio was on the phone. "I heard an interesting rumor today, Francis. I heard that one of your primary suspects, that Xenakis fella, is the husband of your little lover from the grocery store. Is that a fact?"

"Sounds like you already know that it is."

"We're going to give him a good look," he said. "We think he might have killed Daubner."

"That's laughable," I said. "He's the mildest guy in town."

"We've got motive. Everyone in town is talking about his transition from social worker to wiseguy. What do you think would happen if we arrested him?"

"Nothing. It's all circumstantial. He'd beat it. He's got a good lawyer, and you have no evidence."

"That isn't what I mean, Francis. What would happen if we arrested Xenakis and had a trial in which your little girlfriend testified? Think anyone's reputation would take a hit?" He chuckled.

"You'd put an innocent man through a murder trial to get back at me?" I asked.

"In a New York minute, Francis. In a New York fuckin' minute."

Okay, here's the truth. I know Smoochie didn't kill Daubner. I never even considered arresting Smoochie until I saw the look on my dad's face when he was in my office. It made me think that somehow Dad knew everything that went on in my office. If that was so, then he knew that Daubner had been blackmailing me.

Remember earlier when I said that little Mildred Goins had demanded a lawyer and wouldn't talk to us about shooting her husband? That was true, but I was the one who put the idea in her head. I felt sorry for her and tried to cut her a break. Allison said that move would someday come back to haunt me. She had been right.

Mildred got drunk in the Starlighter Bar one night and ended up giving Daubner head. He videotaped it. But that wasn't the only thing he got on camera from Mildred. He started squeezing me for cash about a year ago, after he gave me a copy of a tape of her telling the entire story of how I let her off the hook in the murder of her husband. "Boy, how terrible would it be for this to fall into the wrong hands?" he said. It might not have been enough evidence to get an indictment against me, but it would certainly have sunk my political aspirations.

Ohio sheriffs have access to the Furtherance of Justice Fund, which they can use at their discretion. I pretended that I was using Daubner as an informant, but the payments were actually hush money. Allison knew something was wrong, because she takes care of my books, and she could see there was more money than usual heading out of the department. She asked me about it a couple of times, and I dismissed it.

I had destroyed my copy of the videotape immediately. The reason I was so thorough in going through Daubner's house was to find the original. I couldn't find it.

I knew the FBI was going to show up, and if the tape was hidden in that house, I didn't want it falling into their hands. That's why I slipped back later that night and torched it.

I knew when I went home after searching the house that Deputy Fairbanks would disobey my direct order and leave his post. He just couldn't help himself. Toots had told me that he had been hanging around the diner where his second ex-wife, Thelma—a hefty bleached blonde who wore thick orange makeup and whose perfume overwhelmed the odor of the diner's grease pit—worked the graveyard shift. Toots had gotten a highly reliable report that Fairbanks was taking his lunches at the diner and on slow nights servicing Thelma in the kitchen. As the sheriff, you get to know your people. Although the mental image of Fairbanks mounting Thelma on the prep table made me want to avoid eating in the diner, I knew I could rely on him to do that, at least, without screwing up. I was hiding in the weeds. The minute Fairbanks's cruiser left the driveway, I moved in.

Chief Fair is a bozo. He couldn't find the source of a fire if it left smoke rings around his ass. That's why I wanted him in charge. I studied arson at the academy. It would take an expert arson investigator to figure out how I set Daubner's house on fire.

So I wasn't really worried about getting caught. Okay, I was, but I figured the odds were in my favor. My big concern right then was my dad. I think he had found out that Daubner was blackmailing me and had killed him for it. This was really bad. The FBI was snooping around, and Vincenzio would have loved a very public and embarrassing trial, in part to humiliate me and ruin my political aspirations, but also to get back at Allison. Things were so bad, in fact, that I was considering arresting Smoochie on a trumped-up murder charge.

I walked over to Toots's office. "We need to talk to Smoochie."

Toots called information for the phone number at Dago Sam's, then pecked it out. "Sammy, Toots Majowski here. Don't give me away. Is Smoochie Xenakis over at your place? Uh-huh, okay. Thanks, Sammy." He hung up the phone. "He's over there making two-dollar bets and acting like a high roller."

We drove over and parked across the street. From our vantage point, we could see Smoochie through the grimy front window of Dago Sam's. When he came out, twirling a toothpick between his tongue and upper teeth, I pulled the car up in front of the shop, blocking him in, and Toots stepped out. "We need to talk some more, *Mr. Xenakis*," Toots said.

Smoochie pinched the toothpick and flicked it into the street. "You boys know the drill," he said in his wannabe-mafioso voice. "You want to talk to me, you need to contact my—"

Toots clamped one of his huge paws on Smoochie's trapezoid muscle and the man wilted, squealing as Toots threw him into the backseat.

"What are you doing? You're not allowed to do this. My lawyer's going to hear about this."

"No, he's not," Toots calmly said as he slid in next to Smoochie.

"Under advisement of counsel, I must—"

"Say it," I told him. "Say you must regretfully decline to answer the question one more time, and I'm going to have Toots hit you square in the face."

Toots, I knew, would enjoy such a directive. I drove out to Route 22 and pointed the sedan west. No one spoke. I got off Route 22 near Bloomingdale and pulled onto a dirt road near an old strip mine. We got out of the car and marched Smoochie through a thicket of briars toward the banks of a bass pond in the bowels of the scarred earth.

"These jaggerbushes are ruining my suit," he said.

"Shut up," I said. "I don't care about your damn suit." I was puffing for breath when I got to the pond. "Goddammit, Smoochie, I don't know what kind of game you're playing, but you're about to become the prime target of the FBI, which also is investigating Daubner's death."

"I'm not afraid of—"

"Punch him, Toots."

"No!" Smoochie squealed, throwing both hands over his face and backing up to the water's edge. "Okay, I'll stop," he said through his hands.

"That's your last warning," I said. "You see, Smoochie, the boys from the FBI don't know that you're a harmless social worker pretending to be a ruthless killer. They don't know that this is all an act. They think you're a very sinister man who shot up one of their informants." I paused a moment to let the words sink in. "Do I need to tell you how much the Federal Bureau of Investigation might frown on that?"

"No."

"People in Steubenville love to talk. Those FBI agents are going to find out that Daubner beat you up, and that he and Dena Marie were having an affair. When that happens, they've got motive."

"But he doesn't have any evidence, because I didn't do it," he said in the panicked voice of the old Smoochie. "They don't have anything on me."

"They don't need anything, you dumbass. They'll squeeze your balls so tight that you'll confess and believe you did kill him. Or they'll simply phony something up."

"The FBI would never do that."

"That would be a very bad assumption on your part. Let me explain something to you, Smoochie, and I'll deny to my dying day that I ever said this. The lead FBI agent on this case is a guy named Alfred Vincenzio. He doesn't like me. In fact, he hates my guts. There is nothing in the world he would like better than to embarrass me by solving a homicide in my backyard. And if you think for one minute that it would bother him to hang you out to dry to achieve that, you're sadly mistaken. In fact, this guy will go out of his way to make me look bad. If you happen to be the poor sap who pays the price to make that happen, so be it."

"How so? How could that make you look bad?"

"They'll get me up on the witness stand and try to make me look stupid—incompetent. He wants to ruin me politically."

Smoochie nodded, then swallowed hard. "Do you think he might ask you if the rumors about you sleeping with my wife are true?"

I could feel my face go flush. "He might."

"They're just rumors, though, aren't they, Sheriff?"

I struggled to swallow. "That's right, Smoochie. Rumors. Vicious rumors. You know how this town is. People talk."

"Yeah, people talk. What do you want me to do when the FBI agents want to ask me questions?"

"Tell them the same thing you told us. Tell them to call your attorney. Don't say anything they can twist around. If you want Dena Marie and the rest of the Ohio Valley to think you killed Rayce Daubner, that's fine. I'll even tell her how dangerous I think you are, but stay the hell away from the FBI."

CHAPTER TWENTY-EIGHT
VINCENT XENAKIS

A green sedan with federal-government license plates was parked in front of my house. I had been putting on a pretty good show around town, but at that moment you couldn't have pulled a needle out of my ass with a bulldozer. I worked up a little spit in my mouth, slammed my car door, and walked toward the house. In the living room, I found Dena Marie sitting on the ottoman, facing the two FBI agents who were seated on the couch. She looked startled to see me and said, "Oh, Vincent, these gentlemen are here to talk to you. They're from the Federal Bureau of Investigation." She said it as though it might be an honor for me to speak to two such distinguished men.

The younger of the two, the white guy, stood to shake my hand. As I pulled off my suit jacket I said, "I know who they are." I walked across the room and stood behind Dena Marie. "Whatta ya want?"

"We're investigating the death of Rayce Daubner," the white guy began.

I cut him off. "That's what you're *doing*. I asked you what you *want*."

The white guy's jaw tightened. The black guy said, "You've got a smart mouth on you, junior."

"Who pulled *your* chain?" I asked. It was exhilarating. I was no longer afraid. I was enjoying taunting the agents. The black agent chewed at his lower lip, and his nostrils flared.

"We need to ask you a few questions," the white agent said.

"You know, Agent . . ."

"Vincenzio."

"Uh-huh. Agent Vincenzio, you know, isn't this heat a motherfucker?"

"The heat?"

"Yeah, this heat and humidity. It gives me an ungodly rash on my balls."

Dena Marie turned, her mouth agape.

"What the hell does that have to do with anything?" Vincenzio asked.

"Nothin'. I just figured you might like to talk about the weather, 'cause I'm not talkin' about Rayce Daubner. I'd like to help you, but I'm under pretty strict orders by my attorney not to talk to you gentlemen. All I'm allowed to talk about is the weather, which, as I said, is giving me a rash on my balls." I reached for my wallet and pulled out Daniel Sabatino's business card. I held it toward Agent Vincenzio, who made no move to take it. I released the card, and it helicoptered to the carpet. "You can call him if you like. But do it from the pay phone down the street."

"You are making a huge mistake, my friend," the black agent said.

"Take your threats, your partner, and your fat black ass out of my house, or I'll have to call the sheriff and have him do it."

The two agents looked at each other for a moment. As the black agent pushed himself off the couch, he looked at Dena Marie and said, "Mrs. Xenakis, you've been a big help. Thank you so much."

Dena Marie gave the slightest of nods. I followed the two men to the door and locked it behind them. I turned and walked across the hardwood floor to the living room. My steps were slow, methodical, intentionally allowing my heels to click on the floorboards. Dena Marie was still sitting on the ottoman, her knees tucked under her chin, looking like the honor student who had been caught cheating on a math test. "What did he mean by that, Dena Marie?" I asked. "'You've been a big help?' What did he mean by that?"

She lifted her brows and gave the faintest of shrugs. "I don't know."

"You don't know? That's interesting. You were here, weren't you?" She kept her eyes focused on the carpet. The power I felt over her aroused me. Never once in our relationship had I been in such complete command. "I would hate to think that you were telling the FBI that you think I killed Rayce Daubner. I would really hate that. You wouldn't do that to your husband, would you, Dena Marie?" I moved in front of her so the growing bulge in my pants was evident. I cupped her chin in my right hand and lifted her face upward. "I'll ask you again. You wouldn't do that, would you?"

"No, of course not."

"Good. Where are the kids?"

"At my mom's."

"Excellent. Come with me." I slipped my hand under her arm and gently tugged upward. She followed, and we walked to the bedroom. There was no tenderness involved. I clawed at her clothes and she responded, plunging her hand into my pants. Inside of sixty seconds we had torn off each other's pants and I was inside her.

It terrified me . . . a little. Never in my life had I dreamed of taking a woman the way I was taking Dena Marie. For the first time in my life, I was in charge. I wasn't begging. I was taking what I wanted from my wife. My brain would not quit racing. My brother had been right. Dena Marie believed I killed Rayce. My boss believed it. They were all afraid, and Jesus help me, I was loving it.

Sex lasted longer than usual. I was so consumed with my power that I hadn't really been focused on the act. After I came, I quietly got out of bed and began getting dressed. Dena Marie lay silent, flushed and spent. Her breasts heaved with short breaths. "Where are you going?" she asked.

"Out."

"Out where?"

"Out. Out is out. I have some people I need to see."

"Who?"

I looked briefly at Dena Marie, then headed for the door. "I'll be late. Don't wait up."

In reality, I had no one to see or any place to go. I went out and drove around Jefferson County for three hours, thinking and smiling. As my brother had said, sometimes the world can be a beautiful place.

CHAPTER TWENTY-NINE
SHERIFF FRANCIS ROBERSON

Clarence Schnitke had given me the bottle of Scotch whisky as a gift for not arresting his sixteen-year-old son, who I found drunk in the back of the family minivan at Friendship Park near Smithfield. He was incoherent, and vomit covered his T-shirt, jeans, and tennis shoes. I should have charged him with underage consumption of alcohol, and would have, except he smelled so bad that I didn't want him in my cruiser. Besides, Clarence could be meaner than hell, and I imagined the punishment he meted out would be far greater than anything the boy would have received in juvenile court. I had the dispatcher call Clarence, and he came out in blue jeans and bedroom slippers to pick up his son. A week later, he dropped off the Scotch as a gesture of thanks, and I'm certain that he didn't see the irony in the gift.

I'm not a Scotch man. I like beer and an occasional merlot. But I really needed a drink, and it was the only thing I had in my office. I filled my coffee mug half full and took two hard swallows. It smelled like pine sap and didn't taste much better, but it had a bite, and that's what I wanted.

Across the street, the big goon—General Something-or-other—who wanted to start his country with Johnny's money leaned against the passenger side of his car, legs crossed at the ankles, his massive arms folded across his chest. The little preacher sat on the fender, his face purple from the beating Johnny had given him through the bars of the jail cell. The general's face was devoid of emotion as he peered at my office window.

On my desk was a sheet of paper. It was an order signed by Judge Lester T. Pappas releasing Johnny on his own recognizance. The only stipulation was that Johnny not leave Jefferson County. The judge knew exactly what he was doing. He had talked to "the general" and knew the behemoth would be waiting for Johnny. It was the perfect way for the judge to exact revenge on Johnny for his courtroom outburst while keeping his hands clean. He was adroitly shoving the antelope into the cage with the lion.

The lobby door skidded open, and a moment later Toots walked in with Johnny. Two cups sat on the corner of my desk. I poured Scotch in both, making no attempt to stop pouring as I went from one cup to the other. "Have a drink, boys." I set the bottle on the desk and leaned back in my chair, my elbows digging into the wobbly armrests. "Do you ever think about the decisions you've made in life? You know, decisions that you later regretted."

Johnny snorted. "You're asking *me* that question?"

"I've been thinking about that a lot lately. I've been thinking about the events that occurred and the decisions I made that put me in this chair at this moment. I just wonder how things could have been different if Beaumont T. Bonecutter hadn't screwed up and I'd never gotten the call to come back to Jefferson County. If that hadn't happened, I wouldn't be sitting here with a knot in my stomach the size of a softball."

Johnny blinked and took a hit of the Scotch. "You're the sheriff, for God's sake. You've got the position you always wanted, the launching pad for your political future. I just spent seven years in the federal penitentiary. If you're looking for sympathy, you're looking in the wrong place."

I could feel myself fighting a grin. "One day, I'm this up-and-coming FBI agent—the star of the Minneapolis field office. The next thing I know, I've got an unsolved murder and arson on my hands. My former FBI brethren are in town attempting to link me to the murder. My wife is pissed because I dragged her to Steubenville and then rewarded her by straying off the reservation with the crazy lady down at the grocery who, in spite of everything, still gives me a boner every time she walks in here. My political aspirations are about to be flushed down the toilet." I held out my cup to Johnny and Toots in a mock toast. "Yes sir, things are going well." I shoved the release form across the desk to Johnny. "Things are about to get worse for you, too, my friend. I've got to cut you loose, and the Aryan Welcome Wagon is waiting for you across the street."

Johnny looked at the paper, then walked over to the window and peeked out. "Crap. I knew this was coming. Can you ignore the order?"

"Hardly," I said. "It's a court order. I couldn't hold you if I wanted to. You're free to go."

"I don't want to go."

"You can't stay here."

Johnny turned and took two steps toward me. I put my hand on my holstered pistol. "Don't even think about it," I said. "You hit me in the nose again and I swear to Jesus I'll shoot you dead."

He stopped and frowned. "That wouldn't do much for your political aspirations."

"Maybe. Maybe not. There are a lot of people out there who might consider shooting you a public service. I'd probably pick up a few votes."

"Come on, Fran, you can't send me out there. I'll be toast."

I took my hand off the holster and sipped from my Scotch. "Let me think about this for a minute." When I pinched the bridge of my nose and immediately remembered why it was so sore, I lifted my head and said, "I've got nothing. How about you?"

"You're supposed to be the smart one, for Christ's sake."

Toots stood up and said, "I'll get him out of here."

"What about those two?" I asked.

"I'll take care of them later."

CHAPTER THIRTY
JOHNNY EARL

Deputy Majowski led me through the labyrinth of tunnels beneath the county building until we surfaced in the bullpen, a fenced-in area next to the underground garage where prisoners are kept until they're processed and taken to a cell. I followed Majowski across the parking garage. The clicking of the heels of his cowboy boots echoed off the walls. He didn't say a word until we got to what I assumed was his personal car. He opened the back door and pointed to the floor. "Get on the floor and stay down. I'll tell you when it's safe to get up."

We pulled out of the garage, and the rear end scraped on the concrete as it crested the ramp and turned left on Fourth Street. "Are they following us?" I asked after a few seconds.

"Shut up," he said.

I tried to concentrate and map our route in my brain. We must have driven fifteen minutes before I finally asked, "Where are we going?"

He didn't answer, but within a few seconds of the question I sensed the car slowing, and then everything around me grew dark. The next sound I heard was that of an automatic garage door closing. "You can get up," he said.

"Where are we?"

Again, he didn't answer. I looked around at the inside of the garage, which I assumed to be his. I sat for a few seconds until Majowski opened the door. "Come on in," he said.

I followed him through the door that led from the garage to a mudroom. The house was immaculate but old, having the look of someone's grandparents' home. "Have a seat," he said as he passed through the kitchen. I pulled out a chair and sat down. The entire house groaned under his weight as he trudged up the stairs. A few minutes later, he reappeared in the kitchen, holding a revolver with a handkerchief wrapped around the handle. My heart raced as my ass puckered.

"You know what this is?" Majowski asked. I tried to work up enough spit to swallow, but nothing would come. "Come on, Johnny, it's not a tough question."

"I spent several years dealing cocaine. I'm familiar with handguns. That's a thirty-eight."

"Very good. And do you know what's special about this particular thirty-eight?"

I shook my head. "I haven't a clue."

"This is the service revolver that was used to propel a bullet into the head of Rayce Daubner."

Again, I swallowed. This time it was painful, like trying to swallow steel wool. "You killed Rayce?"

Majowski held up his free hand, waving a palm at me. "Now, let's be very clear—I never said that *I* killed Rayce. I simply stated that this is the gun that was used to kill Rayce. Big difference."

"Uh-huh. Are you going to use it to kill me, too?"

"Don't think for one minute that the thought hasn't crossed my mind. Let me tell you a little story. I never had the opportunities that you had. My dad was dirt poor, and I couldn't carry a football or hit a baseball, so I went to the army and ended up wading through rice paddies in Vietnam. When I came back, I went to the police academy. It wasn't really what I wanted to do, but I sure as hell didn't want to go to the steel mill or the coal mine, so I became a cop. It's been a good living, and I've done a good job, but I always figured that with a few breaks I could have done more. But it didn't work out, and I ended up as a county mountie in Steubenville, Ohio. It's an honest living, but it's not exactly the pathway to being a CEO. Then your buddy Francis becomes sheriff. He needed me to help him get settled, show him the ropes, you know? And, fortunately, we hit it off. I know he's got political aspirations, and he tells me if he gets elected to Congress, he wants me to come along as his aide. Someday, maybe he gets to be governor. I'll be his chief of staff. All of a sudden, my future is looking pretty damn good. That is, until you got out of prison and that lowlife Rayce Daubner ended up a corpse."

"I didn't kill him, you know," I blurted out, then choked back a nervous laugh. "But then, how could I? You have the gun."

He smiled, and his lips disappeared behind his moustache. He bounced the handle of the pistol in his hand and squinted down the sights. "Did you know that Daubner was blackmailing the sheriff?"

"Of course not. How could I have known that? What for?"

"That doesn't matter. What matters is that two weeks ago I was prepared to ride his coattails all the way to the governor's mansion. Now it looks like the only way he'll get to Columbus is if he gets sent to the state penitentiary. And nothing would make those FBI boys happier." Toots worked his hand around the revolver until the handkerchief covered the barrel and his hand covered the handkerchief. He then held the gun out to me. Relieved that he wasn't going to shoot me, I took a few cleansing breaths but made no attempt to take the gun. "Take it," he ordered. "Take it, goddammit!" he yelled. I lifted the pistol out of the handkerchief. "Do you understand what I want you to do?"

"I don't have a clue."

"Do you like that little preacher?"

"I hate his guts, but I don't think I want to shoot him. I'm reasonably certain that would be a violation of my parole."

"I saw that little prick hanging around town before the general showed up. I couldn't figure out why he was here, but he was obviously on a scouting mission for his boss. I suspect he was trying to keep an eye on you. He's a sneaky little turd. So here's how this will go down. When I get back to the sheriff's office, I'm going to arrest the preacher."

"For what?"

"I don't know yet. I'm going to talk to him, and I'm reasonably certain that he'll say something to me that I'll find extremely offensive. The car is in his name. I checked. I'll toss him in jail and have the car put in the impound lot. I want you to take the gun and hide it in his car. And for the love of Christ, wipe your fingerprints off before you plant it. Tomorrow morning, I'm going to ask the sheriff to get a warrant to search the car. He'll resist because he won't see the value. I'll work on him. We'll get the search warrant, and when we do, I want that revolver in the glove box or tucked into the backseat or under the spare tire. I don't care where you put it, but I want it in the car. The sheriff's going to find it and arrest the preacher for the murder of Rayce Daubner."

"Help me out here," I said. "What's my motivation?"

"Your motivation is that the FBI is crawling all over Jefferson County trying to solve this case before we do. They want to embarrass the sheriff and kill his political aspirations."

"I still don't understand how this involves me."

Majowski's jaw set, and his eyes narrowed to slits. "Because if you don't, I'm going to set you up to take the fall. I'll put my hand on a Bible and swear that you confessed to me. I'll even say I saw you with the murder weapon in your hand."

"Maybe I'll just shoot you right now."

"Maybe you will, but it won't be with that gun. It's not loaded, dipshit."

I exhaled a long, exasperated breath. "Okay, so I plant the gun and you arrest the preacher. That doesn't help me. The general is the dangerous one, and he'll still be on the street."

"You're not getting this, are you? This isn't about you. This is about Francis Roberson. You help me, and I'll get the assault charges against you dropped. How you deal with the Nazi is your business."

"Why would the preacher want to kill Rayce?"

"We'll say it was over drugs. We'll say Rayce stole the revolver and the preacher got his hands on it and killed him."

I shook my head. "God, that's lame. It makes no sense. There's no connection between the preacher and . . ." My voice trailed off. For one of the very few times in my life, an idea came to me at the exact moment that it was so badly needed. "When you get back and the preacher mouths off to you, is there any chance that the general might start running his mouth, too? Maybe both of them will end up in jail?"

"Why?"

"I'm not asking for much. Humor me."

He stared at me for a long, hard moment, then said, "I'm sure the general might also have something to say that offends me."

"Good," I said. "Now, this is what else I need . . ."

CHAPTER THIRTY-ONE
VINCENT XENAKIS

Conversing with the president at Ohio Valley Hospital was strictly forbidden by my boss. Douglas Oswald used our chain of command as a way of creating a buffer and taking credit for my accomplishments, thus enhancing his status within the senior management team. The president of the hospital was Roland Clemens, an affable, outgoing man with a ready smile and a squat nose that wouldn't support a pair of eyeglasses. Clemens was well known for his M.B.W.A. Program, which stood for Management By Walking Around. He loved strolling the halls of the hospital, talking to patients, nurses, doctors, and janitors. In spite of this, I had never had a single conversation of substance with the man, and he had been president for my entire tenure at Ohio Valley Hospital.

Mr. Clemens had appeared rattled after the article in the paper listed me as a suspect in Rayce Daubner's murder. That wasn't hard to understand. Having a suspected murderer as your assistant director of social services would make any hospital administrator uneasy. That played to my advantage. I sat in my car at the south end of the parking lot until I saw him drive into his reserved parking space, then I timed my walk to the building so I could meet him at the front entrance. "Good morning, Mr. Clemens."

The omnipresent smile disappeared, replaced by a look of surprise as he saw me walking under the portico beside him. "Oh, ah, good morning, Smoo . . ." He blinked twice and swallowed once. "I'm sorry, but I don't think I know your real first name."

I arched my brows. "Really? It's Matthew. Matthew Vincent

Xenakis. My friends call me 'Vinnie.'" I winked. "You're my friend, aren't you, Mr. Clemens?" I laughed before he could answer. "Since you're my friend, you can call me 'Vinnie,' too." I followed him through the lobby outside his office and entered his private lair without an invitation. "We haven't had a chance to talk lately, and I wanted to ask you how the community outreach on my childhood obesity program was going."

"*Your* childhood obesity program?"

"Yes, *my* childhood obesity program. It was my idea. I created it and wrote for the grant. I assumed that Mr. Oswald told you that."

He looked at me for a moment, then pressed a button on his intercom and asked his secretary to bring him the file on the program. When she did, he pulled the report and accompanying cover letter and pointed to the second paragraph, which read:

It is my opinion that Ohio Valley Hospital cannot simply be a spectator in the growing problem of childhood obesity. In order to combat the problem and put our hospital on the battle lines, I have created a program for fifth- and sixth-graders that will educate them on the dangers of obesity, encourage good eating habits, and provide a sound fitness regimen.

I nodded. "That's interesting. That sounds like the exact verbiage I used in my memo to Mr. Oswald when I explained the importance of the program to him." I opened my briefcase and pulled my own file folder. I handed him a copy of the memo I had sent Oswald when I first proposed the program. "You'll see by the date on the memo that I sent it to him eight months before he came to you with the proposal. The second paragraphs are identical." As he compared the paragraphs, I pulled a draft copy of the program from my briefcase. "Here's the draft of my program. I'm sure you'll find that it's virtually identical to the one he passed off as his own. Also, here's my application to the Crocetti Foundation for the grant." I allowed him a few seconds to review the documents and asked, "What about the community immunization program?"

"What about it?" Clemens asked.

I could feel my jaw tighten, and it was not a show. It was true anger. "Did he tell you it was his?"

"Yes."

"It wasn't. It was mine." I reached into my briefcase and tossed another folder on his desk. "The documentation is there. I suppose I don't even need to ask about the teen pregnancy education program?"

It was Mr. Clemens's pet project, an effort by the hospital to educate high school freshmen about the dangers of unprotected sex and the responsibilities of raising a child. The hospital purchased real-life dolls equipped with computer chips to cry and require attention, as well as monitor their care. Each freshman was required to take one home for a weekend and was graded on the effort. The program had won the hospital and Mr. Clemens many accolades.

I slapped another folder on the desk. "Mine, too. Mr. Clemens, are you telling me that you had no idea that these were my programs?"

He looked as though he had been caught masturbating. "No, I just assumed they were Mr. Oswald's work. His name was on the reports. He never mentioned your name. Why didn't you say something before now?"

"Before now, I was just trying to be a good soldier. What's the phrase you like to use, Mr. Clemens? 'Be a good team player.'" I snapped my briefcase closed. "Well, I've been a good team player, and you see where it's gotten me." I walked out without saying another word. Mr. Clemens sat behind his desk, his mouth open.

Shirley was already at her desk when I entered the offices of the social services department. "Shirley, when Mr. Oswald comes in, please tell him I want to see him in my office."

She squinted. "You want to see Mr. Oswald in *your* office?"

"Did I stutter?"

"No, sir."

"Thank you, Shirley," I said, closing the door behind me. I bit on my finger to keep from laughing aloud. Sweet Jesus, I loved the new me. I peeled off my suit jacket, revealing a tight vest over a crisp white shirt and a maroon and gold necktie in a tight Windsor knot. The vest and tie, I believed, added a level of authority that was called for in this situation.

When I heard Shirley and Oswald talking in the lobby, I slipped a toothpick into the side of my mouth and pretended to be talking on the phone. He rapped three times on my door and then pushed it open a few inches. I waved him in while continuing my pretend telephone conversation. "Look, this is very simple, either he gets with the program or . . . exactly . . . I don't have the time for this kind of nonsense. That's right. Handle it, or I will. Listen, I've got someone in my office. I'll call you back." I motioned toward an open chair, and Oswald sat. "Do you have my performance review?" I asked.

He fumbled with the clasps on his briefcase, then produced the document. Unsmiling, I read over the evaluation. It was stellar. I exceeded expectations in nearly every category, and Oswald had recommended me for a 12 percent merit raise. Without a word, I nodded and signed the document. I handed him the pen and pushed the evaluation toward him but kept my fingers on the paper. After he had signed, I pulled it back.

"I'll need to take that to human resources," he said.

Slowly, I folded the review twice and slipped it inside my vest. "I'll take care of that." I turned in my chair to face him directly. "I had a conversation with Mr. Clemens this morning."

"Mr. Clemens?"

"Please don't make me repeat myself."

His face was glowing red, and beads of perspiration began to appear around his hairline. "What about?"

"Well, you'll be happy to know that I didn't tell him about you going doggie on Mrs. De La Torre, if that's what you're worried about."

Two years earlier, I had left the office late on a Friday afternoon. I was twenty minutes away from the office when I remembered that I had forgotten to hand in my weekly time sheet, which Oswald insisted be on his desk before the weekend. I returned to the office and, assuming he had gone home for the day, walked into his office without knocking. Annette De La Torre, the head of the payroll department, was bent over his desk, and Oswald was servicing her from behind. I said, "Here's my time sheet," set it on the credenza, and left. Until now, neither of us had ever mentioned it.

Oswald had assumed I didn't have the courage to blackmail him. And he was right . . . until now.

"I gave you a twelve percent raise, goddammit," he growled between clenched teeth. "What else do you want? That's the most I can possibly give."

"Here's the thing, Dougie. It's not always about the money, if you know what I mean. Sometimes it's simply a trust issue. For example, you trust your spouse to be faithful—and just so you know, I'm not talking about you at the moment—and they let you down. You know what I mean? Did you know that my wife and Rayce Daubner were having an affair?"

He shook his head. "Of course not. How would I know that?"

"Really? I thought everyone in town knew."

"I don't concern myself with other people's personal lives."

"That's good, but just so you know, when someone you trust violates that confidence and commits the ultimate betrayal, it makes you very, very angry. How can there ever be trust in a relationship after that? I ask you that question, because it's not unlike the situation you and I are in right now. See, I trusted you to do what was right. But this morning, I found out that you've been unfaithful to me. I asked Mr. Clemens about all the programs I had created for this hospital, and lo and behold, they all have your name on them. Mr. Clemens had no idea that those were my programs. You had taken all the credit." I paused a moment for the words to sink in. "Do you see how that can just suck the trust out of a relationship, Dougie?"

"Well, as the head of the department I felt it was—"

I held up a hand, and it silenced him. "If you are about to justify taking credit for my work, save your breath. We're well beyond that." I reached into my top desk drawer, pulled out a sheet of paper, and slid it across the desk. "Sign that. I'll turn it in with my review."

"What's this?"

"I know you can read, Dougie, I've seen you do it."

The letter was to the point.

August 14, 1989

To whom it may concern:

I am hereby tendering my resignation as director of social services for Ohio Valley Hospital, effective immediately.

Signed,
Douglas Oswald

He pushed it back toward me. "How dare you. I'll not be black-mailed. I'm not signing this."

I took my index finger and slowly pushed it back toward him. "I do believe you will."

"I told you, I'll not be blackmailed. I'll talk to Mr. Clemens. I'll tell him that you were doing those programs under my direct supervision. He'll never fire me."

"You don't seem to have a grasp of your actual problem. It's not about Mr. Clemens." Again, I paused to let the words settle. "It's about *me*. You see, Dougie, the last person who didn't listen to me was a man who was sleeping with my wife. I went to his place to talk to him, like a reasonable person, but he just didn't want to listen." I leaned closer. "That man? He'll never sleep with my wife again. In fact, he'll never sleep with anyone's wife again. That man made me angry. And, right now, I'm very angry with you, Dougie. Why, it's as though *you* were the one having an affair with my wife. Are you understanding now?" He swallowed hard and nodded. "Good boy. Now, sign the paper."

CHAPTER THIRTY-TWO
DENA MARIE CONCHEK ANDROSKI XENAKIS

I am a sick puppy—one magnificently disturbed human being. The whispers that people didn't think I could hear are all true. The accusations of mental illness were dead on. I'm nuts. Or, as Johnny Earl once so eloquently phrased it, I am "stone crazy."

I love my husband. Absolutely love him. Adore him, in fact. I can't wait for him to come home from work. I'm sending the kids back to my mother's. Never before have I met him at the door with a cold beer and a blow job, but I will start a new tradition tonight. And I'll be wearing the dress he bought me, the blue one with the wide white collar that makes me look like the pickled old biddies in the church choir. But he likes it, so I'm going to wear it. The strip steak and mashed potatoes—his favorites—will be ready. I will cut his meat and spoon-feed him the potatoes, naked, if he likes.

In the years we've been married, he has never treated me as badly as he treated me the past few days. He's rude, crude, and demanding. His answers are short, and there's a vileness in his tone. He virtually dragged me to the bedroom and took me as though I was a street whore, penetrating me without a kiss or a touch, grinding at me like he was late to catch a plane, ejaculating, then rolling off and looking at me in disgust.

And oh, sweet Jesus, I am moist in my panties at the thought of him climbing on top of me again tonight. I will suck him hard then let him take me. He'll pull my hair back until my forehead is pressed against the headboard, then press my ankles to my ears and ride me into the sheets.

What in God's name is wrong with me? What went wrong with my wiring? When he was a saint, I couldn't stand the sight of him. Now he acts like a bastard, practically a Rayce Daubner reincarnate, and I love him. I crave him. I know he killed Rayce. No matter what anyone says, I know he killed him. For years, I believed that he was just a wimp. But he's not; he's a killer.

I'll do anything to keep him. This morning, I watched as Vincent—I'll never dare call him "Smoochie" ever again—drove his car away from the house and headed for his job at the hospital. As soon as the taillights disappeared onto Kennedy Avenue, I got dressed and went down to the sheriff's office. I had to protect my man.

CHAPTER THIRTY-THREE
SHERIFF FRANCIS ROBERSON

My life was becoming a recurring nightmare. As I entered my office at 7:30 a.m., Dena Marie Xenakis was pouring water into my coffeepot. She smiled and said, "I thought it would be okay to make some coffee."

"Dena Marie, what are you doing here . . . again?"

"Mr. Majowski let me in. I told him I needed to talk to you, and he said I could wait in your office."

"Toots let you in?" I peeked over toward his office; the door was half open and the light on. That was odd. Toots never arrived at work before nine. Allison must have heard Dena Marie's voice, because the familiar heel-to-toe, click-clack of her shoes started toward my office. I pushed the door closed before she could get close enough to give me the finger. "Dena Marie, I know you're trying to be helpful by getting your husband arrested for murder, but you're making my home life a living hell."

"Not anymore. I wanted to tell you that you can call off the dogs. Vincent didn't kill Rayce. I'm truly sorry for the confusion."

I set my briefcase on the floor behind my desk, and I could feel my forehead wrinkling in the same perplexed furrows that were once brought on by my advanced calculus class. "Vincent?" I asked.

"My husband," she said.

"Smoochie?"

"Please don't call him that. His name is Vincent."

I nodded. "Yes, so I've heard." I eased myself into my chair.

"Coffee?" she asked. I grabbed the mug from the corner of my desk and held it toward her. "Cream?"

"Black," I said. "Listen, Dena Marie, this is quite the turn of events. Just a couple of days ago, you were in here pleading with me to arrest him. In fact, you said something like, 'He killed Rayce. I know he did.'"

She sashayed over to one of the chairs in front of my desk, sat down, and rolled her eyes. "Things change. I mean, what was I thinking? Vincent? Commit a murder? It's laughable, don't you think?"

"I don't know, Dena Marie. I thought it was laughable the first day you walked in here. But that's when he was the old doormat Smoochie Xenakis. Now that he's Vinnie the Shark, I don't know. It would seem to me that Vincent is more likely to have murdered someone than Smoochie. He might warrant a second look." I crossed my ankles on the corner of my desk and interlocked my fingers behind my neck. For the first time in several days, I was smiling and actually starting to enjoy this. "This is all very interesting, don't you think, Dena Marie? I mean, why is it that when he was good ol' Smoochie, you couldn't wait to get rid of him? But now that he thinks he's Michael Corleone, you want to protect him?"

"I've always loved Vincent. I was just a little confused."

"Confused?" I dropped my legs from the corner of the desk and took a sip of the steaming brew. "Dena Marie, in all candor, I'm not the one you need to be concerned about."

"What do you mean?"

"There are two agents from the Federal Bureau of Investigation running around the county, investigating the murder. Rayce Daubner was a federal informant, and they're investigating—"

"I know. I talked to them last night. They were at the house."

She had my full attention. "You talked to them? What did you tell them?"

"Same stuff I told you earlier, mostly. I don't think they believed me, though."

"I want to make sure I have this straight. Last night you wanted him in prison; this morning you don't?"

"Something happened last night to make me change my mind."

"Did they ask Smoochie—er, Vincent—any questions?"

"They tried, but he started talking about some rash on his testicles. He called the black guy a fatass and they left."

"Good boy, Vincent."

"Why would you say that? Don't you want their help?"

"They're not here to help, Dena Marie. They're here to stick someone with the murder so they can cram it up my ass sideways. It's a long story, but it would certainly behoove Vincent not to talk to them."

Her left eye closed slightly as she absorbed this. "Did you warn Vincent about this?" I shrugged and nodded once. "You're protecting Vincent, even though he probably killed Rayce?"

"You're making my migraine return."

She pressed her right palm to her breasts and said, "You're protecting Vincent because you love me so much, aren't you, Francis?"

It was at that instant that the appeal that had held sway over me seemed to vanish, dissipating like the white smoke escaping from the stacks at Wheeling-Pittsburgh Steel. She seemed childlike—infantile, all wrapped up in her own little world. And now, for whatever reason, she was in love with her husband.

"Yes, Dena Marie, that's exactly why I'm protecting him. Ours is a forbidden love that can never be, so I'm willing to do everything in my power just to make you happy."

She pressed two fingers to her lips, mouthed the words "thank you," and left.

Dena Marie wasn't gone from my office thirty seconds before Toots walked in, a purplish mouse under his left eye and the front of his shirt held together by two safety pins. "Sorry for letting the crazy lady in here, boss. She was here at seven o'clock and would . . . not . . . shut . . . up. She was prattling on about how she needed to see you and how

Vincent wasn't guilty and how she'd just die if Vincent ever went to prison. I let her in your office so I didn't have to listen to her anymore."

"What in Christ's name happened to you?"

"We had a little incident last night."

I covered my face and massaged my eyeballs. "I really don't need another incident, Toots. What was it?"

"I had a little run-in with the friends of the Third Reich." He dropped a folder on the desk. "They're in the jail. I arrested them both for aggravated menacing and assault on a police officer."

"What the hell happened?"

"They were out front when I got back from dropping off Johnny. They started running their Nazi mouths, and I told 'em they had about two seconds to clam up or they'd be eating cold oatmeal for breakfast as the guests of the Jefferson County Sheriff's Department. The big one said, 'You ain't near man enough, porky.' I didn't mind that assault on my manhood, but that 'porky' comment went right up my spine. I walked over to them and put a finger in that little preacher boy's face, and he shoved it back up in my face. Then the fight was on."

"You got in a fight with those two and all you got was a little shiner and a torn shirt?"

"I gave the preacher a backhand and knocked him clear off the hood of the car. The goon and I wrestled around a little. He elbowed me in the eye, so I clubbed him. No shit, Fran, I smacked him in the head and my nightstick bounced back like I'd hit a chunk of granite. It almost flew clear out of my hand. I gave him a mouthful of pepper spray, and he settled right down."

"Oh, Jesus. Did they need medical attention?"

"No."

"No, they didn't? Or, yes they did but you elected not to bother?"

"Probably the latter. They can go to the hospital when they get to their new country." Toots took the chair Dena Marie had been sitting in and touched at the puffy spot under his eye. "It doesn't detract from my natural good looks, does it?"

"How could it?"

He grinned for a minute, then his expression turned serious and he got around to the reason for his visit. "You don't suppose those two had anything to do with Daubner's murder, do you?"

"Anything's possible."

"When Daubner got out of high school, he bragged that he had joined the Ku Klux Klan, and for a long time he had a Confederate flag hanging outside of his house."

"Why would that make him a target? Wouldn't that endear him to them?" I asked.

"In most cases it would." Toots pulled his pocketknife from his pants pocket and slowly began working the blade beneath his fingernails, deliberately making me wait for his point. "Yes sir, it would in most cases. Let's say, for example, that Daubner had somehow gotten himself involved with the goon and his Aryan Republic of New Germania, which is not a total stretch, since we know that Daubner claimed to be a Klansman."

"Go on."

"Johnny Earl gets sent to prison and ends up in the same cell as the would-be chancellor of the new republic. Earl and Himmler talk. Earl tells him about getting set up on a drug deal by a federal informant. Himmler asks who it was and Earl tells him, some guy named Rayce Daubner. Himmler knows Daubner because they ran around together wearing white sheets and burning crosses. Maybe Daubner was supposed to be a citizen of New Germania, but now Himmler knows that he's actually a federal informant."

"You think that Himmler and the preacher came to Steubenville to get rid of the traitor?"

Toots made an imaginary pistol with the thumb and index finger of his right hand and shot me as he winked. "I'd say that scenario is a hell of a lot more likely than anything else we've got."

I felt a tingle in my balls. The tingle spread upward, to my stomach and nipples and ears. "Has he been around town that long?"

Toots shrugged. "I don't know. Just because we didn't see him doesn't mean he wasn't around. We know the goon was in prison, but he could have sent the good preacher on a mission."

"It could have happened."

"Of course it could have happened. I impounded their car. Why don't you get a search warrant for it? If they're heading to their new country, chances are that's where they're keeping all of their possessions. Maybe there's something there."

CHAPTER THIRTY-FOUR
ALLISON ROBERSON

Toots Majowski walked into the radio room and leaned over my desk. "Make sure he understands the importance of the discovery," he said in a barely audible tone.

"What happened to your eye?" I asked.

"The discovery, goddammit, make sure he knows it's important."

"What discovery?"

He turned and started back to his office. When he got to the doorway, he looked at me for a tense second and mouthed, "the discovery!"

A few minutes later, Frannie came excitedly out of his office. "I'm going to see Judge Pappas to get a search warrant," he said.

"For what?"

"That little Nazi preacher's car."

When I heard his footfalls fade down the hallway, I got up from my desk and walked over to Toots's office. "What happened to your eye and your shirt, and what the hell is this all about?"

Toots looked up from the paperwork in which he was pretending to be engrossed. "I got into a little scrape is all."

"Why is Fran going after a search warrant?"

"Apparently he feels there might be something of interest in that car."

"*He* thinks there might be? And what discovery is going to be so important?"

He blinked twice and said, "You'll know it when you see it." Then he went back to pretending to be busy.

Fran was back in less than thirty minutes. I couldn't remember the last time I had seen him so excited. He rapped twice on Toots's door-jamb. "Got it; let's go."

As they were about to walk out of the office, Toots said, "Allison, why don't you come with us? We could use another witness, just in case we find anything."

Fran went to the evidence room and returned with a set of keys to the preacher's car. We walked down to the bullpen and hopped into Fran's cruiser for the short drive across town to the county impound lot, which was located in a corner of the county highway department's fenced, two-acre gravel lot on Hopedale-Steubenville Road. Fran unlocked the front door of the sedan. "I'll start with the trunk," Toots said, taking the keys from Fran.

I stood near the front and watched as Fran searched all the obvious places—in the glove box and ashtrays, above the sun visors, under the seats and dash and floor mats, and between the seats. "You find any-thing, Toots?" he asked.

"Couple duffle bags of military fatigues and a stack of skin magazines."

"Odd items for a man of the cloth to be carrying around in his car." Toots kept his head buried in the trunk. "How about you?"

"Nothing." Fran crawled off the seat and walked back to where Toots was working. I followed him. His excitement had waned. I could have told him that the little preacher couldn't possibly have killed Rayce Daubner, but he wouldn't have listened. Once Fran gets his mind set on something, there's no changing it. Beads of sweat were peppering Toots's forehead when he backed out of the trunk. "It's like a landfill in there."

Fran lifted the stack of porn magazines out of the trunk and dropped them on the gravel; they fanned out like fallen dominoes, portions of taut skin everywhere. He pulled the duffle bags out one after the other and dropped them on the gravel. Dirt and clutter littered the floor of the trunk. Nothing but trash. "Damn," he said. Then, with the back of his flashlight, he reached in and flicked at a yellowed newspaper. Beneath it was a circular crease. "Toots, did you check the spare wheel well?"

"Not yet. I hadn't dug down that far."

Fran peeled off the carpeted circular cover, dumping trash onto the side of the trunk. He froze for a moment. He looked at me, then back into the spare wheel well. I leaned in closer. Stuffed in the crater of the spare wheel was a white towel with a blue stripe down the middle. The towel had been neatly folded several times. He lifted the towel, bobbed it in his hands a few times as though gauging the weight, and delicately began peeling away the terrycloth. When the last flap was removed, it revealed a steel-blue revolver.

I gasped. "Oh my God! That's your service revolver!"

"Toots," he said. With a trembling hand, Fran showed his chief deputy the revolver. Then he lifted the dangling end of the towel and stretched it out. Printed in white block letters down the middle of the blue stripe were the words "Valley View Motel."

Fran looked at Toots, who said, "When I booked them in last night, that's where they said they were staying."

"Mother of Christ," Fran said.

To me, everything else seemed like it should be a formality. Fran would send the weapon and the slugs the coroner had dug out of Rayce Daubner to the state forensics lab in Columbus to verify our suspicions that the .38 was the gun used in the murder. I can't even begin to tell you how relieved I was about this. I'd been extremely worried that this entire debacle was going to trash Fran's political aspirations. And let's be honest: My real concern was that I'd end up stuck in Steubenville. A lot of politicians' wives support their husbands' political careers because they enjoy the residual benefits and being in the spotlight. Me, all I want is to get the hell out of that monstrosity of a house and this filthy little town.

Fran went back to Judge Pappas and secured another search warrant for room 7 at the Valley View Motel. I followed Fran and Toots to the property room, where they took the key attached to the plastic green fob from the envelope that contained the personal property taken from the Reverend Wilfred A. Lewis when he was processed into the jail. When we arrived at the Valley View, the cleaning lady was standing between rooms 7 and 8. The door to room 7 was slightly ajar, and she was plucking little soaps and a mini bottle of shampoo from the cart. "You haven't cleaned room 7 yet, have you?" Fran asked.

"Just finished," she said, grabbing some clean towels. Her face was deeply creased. Her gray hair was pulled back in a bun, and several wild whiskers sprang from her chin. "I just need to take these in."

"I'll take them," Toots said, compressing the towels and toiletries between a pair of thick hands. "We've got some work to do in here. Did you empty the trash from this room?" She pointed to a clear plastic bag tied to the front of her cart.

Fran untied it and said, "Thanks."

The room was surprisingly neat. Several pressed shirts hung in the closet. There were two shaving kits on the vanity, and several pairs of shoes were lined up against the wall. On the corner table sat a manual typewriter and a stack of papers.

"Look at this," I said, reaching for the stack of papers.

"Don't touch it!" Toots yelled, causing me to jump.

"Christ, Toots, what's wrong with you?" I asked.

"Sorry, Allie, but that might be important. We don't want to contaminate it with your fingerprints."

On the top sheet were the words:

Operation Adolph Lives
Manifesto for
The Aryan Republic of New Germania

"This looks big," Toots said. "I've got some rubber gloves out in the car. Let me get them." He returned with two pairs of latex gloves, which he and Fran tugged on. Gently taking the cover page by the corner, he flipped it faceup on the table, revealing a preamble and numbered proclamations that resembled a to-do list.

1) The Aryan Republic of New Germania shall be founded. Its capital shall be called New Berlin and shall be formed in the mountains of what is now western United States.

2) An Army will be formed.

3) Jews and niggers, or any half-breed containing nigger blood, shall not be admitted under any conditions.

4) The current president of the United States will be assassinated.

5) Any government official or undesirable interfering with the establishment of the Aryan Republic of New Germania will be considered an enemy of the state and executed.

6) Through expansion, the Aryan Republic of New Germania will take control of all lands currently in the control of the United States.

Beyond the line items were detailed plans for assassinating the president and every member of Congress and taking control of the government. "Nothing but a bunch of gibberish," Fran said. "It's just the ranting of a crazy man."

Toots looked at me, the skin stretching tight across his jowls.

I recalled his earlier admonition: *Make sure he understands the importance of the discovery.* "Gibberish? Are you kidding me?" I asked.

Fran's forehead creased with lines of confusion. "What?"

"You can't possibly be that thickheaded, Frannie. You have an ex-convict who spent time in a federal prison who writes a manifesto plotting the assassination of the president of the United States and the overthrow of our government, and all you say is it's 'a bunch of gibberish'?"

Fran looked at Toots for help. "Think big, Mr. Congressman," Toots said.

Then Fran rolled his eyes. "Give me a break. Do you really think anyone's going to believe this goofball could actually assassinate the president?"

For the first time in my life, I hit Fran. I slapped him hard across the left ear with an open hand. "Yes, goddammit! That's exactly what I think, you moron. This is your chance. You've already got them on murder. Now you can get them on conspiracy to kill the president." He cupped his hand over his reddened ear. His jaw tightened, and for a moment I thought he might hit me back, but I didn't stop talking. "Let me spell it out for you. I think the lead paragraph in the newspaper would read:

"'In the midst of a murder investigation of Ku Klux Klan member and white supremacist Rayce Daubner, Jefferson County Sheriff Francis Roberson uncovered a plot to assassinate the president of the United States by the radical leader of a separatist group attempting to start a new country—the Aryan Republic of New Germania—in the mountains of the American West.'"

"I don't know," he said.

I raised my arm again and said, "So help me Jesus, Francis, if you fumble the ball on this one, I'll—"

"Hey, look at this," Toots said, pointing to a page near the back of the manifesto.

The last several pages of the document listed names and addresses. On the first page was a listing for

Daubner, Rayce; Steubenville, Ohio

"Bingo. There's your connection," Toots said. "He somehow got involved with these guys, and they found out he was a federal informant. It makes sense. Himmler was a cellmate of Johnny Earl. He tells Himmler the name of the guy who set him up for the drug fall, and Daubner happens to be on Himmler's Christmas card list. They murdered him because they assumed that he was a traitor to the Aryan Republic of New Germania."

Fran looked at me this time. "That's it," I said. "You've solved a murder and saved the life of the president. You're going to be a hero."

"I've got a friend who works for the Secret Service in Columbus," Toots said. "I think you should let me call him. They're going to be very interested in this."

"Do you really think so? I mean, do you really think they'll view this guy as a legitimate threat?"

"Don't make me hit you again," I said. "It doesn't matter how much of a legitimate threat he is. He was going to attempt an assassination on the president, and you foiled the plot."

Again he looked at Toots, who shook his head. "You're about to be a national hero, Sheriff. You're about to be the guy who saved the president's life—the former FBI agent who gave up a glamorous career with the agency to return to Jefferson County, Ohio, because he loved the people and wanted to be their sheriff. Play this right, and it's your ticket to the United States Capitol."

CHAPTER THIRTY-FIVE
SHERIFF FRANCIS ROBERSON

Early the next morning, as I entered the jail, Alaric Himmler lifted his head off the cot for a second, then dropped it back into the hammock created by his interlocked fingers. The preacher got up and walked to the front of the cell and started yelling, "This is a crock of horseshit. You've got no right to keep us in here."

Fritz Hirsch was grinning and pressing his face between two cell bars. "Uh-oh, it's the man of God, and he's in a rhubarb with the head referee. He's blowing snot bubbles, he's so upset. But I'm telling you, folks, this referee is not going to budge. He's a mule."

"And tell that crazy son of a bitch to shut his mouth," the preacher shouted. "He's driving us crazy; he announces every move we make."

I looked over at Fritz and couldn't help but grin. "Fritz, that's enough."

"Oh my, sports fans, the preacher has just gone crying for mercy to the referee. This game is over. It's over. Fritz wins! Fritz wins! Fritz wins!"

"Who else has been using your car?" I asked the preacher.

"No one's used that car but me and the general. Now, how long are you going to keep us in here on these garbage charges? We didn't do nothing. That fat slob of a deputy provoked an argument with us, then arrested us. That's baloney."

"You're telling me that you haven't let anyone take that car out on a joyride? The only ones who have been in it are the two of you?"

"Are you hard of hearing, too? No one drives my car but me."

I nodded to show I understood. From my briefcase I retrieved the plastic evidence bag containing the .38 caliber revolver. "We found this in your car. Any idea how it got there?"

"You didn't find that in my car."

"Oh, but I did. It was in the trunk, wrapped in a Valley View Motel towel."

"Well, if you did, then you or someone planted it there, because that's not my gun."

"Oddly enough, it's mine."

The preacher squinted. "Are you on drugs or something?"

"This is my service revolver. It was stolen out of my office a few months back. Rayce Daubner stole it. *You* used it to murder Daubner."

"What? I never murdered anyone in my life. I never touched that gun, and I don't even know who this Daubner guy is."

"Really? That's very interesting, because his name is in the back of the manifesto that I found in your room at the Valley View Motel."

This brought the general to his feet. "I know every man on that list. There was no Rayce Daubner."

I pulled a photocopy of the page with Daubner's name on it and held it up.

The general looked at me, and the skin around his eyes tightened. "This is a setup."

"Are you telling me you didn't type this list?"

"That's exactly what I'm telling you."

"The font on the manifesto matches the font on the Underwood typewriter in your motel room."

"There is no typewriter in my motel room."

"Not anymore. I've confiscated it as evidence. You boys are under arrest for the murder of Rayce Daubner and, coming soon, conspiracy to kill the president of the United States."

I called the FBI office in Pittsburgh and asked them to deliver a message to agents Vincenzio and Norwine. "Will they know what this is in reference to?" the secretary asked.

"Most definitely," I said.

Twenty minutes later, Vincenzio called. "Looking for some help on your investigation?" he asked, a mocking edge in his voice.

"What investigation would that be?" I asked.

"There's only one that you ought to be concerned about, Francis."

"Oh, you mean the Daubner murder? Tsk. Where's my head? That's what I was calling you about. We made an arrest, and we're going to hold a press conference at the courthouse tomorrow morning at nine. I thought maybe, since you're so interested in this case, you'd want to stop by."

"You made an arrest in the Daubner murder? Who?"

"You know, with Rayce being an informant for the feds, I thought you might be interested," I said, ignoring his question.

"Who'd you arrest?"

"I thought you'd be interested, particularly since his being an FBI informant is apparently what led to his demise."

"Bullshit. This had nothing to do with his role with the FBI. Who did you arrest, goddammit?"

"I'm sorry, Agent Vincenzio, but we're not releasing that information at this time. However, you're welcome to attend the press conference in the morning; it's at nine o'clock at the sheriff's department and—" That was all I got out before he hung up on me.

Allison had appointed herself to arrange the press conference. I was surprised at how quickly she did it and how many reporters agreed to attend. There were reporters from the Steubenville *Herald-Star*, the Wheeling *Intelligencer*, the *Ohio Valley Journal,* the Steubenville and Wheeling television stations, and three local radio stations. Seated at the table at the front of the room were myself, Toots, and Jason Sinclair of the Secret Service field office in Columbus. In the seats behind the media were Agents Vincenzio and Norwine, a handful of court watchers, and the two public defenders who had been assigned to Himmler and the preacher.

While the reporters were getting settled, Vincenzio came up and sneered. "This changes nothing, Roberson," he said in a low voice so that only I could hear. "I don't believe for one minute that these two killed Daubner. This is just a sham to get the heat off you, but I'll tell you right now it isn't going to work. In fact, this makes things even better, because once I pin this murder on your old teammate or that doofus social worker, your butt will be mine, too."

I looked at him and smiled. "Alfred, in fifteen minutes, you'll be happy just to get out of Steubenville without making a total ass of yourself. Now, why don't you have a seat? We're ready to get started." Once the last radio reporter added his microphone to the bouquet of instruments at the lectern, I stood to begin the press conference.

I introduced myself, Toots, and Sinclair, then, as camera flashes lit the room, I said, "I'm going to read a statement, then Agent Sinclair will make a statement, after which we'll open this press conference for questions.

"On July 21, 1989, Steubenville resident Rayce Daubner, age thirty-five, was found murdered in Jefferson Lake State Park in Jefferson County, Ohio. Mr. Daubner had been shot to death, and forensic tests determined that the murder weapon was a thirty-eight-caliber handgun. Two days ago, a thirty-eight-caliber revolver, which had been stolen from the sheriff's office several months ago, was recovered in a car owned by the Reverend Wilfred A. Lewis, whose last known address was in Terre Haute, Indiana. Tests conducted by the Ohio Bureau of Criminal Investigation and the United States Secret Service have determined that the thirty-eight-caliber handgun recovered from Reverend Lewis's car was the same one used in the shooting death of Mr. Daubner. Reverend Lewis and an accomplice, Mr. Alaric Himmler, have subsequently been arrested and charged in connection with Mr. Daubner's murder. Reverend Lewis, Mr. Himmler, and Mr. Daubner were members of a white supremacist group known as the New Order of the Third Reich. Evidence found at a motel room being used by Reverend Lewis and Mr. Himmler revealed information linking the three men. We believe that Mr. Daubner and the suspects had a mutual interest in the New Order of the Third Reich. Furthermore, we believe Mr. Daubner was murdered after it became known to Reverend Lewis and Mr. Himmler that Mr. Daubner was an informant for the Federal Bureau of Investigation. How the suspects came into possession of the murder weapon is speculative at this point, but Mr. Daubner had been a suspect in the weapon's theft from the Jefferson County Sheriff's Department. We have yet to determine which of the two suspects pulled the trigger. Reverend Lewis and Mr. Himmler are currently being held in the Jefferson County Jail. Their arraignment on murder charges is scheduled for nine o'clock tomorrow morning in Jefferson County Common Pleas Court, the Honorable Judge Lester Theodous Pappas presiding."

I looked up and made eye contact with Vincenzio, who sat and glared. As I returned to my seat, Agent Sinclair stood and walked to the lectern. "Good afternoon. In the course of his investigation of the murder of Rayce Daubner, Sheriff Roberson uncovered a plot by Reverend Wilfred A. Lewis, Mr. Alaric Himmler, and their white supremacist organization, the New Order of the Third Reich, to assassinate the president of the United States." At that instant, heads in the audience snapped up, and the color drained from Vincenzio's face. He looked at me, and I winked. "Through the diligent work of Sheriff Roberson and Chief Deputy Majowski, this plot was foiled. It was believed to be a legitimate threat to the president and other members of the United States Congress. Sheriff Roberson obtained the manifesto of the New Order of the Third Reich, which detailed plans to assassinate the president and establish a new country in the western part of the United States. We have determined that the typewriter found in the motel room rented by Reverend Lewis and Mr. Himmler was the same one used to type the manifesto. I cannot divulge details of the plans, but suffice it to say, we are very grateful for the outstanding police work conducted by Sheriff Roberson, Chief Deputy Majowski, and the rest of the Jefferson County Sheriff's Department. Without their initiative and thoroughness, we could have been facing a tragedy of mammoth proportions. This case will be turned over to the federal prosecutor, who will seek indictments for conspiracy to kill the president." He looked at me, and I nodded. "Okay, are there any questions?" Sinclair asked.

Eight hands flew up in unison. I joined Agent Sinclair at the lectern. We were peppered with questions as the reporters tried to decipher the story that had just been dropped on them. Marshall Hood of the *Intelligencer* asked, "How do you know that Mr. Daubner was a federal informant?"

"I was informed of this fact by the Federal Bureau of Investigation after Mr. Daubner's death." I glanced at Vincenzio. "In fact, we have FBI agents Vincenzio and Norwine in attendance today. They have been in town conducting a separate investigation of Mr. Daubner's murder. Gentlemen, would either of you care to comment on your relationship with Mr. Daubner?"

It was one of the few times in my life when the perfect response came out of my mouth at the right time. They say there is no greater revenge than success, and at that instant, Alfred Vincenzio realized that I had beaten him again. He walked out of the room and left Steubenville.

CHAPTER THIRTY-SIX
VINCENT XENAKIS

I can't believe he signed the paper and resigned. What a dunce. It was a total bluff. I didn't even think of it until I walked into my office. I had pecked it out on the computer about four seconds before he walked into the room.

An hour after Oswald left my office, I walked into the staff meeting with a never-before-felt confidence. I took my former boss's usual seat at the executive table and without comment began pretending to organize and study my papers. I could feel the eyes upon me. When Roland Clemens entered the room, he arched his brows in my direction and asked, "Isn't Mr. Oswald coming?"

"No," I replied.

"Is he ill?"

"No."

Mr. Clemens wiped at the corners of his mouth and asked, "Well, why isn't he here?"

I had hoped to make the announcement more dramatic, but I simply slid the resignation letter across the glass-topped table to Mr. Clemens. "Mr. Oswald resigned this morning. He asked that I give you his letter of resignation."

"What? He resigned? Just like that?"

"Effective immediately," I replied, looking at my papers and fighting off the urge to smile. "He's elected to pursue other interests." I stared at Mr. Clemens until the silence became uncomfortable and he began the meeting. I gave an update on the social services department, making several references to my programs, acting as if I had been in charge of the department for years. When Mr. Clemens had adjourned the meeting and was gathering his papers, I said, "Mr. Clemens, could I have a minute with you, please?" When the room had cleared, I handed him an envelope containing my performance evaluation. "It's my annual evaluation. Mr. Oswald was kind enough to complete it before he resigned. I assume that you'll take care of getting that to human resources and approve the salary increase."

He nodded and slipped it into his leather portfolio. "Be happy to," he said.

"Good. Very good. Now, on another matter. You'll be needing to hire a replacement for Mr. Oswald. Given my years of service to the hospital and the fact that for all intents and purposes I've been running the department, I would think that an executive decision is in order to simply appoint me as the new director of social services."

He swallowed, smiled, and said, "I certainly don't see any problem with that, Vincent." He forced a laugh and patted me on the back as though we had been close friends for years. "No, in fact, I think that's an excellent idea. I'll talk to human resources and send out the memo immediately."

"Thank you, sir."

I went back to the office and told Shirley to take the rest of the day off but come back in the morning ready to work. "I've got big plans for this department," I told her. After lunch, I would call housekeeping and have them move my things into Oswald's former office. It tickled me to think how angry it would make Oswald when he learned that I had taken over his job and his office. I shut the door to my office and turned on the local radio station.

I leaned back in my chair. I closed my eyes and smiled, reflecting on the good fortune that had made me a suspected killer, when the music on the radio was interrupted by a special news bulletin.

An excited news reporter said, "Jefferson County Sheriff Francis Roberson is being credited with foiling a plot to assassinate the president of the United States. Details of this dramatic story were released at a press conference today in which Roberson also announced the arrests of two white supremacists in connection with the recent murder of Rayce Daubner of Steubenville."

My eyes flew open.

Crap!

CHAPTER THIRTY-SEVEN
CONGRESSMAN
FRANCIS ROBERSON

I thought Toots was full of baloney when he was yammering on about me being the next American hero. The manifesto was simply so much gibberish—the ramblings of a lunatic. But I'll be damned if Toots wasn't right. The morning after the press conference, reporters from every major media outlet in the country were crawling all over Jefferson County—the *New York Times*, the *Washington Post*, the *Chicago Tribune*, the *Boston Globe*, *Newsweek*, *Time*. It seemed like there was a camera or a microphone in my face all day. I can't tell you how many interviews I did, but I was hoarse by mid-afternoon. Allison sensed that there would be a lot of reporters in town, so she had me dress in my complete sheriff's uniform, sans the tie. She said that gave me a more honest, down-home look.

Before she sent me out the door that morning, Allison kissed me on the cheek and said, "Francis, if you downplay this, I swear you'll never get another blow job in your entire life."

"It seems that we're heading that way anyway," I responded.

She arched her brows. "Be a good boy and play nice with the reporters, and we'll fix that tonight."

Perfect. That was better than being a national hero. I did the interviews as though I believed Alaric Himmler to be a threat to the American way of life. My photo ended up on the front page of every major daily in the country the next day, along with mug shots of Himmler and the preacher. I got great spreads in *Time* and *Newsweek*. The headlines and leads varied, but mostly they talked about how the sheriff from little Jefferson County, Ohio, foiled a white supremacist plot to overthrow the government and assassinate the president. A few days later, one of those network news magazines came to town and spent an entire day with me—interviewing me in the office, interviewing me walking down the street, interviewing me on the high school football field with my old coach, taping me walking around the charred remains of Daubner's house. It ran the following Tuesday. On Thursday morning, a representative of the Democratic Party was in my office.

Now here's the kick in the head: not the local Democratic Party, but a member of the national Democratic Party asking me to consider running for the US House of Representatives. He said that I was a national hero and that I was a lock.

Of course, I agreed. The next thing I knew, I was meeting with consultants who coached me on everything from what clothes to wear to what food to order in restaurants to how to wear my hair. In about three days, they had me in full campaign mode.

I ran unopposed in the primary and won the general election in a landslide. The incumbent Republican garnered just 32 percent of the votes to my 68 percent. It was the widest margin of victory in the history of the district. I appointed Toots my chief of staff and began looking for office space in Steubenville.

Life is funny. I didn't wrongly go to prison for Daubner's murder, or even rightly for torching his house. Instead, it was the good preacher and Himmler who would never again see the outside of a penitentiary. By the time you added up their state and federal times, they were both looking at a couple hundred years in the can. I was reasonably certain that we would never hear from them again.

A few days after the election, on a Friday afternoon, Toots and I were sitting in my office sipping whisky, smoking cigars, and talking about the funny bounces life sometimes takes. There were some things on my mind that I had been wanting to ask Toots, but I had been avoiding the conversation because I didn't really want to hear the answers. However, with the election behind us, I was feeling a little more at ease.

"Toots, don't you think it was odd that the general had his manifesto, the very document that put him in prison, and one that implicated him in the death of Rayce Daubner, sitting right out on the middle of the desk in the hotel room? There's the cleaning lady going in and out, and yet he leaves it right out in the open where a blind man could have found it. Didn't that strike you as odd?"

"Who knows what was going on in his head?" Toots said. "He's a total whack job, and so is that little preacher."

"True. I guess you never know, do you?" I looked out the window for a long moment, then back at Toots. "You didn't kill Rayce Daubner, did you, buddy?"

He snorted and laughed. "Sheriff, would I do something so asinine as to risk my career? Give me a little credit, please."

I nodded and waited to see if he was going to elaborate. He didn't. "Toots, you didn't answer my question. Did you kill Rayce and plant the gun in the preacher's car? When I was working in the front of the car, looking under the seats, you didn't slip the pistol into the trunk, did you?"

Toots leaned back in his chair and shifted his butt. "This conversation is making me a little uncomfortable, Congressman."

"I've got to know, Toots."

"Sheriff, my right hand to God, I was nowhere near that car after it hit the impound lot. And if that sounds evasive to you, then let me clearly state this once and for all: I did not kill Rayce Daubner, and I did not plant that gun in his car. You have my word. I swear to Christ. Besides, do you think I went to the motel room and planted the manifesto and the typewriter with the matching font, too?"

I smiled, relieved. "I guess not."

On a Friday evening a couple of months after winning the Democratic primary, I saw the Xenakises—Dena Marie and Vincent—at the

Federal Restaurant in Steubenville. It wasn't an accident. I knew they would be there and eating in one of the little alcove booths that offer the most privacy. Dena Marie was in a scarlet cocktail dress, and Vin— as his friends now called him—was in a black suit with a vest and an open-collar white shirt. As I got ready to leave the restaurant, I caught Dena Marie's eye.

I turned to my wife and said, "Sweetheart, how about waiting for me by the door? I have a little business to take care of." She looked over at the booth where Dena Marie was sitting, and her brow furrowed. "It's totally on the up and up, and it won't take but a minute, I promise."

Vin and Dena Marie both saw me approaching the table. She sat uneasily, nervously working the napkin in her lap into a ball. He pushed a too-large piece of steak into the side of his mouth and said, "Well, well, well, if it isn't Jefferson County's revered sheriff and future representative to the United States Congress. To what do we owe this honor, Sheriff?"

I put my hands on the plaster sides of the alcove opening and leaned in toward the table. "I want you to hear this from my mouth, Xenakis. I know those two boys who went off to prison couldn't have pulled off the murder of Rayce Daubner by themselves. They weren't that smart."

He looked at me for a long moment, continuing to work the steak. Talking around the lump of beef, he asked, "What are you saying, Sheriff?"

"They had help. Someone had to hatch the plan." I leaned in closer. "I'm not sure they even had the guts to pull the trigger."

He smiled. "Sheriff, can I offer you a glass of wine?"

I whispered, "I know you killed him."

"This heat is a motherfucker, don't you think?" Vincent said.

Dena Marie pressed her napkin to her lips, her eyes darting between me and her husband. "I don't know how it went down, but I know you were there. I don't have the proof yet, but I know in my gut that you were there." I turned to Dena Marie. "Dump this guy, Dena Marie. He's trouble. Big trouble."

"Sheriff, my lovely wife and I are trying to enjoy a rare evening out.

If you need to talk, perhaps you'd like to give my lawyer a call. I'm sure he would—"

My jaw tightened. "These other rubes might fall for that social-worker routine of yours, but you're not fooling me for one second. Not one. I'm on to you, Vinnie. Just because I'm not going to be sheriff anymore, don't think that I'm not going to be keeping an eye on you. Daubner was a loathsome human being, but he didn't deserve to die like that." I pushed myself upright and let my hands drop from the plaster. "Wise up, Dena Marie. Get out while you have a chance." I looked at Vincent and said, "I'm going to make it my life's work to see that you join the rest of the scum behind bars."

"You talk a good game, Sheriff. Give it your best shot. By the way, can I give you the name of my tailor? If you're running for Congress, you really could use one."

I turned and walked away.

"What was that all about?" Allison asked after we had gotten in the car and were on our way home.

"I was just doing a favor for an old school chum." She stared, not satisfied with that murky explanation. I elaborated. "I was helping Smoochie—Vincent—with a marriage problem. He really liked being a suspect in Rayce Daubner's murder. When Dena Marie thought she was married to a killer, she suddenly found this new respect for him. When we charged Himmler and the preacher with the murder, Vincent was worried that Dena Marie would lose interest because—"

"Because her husband wasn't a murderer?" Allison asked. "She fell more in love with her husband because she thought he had killed a man?"

I shrugged. "I think she likes the idea that he's dangerous. Vincent liked it, too. It was the first time in his life that people showed him respect. I went over to the table and told him—really, I was telling her—that I knew he was involved in the murder and that I'd be keeping an eye on him. Now that Dena Marie thinks that I think her husband's a killer, they'll be together forever. It'll give her lots to talk about down at the A&P."

Allison shook her head. She peered out the window, seemingly mesmerized by the lights of the steel mills that shimmered off the dark waters of the Ohio River. "Do you really think anyone else was involved in Rayce's murder?" she asked.

"I don't know, Allison, and at this point I don't care. Why, do you have any suspects in mind?"

She looked at me and grinned, tilting her head in a way that made her look both mischievous and beautiful. She caressed my arm and gently laid her head on my shoulder. She was my angel.

CHAPTER THIRTY-EIGHT
ALLISON ROBERSON

I killed that son of a bitch.

I did a sloppy job of it, and I'll be the first to admit that, but it was the first time I had ever shot anyone to death, so cut me a little slack. I didn't intend to shoot him. Okay, that's bullshit. I meant to kill him all along. If he had thrown his hands in the air and produced the videotape he was using to blackmail my husband and promised to leave town forever, maybe I wouldn't have shot his sorry ass, but he didn't. He did exactly what I knew he would do, so I pulled the gun and announced that I intended to kill him. That's when I shot him in the kneecap. He dropped to the dirt, yelled, and called me a fuckin' cunt. That's when I squeezed off a second round and took out a chunk of his shoulder. By that time, he was royally pissed off. He struggled to his feet and lunged at me. He was just a few feet away when I put one in his chest. The bastard was so full of evil, he just wouldn't die. He rolled around in the dirt, looking at me, moving his lips, trying to call me names, twitching and moaning. I got a little closer to him, pointed the gun at his head, closed my eyes, and squeezed the trigger.

The last shot was the one that knocked me off-balance. I fell and tumbled to the bottom of the ravine. The contents of my purse spilled everywhere. I wrenched my wrist but otherwise survived unscathed.

I ought to back up a little and give you the full story.

Sheriffs in Ohio have what is known as the Furtherance of Justice Fund. This is money equal to half the sheriff's annual salary that can be used at his discretion for law enforcement purposes. The sheriff has complete control over this fund and how it's spent, and I'd imagine that it's a great opportunity for abuse. However, my husband Francis is famously anal and kept track of every penny . . . until last year. That's when I noticed that a significant amount of money was being drained out of the fund. When I questioned him about it, he became very defensive and said that as the sheriff there were certain things he needed to spend money on to keep peace in the county. He said he was using it to pay an informant and that's all I needed to know.

At first, I thought he was spending it on that little tart Dena Marie Xenakis. But about the same time, Rayce Daubner started spending more and more time in Fran's office. The withdrawals from the fund, I noticed, coincided with Rayce's visits. I went into Toots's office and closed the door. "He's in trouble, isn't he?"

Toots rolled a pencil between his thick fingers and nodded once. "Yep."

"What?"

"Mildred Goins." My stomach seized up. I had been with Fran and Toots the night they went to Mildred's home after she had put a deer slug in the chest of her husband. Fran had, essentially, coached Mildred on what to say to investigators in order to stay out of jail. I knew it was going to blow up in his face.

I sat in the chair in front of Toots's desk as he continued. "Apparently, Mildred got drunked up one night at the Starlighter Bar and started bragging about how she had killed her husband and the sheriff had helped her beat the rap by coaching her on what to say. I probably don't have to tell you who was sitting within earshot at the bar."

"Rayce Daubner."

"He took little Mildred back to his house and videotaped her recounting the entire story in painful detail. He made a copy and came in to the office the next day and showed it to Fran. He said it was going to cost Fran five hundred dollars a week, and maybe after a year or two he'd give him the original."

"What did Fran do?"

"Same thing he always does when he gets worked up—threw up in the wastebasket."

I nodded. "He's got the stomach of a little girl. What's the plan? What's he going to do?"

Toots shrugged. "What can he do? Pay the money and hope Rayce eventually gives up the tape."

"What do you think are the odds of that?"

Toots used the thumb and index finger on his right hand to make a zero.

In late April, Daubner stopped in to see Fran for his weekly blackmail payment. About ten minutes after he arrived, one of the deputies pepper-sprayed an unruly teenager in the lobby. The parents were there, and all hell broke loose. Fran came running out of his office; Daubner followed a few minutes later, smirking at me on his way out. Amid the confusion, I slipped off my heels and walked into Fran's office in my stocking feet. As was his habit, Fran had removed his holster and service revolver, the steel-blue .38, and set them on top of the file cabinet. I had the pistol and slipped out of his office in seconds.

When Fran discovered it was missing, he went into a panic. Of course, he suspected Daubner.

The next time Daubner came to the office, I met him in the hall on his way out. Again, he had that stupid smirk on his face. "I want to talk to you," I said.

"Talk away."

I tipped my head toward the front door. I walked with my arms crossed, refusing to make eye contact until we were on the sidewalk outside of the courthouse. "Tell me, Rayce, how many blow jobs is it going to take to get you to leave my husband alone and give me that tape?"

"Whoa," he said. "Now that's an interesting proposition."

"How many?"

"Let's start with one and figure it out from there."

I knew, of course, that Rayce would never give up the tape. I planned to kill him all along. Our first encounter was at his house. I stopped on my way back from buying a new dress for my niece's baptism. He invited me in and put his hand up to my face, running my hair between his fingers. "This isn't about love and affection, Rayce," I said, knocking his hand away. "This is about making you happy so that you'll quit blackmailing my husband."

He grinned, and I could feel the heat in my belly. I couldn't wait to kill him. He unhitched his pants and sat down in an overstuffed chair in the living room. "If that's the case, come work your magic."

I did. I got on my knees in front of the chair and took him in my mouth. It was the most repugnant act of my life. Given that, I will say that never in my life had I seen another man who was half as big as Rayce Daubner. When he came, he held my hair and forced me to swallow his load. It made me want to kill him even more.

I met him at his house twice more. "No more meeting here," I said as I stood and walked to the door. "It's too risky. I can't afford to have my car seen outside your place."

"You want me to come to your place?" he asked. "Do you think the sheriff would like to watch his wife suck my dick?"

"I'll call you once I have a better idea. How many more times, Rayce?"

He hitched up his pants and worked his belt through the clasp. "You're not even close, darlin'."

I called him the next week. "Meet me at Jefferson Lake State Park," I said.

"It's a big place."

"There are some walking trails on the other side of the lake. There's a path that goes up to the caves."

"Christ Almighty. That's a fuckin' hike."

"I'll make sure it's worth your effort."

The remote section of the park was called "the caves," which were the old entrances to deep-shaft mines that had been sealed up except for the first ten or fifteen feet. For years, high school kids had used the caves for partying and romance on Friday nights after the football games. I was going to use them to kill Rayce Daubner.

He met me on the path, and I said, "There's a real private place up here. I already checked it out." He followed me along a narrow path through a thicket of wild blackberries that led back toward the walking paths. When he crested the ravine, I turned and held the gun on him with both hands.

Incredibly, he just smiled. "What's this all about, sweet lips?" he asked.

I had seen enough movies to know that I should have just shot him, but I felt compelled to answer. "You're scum, Rayce. You'd never give up that tape no matter how many hours I spend on my knees, so I'm going to kill you. Someone might find the tape, but hopefully it'll be my husband when he searches your house for clues about the identity of your killer."

"You're not going to shoot me. You want the tape? I'll give it to you. Follow me back to my house and I'll—"

Boom.

I can't explain why the first shot hit him in the knee. Nerves and inexperience, I guess. The blast echoed throughout the park. He was just getting off the ground when the second shot grazed his shoulder. After that it was impossible for me to miss.

Toots knows that I'm the killer. Just before Daubner's body was transported to the coroner's office, Toots made one last sweep of the area. It was then that he found the antique blue-and-white enameled compact mirror that Fran bought me for Valentine's Day the first year we were married.

I realized it was missing the day after I killed Daubner. I tried to convince myself that I'd simply misplaced it, but I knew what had happened. It had rolled into the high grass when I tumbled down the ravine, and I hadn't seen it when I was gathering my stuff back into my purse.

The day that Fran was in his office, talking on the phone to Marshall Hood of the *Intelligencer*, all upset because the press had found out that he had questioned Johnny and Smoochie, but unaware that

I was the one who had called them, Toots walked calmly up to my desk and asked, "Lose something?" He was holding the compact in his thick right hand, waving it back and forth. I lurched at it, and he pulled it back. "We need to talk, Allison." He placed the compact on my desk, and I snatched it just as Fran walked out of his office, angry and screaming about getting the call from the reporter.

"I just got off the phone with Marshall Hood at the *Intelligencer*," he yelled. "He knows we questioned Johnny and Smoochie; he knew Daubner had kicked the shit out of Smoochie; he even knew Johnny gave me a headbutt to the nose. How in the hell did he find out?" Then he looked me square in the eyes and said, "You're looking awful damn guilty about something."

I was looking guilty, but it had nothing to do with calling the reporter. It was because I had just been busted for the murder of Rayce Daubner. I could feel the red splotches that I get when I'm nervous creeping up around my neck. I went on the offensive and said, "Excuse me? You have the nerve to say that *I* look guilty?" I said it in reference to his fling with Dena Marie. I knew that would get him off my back. "You are treading on such thin ice it's unbelievable."

Fran and Toots met for a while to discuss the likely suspects of the press leak. By the time they had finished, I had cleaned off my desk and was ready to go home. Fortunately, Fran had to run to an emergency Jefferson County commissioners meeting, and it gave me a few minutes alone with Toots.

"I didn't think you had it in you, princess," he said. I didn't speak; I was fighting back tears. "You can relax," he assured me. "I'm not going to say anything about it. He deserved it."

"Did anyone else see the compact?" I asked.

"What compact?" Toots said.

I smiled while tears started down my cheeks.

"Listen," he said, "I don't think anyone's going to get too upset if the murder of Rayce Daubner goes unsolved. But if the sheriff's wife gets arrested for the murder, it's going to severely damage his chances of ever becoming president of the United States."

"He was going to turn that tape over to the FBI and take Fran down," I said. "Fran's a good man. I couldn't just sit back and let that happen."

Toots nodded. "Did you steal Fran's service revolver, too?"

I nodded. "I figured if Daubner was killed with a gun he was suspected of stealing, then it might throw off the detectives. I was going to leave the gun there so you could find it, but I fell down the hill after I shot him, and I panicked. There wasn't any time to wipe the prints off the gun. I just wanted to get out of there."

"Understandable. What did you do with it?"

"It's at the house—in the basement."

Toots's eyes widened. "You have the gun used to kill Rayce Daubner *in your house*? Jesus Christ, Allison, what were you thinking?"

"Apparently I wasn't. I didn't know killing someone was going to be so unnerving."

"Go get it. Now. Do it while Fran is in the commissioners meeting. I'll wait here."

There was virtually no chance that anyone would have found the pistol. I had hidden it in the basement in some soft dirt behind a loose stone in the corner of the foundation. But I did as Toots ordered and had the pistol back in his office inside of thirty minutes. He immediately put it in a manila envelope, slid it into a desk file drawer, and locked it up.

"What are you going to do with it?" I asked.

"Wipe it clean of your prints, for starters. Beyond that, I haven't decided. Allison, I cannot understate the importance of never, ever saying another word about this to anyone. Not Fran. Not me. Don't even mention it in your prayers."

"Trust me. I'll never utter a word. Toots, thank you so much for . . ."

He held up both hands and said, "Forget it. Get out of here. Go get dinner started." I nodded and headed for the door. "One more question."

"Sure."

"Did you burn down his house so that you could destroy the tape?"

"No, I just killed him. I just lucked out when the house burned down."

CHAPTER THIRTY-NINE

JOHNNY EARL

At a few minutes before eleven the morning after Deputy Majowski slipped me the keys to room 7 at the Valley View Motel, I was driving out of Steubenville. The canopy of oak and maple foliage shaded the asphalt, and sunlight flickered through, dancing across my hood as I passed. In my rearview mirror, I could see the stacks of the steel mills and the homes that dotted the hillside. Beyond the tunnel of trees, the road dipped and turned to the right, beginning the long descent down Stony Hollow Boulevard to the floodplains of the Ohio River Valley. Behind me, Steubenville disappeared from my rearview mirror, and from my past.

I crossed over the West Virginia panhandle and into Pennsylvania. Just outside of Pittsburgh, I turned off Route 22 and drove to Raccoon Creek State Park. I walked down to the lake, unsnapped the typewriter case, and filled it with stones. I grabbed the handle with both hands, spun like a hammer thrower, and heaved it into the lake. It splashed, bobbed once, twice, and disappeared, sending ripples across the water.

The Cathedral of the Immaculate Conception is on Merrimac Street in the Mount Washington section of Pittsburgh, about a mile from where I had lived during my days as a drug dealer and apprentice mason. I rented a room at the Hilton near the Golden Triangle and rode the incline to Mount Washington later that same afternoon. The backpack I had slung over my shoulder contained a manila envelope of clippings and mementos, a pair of rubber gloves, a small crowbar, and a claw hammer, both of which were wrapped in hotel bath towels to keep them from clanging in the bag. I arrived at the church at five

forty in the afternoon. I sat in a pew at the back, admiring the tow-
ering masonry that I'd had a minor role in constructing, as well as the
brick vault in the corner that I had built and sealed. Inside the vault
was a time capsule. Two women were praying silently at the front of the
church. I sat with my head bowed until they left.

When they were gone, I walked to the back of the sanctuary and
slipped inside a broom closet. Closing the door gently, I sat in the
corner behind a vacuum cleaner, the backpack on my chest between my
crossed arms. I dozed, listened to the organ and the Mass, and patiently
waited for the evening service to end. Long after the Mass had ended,
I could hear footfalls within the sanctuary. By eleven o'clock, it had
been several hours since I heard the sounds of another human being. I
slipped on the rubber gloves and pushed the door open, slowly, to find
the sanctuary dark except for a dull light shining from behind the cru-
cifix at the front of the sanctuary. I whispered, "Old man, I'm going to
ask forgiveness in advance here."

I have never been a particularly religious man, but I'll be the first
to admit that I was still uncomfortable with what I was about to do.
I quickly took the small crowbar and placed the flattened edge in the
mortar below the first row of bricks. Behind the mortar, I knew, was
the steel plate that supported the top of the time-capsule vault. With
two taps of the hammer, the mortar crumbled, revealing the edge of
the steel plate. Two more whacks with the hammer drove the crowbar
beneath the steel. I worked the bar up and down several times until the
mortar broke away and the steel plate and brick cap broke loose. I slid
the crowbar off the base of the vault, and it fell to the carpeted floor
with a thud that echoed in the sanctuary.

I pulled the steel canister from the vault and twisted off the cap,
revealing four hundred and seventy-two thousand dollars neatly
wrapped in paper bands. I covered the steel canister with the backpack
and turned it upside down, emptying it in a single motion. The overstuffed envelope in my backpack carried the documents the church
had given to me eight years earlier to place in the capsule. On it I had
printed a simple message: *Sorry for the damage.* I placed five thousand

dollars and the envelope back in the canister and dropped it into the vault.

I left through a back door and walked to the incline. Early the next morning, I left Pittsburgh with all my earthly possessions and four hundred and sixty-seven thousand dollars in cash in the trunk of my rusting Camaro.

EPILOGUE
JOHNNY EARL

I was asked to join the local Rotary Club. Isn't that a kick? Once I started my own business and became a successful member of the community, the Rotarians thought I would be a nice addition to their club. A few years ago, I had the skinhead tattoos removed from my biceps with a laser, so there were no outward signs of my previous rank of colonel in the New Order of the Third Reich. I even joined the country club, and last year I placed third in the club golf tournament. I'm not as good a golfer as I was a baseball player, but I'm pretty damn good.

For obvious reasons, I don't talk much about my past. The men at the country club love talking about their past athletic exploits, but I don't say much, as I'm sure it would eventually lead to questions about the time between the end of my baseball career and the starting of my own construction business.

After leaving Pittsburgh with my stash of cash, I drove west, finally settling down outside of Fort Worth. I love Texas and am grateful to have had an opportunity to start over. I put my ill-gotten money in a safe-deposit box, minus enough cash to get an apartment and buy a backhoe, trailer, and dump truck, and began Big Red Excavation.

The business has grown to seven full-time employees, a host of sub-contractors, and so much equipment that I'm having trouble keeping track of my inventory. I still have well over three hundred and fifty thousand dollars of my drug money in a safe in the basement of my new house. I'm not sure how to spend it or introduce it to my invest-ment account without attracting the attention of the Internal Revenue

Service. My business has been so successful that I really don't need it right now, which is a good problem to have.

I haven't been back to Steubenville. There's no reason to go back. Once Mom and Dad saw that I was a legitimate businessman and was unlikely to go back to prison, they moved near me in Fort Worth. Dad helps me out with the business a few hours a week. It gives him something to do, and Mom is happy to get him out of the house.

Francis Roberson was recently reelected to Congress. He caused a big fuss back home when in the middle of his last term he switched parties and became a Republican. I saw him on one of those Sunday-morning television shows after he switched, and you would have thought he was a homosexual coming out of the closet. He said he had been living a lie and wasn't true to himself, blah, blah, blah. He's starting to sound more like every other politician out there. He won the last election by the narrowest margin so far, but his stature in the legislature seems to be growing. He's been mentioned as a possible vice presidential candidate and is reportedly considering a run for governor.

He was in Dallas last year for a fundraiser for a Texas congressman. They're big on law and order down here, and Fran is still a big draw when he tells the story of foiling a plot to assassinate the president. The fundraiser was five hundred dollars a plate, and I went just for kicks. After the dinner, while Fran was shaking hands and yammering on about how much he loved Texas, I went over and sat down at a table where his chief of staff, a slimmed-down and dapper-looking Toots Majowski, was talking with a few of the locals. Majowski nodded at me and said , without conviction, "How ya doing?"

"Good," I said.

He continued to talk to the other men at the table for another minute until the light clicked on. He stopped talking in mid-sentence, looked back at me, and said, "Well, I'll be goddamned. Look what the armadillos dragged in."

Fran had no such recognition problems. He walked over to the table and said, "Jesus H. Christ, if it isn't the great Johnny Earl." He gave me a hug and said to a few of the Texans nearby, "Did you know this guy was probably the greatest athlete to ever come out of Steuben-ville, Ohio?"

I said, "Easy with that athlete stuff, Congressman. Down here they just know me as Johnny the backhoe guy." Everyone chuckled. When their attention turned away, I slapped Fran in the chest and asked, "What the hell do you mean, '*probably* the greatest'?"

Fran and I talk on the phone about twice a year. When we talk, he generally gives me an update on the old gang, including Vincent and Dena Marie Xenakis. They moved from Steubenville to a little farm near Lake Austin after Vincent was promoted to chief operating officer of Ohio Valley Hospital. Over time, he gave up the black suits and toothpicks and slicked-back hair, but rumors still circulated that he had been the triggerman in the murder of Rayce Daubner and that he had set up the preacher and general to take the fall. These rumors were circulated, in part, by Dena Marie, who was still in love with the idea that Vincent murdered Rayce. Of course, he did nothing to dispel these rumors, and whenever Fran saw Vincent and Dena Marie in public, the former sheriff would flash him an ugly glare. Fran said Vincent appreci-ated this, as it helped keep Dena Marie in line.

I don't know who killed Rayce Daubner. Maybe Fran, maybe Fran's dad, maybe Toots, maybe Smoochie. I don't know who torched his house or what they were trying to cover up. None of that matters to me in the least. I'm just amazed that things worked out. Had I stayed in Steubenville, I would have forever been the guy who blew his chance at a pro baseball career, and I would have forever been reminded of my failures. Here, nobody knows that I was a high school legend, and nobody cares.

And, for the first time in my life, I'm okay with that.

ACKNOWLEDGMENTS

Whenever I sit down to write acknowledgments for a book, I always recall the many times when I was struggling alone, writing manuscripts and sending them off to the black hole that is the slush pile at the publishing houses, a place where unsolicited manuscripts go to die.

These days, I have an incredible support team behind me, and I am very appreciative of their efforts. At the top of this list is my agent, Colleen Mohyde. In spite of the fact that she represents other authors—a habit I have continually asked her to break in order to focus solely on my needs—she does a tremendous job on my behalf. She is equal parts life coach, editor, and agent. She does all the heavy lifting and math that I don't want to be bothered with. I would give you her contact information, but she already has enough authors, so please don't bother her.

This is my second book under the guidance of my editor, Dan Mayer. I very much appreciate the support, his easy touch, and the confidence he has shown in my writing.

The duo who publicize my books are Cheryl Quimba and her supervisor, Jill Maxick, Seventh Street's vice president of marketing and director of publicity. They are a pair of five-star performers. I appreciate their hard work and the fact that they silently tolerate all of my suggestions of how they should be doing their jobs.

Also, many thanks to Jade Zora Scibilia, my proofreader at Seventh Street. There are few things as painful as dealing with a neurotic author in the days before a book goes to print. She deftly talked me in off the ledge several times.

I also must thank my sweetheart, Melissa, who supports me unfailingly and so often asks, "Shouldn't you be writing?"

My Ohio River Valley roots continue to be an inspiration for my novels. *A Welcome Murder* is set in Steubenville, which was once the center of steelmaking in the Ohio Valley. When I was a kid, the highlight of my week was the Saturday-morning trip to Steubenville, where the downtown streets smelled of sulfur from the mills and warm sugar and dough from the bakeries. There were movie theaters, five-and-dimes, crowded sidewalks, and great prosperity. Like the denizens of "the 'ville" and the rest of the Ohio Valley, I hope for a day when that prosperity returns.

ABOUT THE AUTHOR

Robin Yocum is the author of the critically acclaimed novels *A Brilliant Death*, *Favorite Sons*, and *The Essay*. In 2011, *Favorite Sons* was named USA Book News' Book of the Year for Mystery/Suspense. It was selected for the Choose to Read Ohio program for 2013–14 and was a featured book of the 2012 Ohioana Book Festival. Yocum is also the author of *Dead before Deadline . . . and Other Tales from the Police Beat* and *Insured for Murder* (with Catherine Candisky). He is the president of Yocum Communications, a public relations and marketing firm in Galena, Ohio. He is well known for his work as a crime and investigative reporter with the *Columbus Dispatch* from 1980 to 1991, during which time he earned more than thirty local, state, and national journalism awards in categories ranging from investigative reporting to feature writing.